The Mic
Her

K R Chapman

ISBN-10:
1532748949

ISBN-13:
978-1532748943

Dedicated to my wife whose support
and encouragement have been unfailing.

To Sue
With my very best wishes
January 2017

K R Chng

AUTHOR'S NOTE

What you are about to read is a true story. The events described occurred in precisely the places mentioned but names of people have been altered to protect family members, some of whom may have perceived the precise detail of some of the events a little differently.

Because the principal characters are deceased and because even when they were alive they were reluctant to talk openly about their experiences, some of the detail has been based partially on conjecture and anecdotal evidence. However, in no way has this detracted from what is in essence a true story of a family's experiences that began during the occupation of France.

Whilst the book essentially follows the lives of one family, and in particular one central character, it seemed important to put their story, and the events that shaped their lives, within the context of their time. Accordingly, reference has been made to widely known people whose experiences create a portrayal of how complex life was under occupation during World War Two.

The lily of the valley, breathing in the humble grass

Answer'd the lovely maid and said: I am a watry weed,

And I am very small, and love to dwell in lowly vales;

So weak, the gilded butterfly scarce perches on my head;

Yet I am visited from heaven, and he that smiles on all

Walks in the valley and each morn over me spreads his hand,

Saying: 'Rejoice, thou humble grass, thou new-born lily flower,

Thou gentle maid of silent valleys and of modest brooks;

For thou shalt be clothed in light, and fed with morning manna,

Till summer's heat melts thee beside the fountains and the springs

To flourish in eternal vales.'

— William Blake

PROLOGUE

I am the family face; flesh perishes, I live on.
— *Thomas Hardy*

It was 9 July but cold and miserable; the rain had been relentless. Puddles collected between the uneven paving stones and a torrent of water was gushing out of a broken down-pipe that was hanging precariously from the wall of the red brick building they were about to enter. The wind had picked up: the zinc down-pipe created a cacophonous sound and its grimy water daubed the wall. As if the very occasion was not sufficient to dampen their spirits, the cold and the rain had made a thoroughly successful job of ensuring they were at a very low point.

Four of them stood huddled together sheltering under an umbrella, not that it kept them dry. The three others were also trying to take refuge from the rain. Nobody spoke. They waited, patiently, nervously. They must have been there for some twenty minutes when a car pulled up alongside them. After a while the door opened and a gendarme in full uniform complete with holstered gun exited the car. He exchanged a few words with the attendant who greeted him at the door, in French so not everyone caught what was said. The gendarme was ushered into the building out of the rain. The others followed, not knowing what to expect. The vestibule was small and there was hardly room enough for everyone. There was nothing on the walls to indicate the function of the building; it was dingy, dark and cold in that place. Perhaps a brighter more inviting room may have helped to warm the atmosphere a little, though perhaps not.

A flight of six or seven concrete steps leading to an open door took the gendarme and his attendant into an expansive space that appeared, at least to those looking from the vestibule, to be completely empty. After a few minutes the attendant came to the doorway and beckoned them. Five of the seven made their way up the steps and into the room, slowly, apprehensively.

She looked as though she was asleep but of course those present knew she would not wake from that particular slumber. The reactions of those in the room varied. Beatrice was sobbing and quite beside herself with emotion and Nathalie, whilst sad of course, held herself together, as much as anything for her son and her step-father. Nathalie's husband, Christopher, was respectful and circumspect, but nevertheless somewhat perplexed, for he could not understand why Beatrice was taking photographs of her mother lying in a coffin.

Time passed slowly, though in truth they were only in that room for a few moments, just sufficient to pay their respects. Christopher was the last to leave and as he did so he paused on the steps as the gendarme brushed past him on his way back into the room. This time his task was to verify the identity of the deceased, and having done so, secure the lid and seal it with wire held in place with wax. As he performed this ritual Christopher became visibly disturbed by an unexpected and curious sensation: he felt himself gasping for air and had to suppress a desire to rush across the room and prise open the lid. He hurried down the steps and joined the others who were by then making their way out of the building and into the hubbub of the street. As they walked briskly through the pouring rain to their respective cars they were in agreement: she had looked untroubled and serene which, given the circumstances of the past few weeks, was good, very good. They drove the short distance to the village church for the funeral service. More waiting under umbrellas in the chilly damp air while villagers joined the family group, offered their condolences, and stood alongside them waiting for the hearse to arrive. As it drove in along the gravel path they were all ushered into the church where they sat waiting for the coffin to be brought in.

The service was short but conducted in a most convivial manner, in fact precisely how a funeral service for a long-serving member of the church congregation should be, except that she was not. She had almost never put foot across the threshold, despite being a long-term resident of the village and claiming good Catholic upbringing. It was very warm inside the church and the smell of incense pervaded the air. At the end of the ceremony the congregation filed slowly past the coffin with each member pausing momentarily before sprinkling it with holy water, hoping to bring relief to the deceased's soul in purgatory, so it is said. They left the churchyard and drove 200 kilometres to Chateau-Chinon where she would be finally laid to rest.

By the time they arrived at the sepulchre the torrential rain had abated, giving way to a fine drizzle. The beautiful view normally seen across the Morvan hills of a typical early afternoon in July was shrouded in mist and it was still cold. In truth, it was miserable. People she knew years ago had gathered, for this was her familial home. The vehicle carrying the body was not yet in sight and so once more there was a great deal of standing around in small groups, under umbrellas or with hooded rain jackets zipped up to the neck. The marble sepulchre was open. It was small but deep; there was room for a second coffin.

'I feel uneasy about her being lowered into that void. It will be sealed over with that marble slab. How will she ...' Nathalie did not finish the sentence but her husband knew exactly what she was feeling for he had felt same as the coffin lid had been secured in place. He put his arm around her shoulders but said

3

nothing. Maybe it was the knowledge that the gendarme had had to verify the body really was dead that had brought about these thoughts; who knows? With the floral tributes amassed with chrysanthemums it became very clear to Christopher why his wife did not like to receive them at Christmas and for birthdays: chrysanthemums were exclusively for funerals in France.

Nathalie caught sight of the hearse. She alerted the others and they all turned to see the vehicle driving ever so slowly out of the mist on its way towards them along the narrow passageway between the rows of graves. It came to a stop and four suited men stepped out and made their way to the back of the vehicle. A trestle table was erected and moved to within a short distance of the open sepulchre. The solid oak coffin was dragged from the back of the vehicle and the four solemn men grasped the handles and placed it ever so gently down on the table. They walked away to allow mourners to gather around the coffin for a quiet moment of private meditation.

Christopher stepped back a little to give room for the close family to move forward. His mother-in-law was dead of course, but what did that really mean? Obviously she was without life in the sense that she could not move or speak and that none of her organs were functioning, but was it possible she was in some way sentient? Whilst unable to converse was it just conceivable she knew what was happening to her? Was she lying there in that cask inanimate but nonetheless aware of those around her, what they were feeling, saying and doing? Perhaps she had sensed her husband's emotion as he stood motionless and speechless whilst beside the open coffin a few hours before. Maybe she was aware her youngest daughter had wept uncontrollably, and just maybe she had been aware too that her son-in-law had looked back into the room at the moment the coffin lid had been lowered and secured. And perhaps she was conscious of how indomitable her eldest daughter had been when, in spite of her own inward feelings of sorrow and grief, others had needed someone more resolute than they were able to be. Ridiculous? Inconceivable? Impossible! But as he stood motionless in the wintry air Christopher's curiosity got the better of him. Perhaps death is not as finite as it is feared to be, but merely a temporary cessation of being before reincarnation. If so, then there will be little doubt his mother-in-law will have a rather more contented second life, making up for the difficult times, particularly those from her early life.

She was now at peace; there would be no more shocks, setbacks or ailments to torment her. No battles to fight and no more suffering. In her last few weeks of life she had known she was going to die, even though those close to her had felt this unlikely. She had been hospitalised and to all accounts had had successful surgery to free a blockage in her oesophagus, but just days after she returned home she was again unable to consume food without vomiting. Her husband had begged her to go back to hospital but her mind had been made up. She was obdurate and nothing was about to alter this. She became weaker by the day and had no resolve to fight for her life.

There can be little doubt that as she lay in her bed for hour after hour day after day, the traumas of her earlier life must have come flooding back to haunt her. She would have been tormented by a collage of visual memories of a twelve year period in her life straddling the war years, through the 1940s and into the early 50s, that had affected her so gravely and that for the rest of her living days had never been far from her consciousness. She endured hardship after hardship and like so many others affected by trauma during that period of time, she would have had no support to help her to cope and move forward. In that brief period in her life she had lived through the testing and onerous hardships endured by her family at the time of the Nazi occupation, the loathsome retribution and purging that had occurred the instant her country had been liberated, and the wretched time in the early years of her first marriage that had left her inconsolable, heartbroken and guilt-ridden. The time was right in her eighty-fourth year for Marie to finally put those odious memories to rest, something she had never managed to achieve whilst among the living.

ground to break up what was rapidly becoming essentially pastoral countryside. From her bedroom window she saw deer feeding nearby, providing her with a clue that there must be plenty of wildflowers in the meadows, and the churned up ground was an indication that wild boar were not too far away. Marie settled down in her new surroundings with her family that first evening very content, and perhaps even a little excited that the next day she would be able to explore the surrounding countryside.

'Oh Maman, I think I'm going to be very happy here.'

'That's good my sweetheart — I want you to be happy. Now come on, it's to bed for you my little flower.'

'Maman, can I go exploring in the countryside tomorrow? Will you come with me? Do you think we'll find any of your favourite flowers Maman — you know those plants with their little white flowers that seem to nod at me as I pass by them.'

'If you mean lily of the valley then we will have to wait some weeks before they pop their heads up above the ground. They hide in the winter and only appear in the late spring when the nightingale arrives'.

'But how do they know the nightingale is there if they are hiding underground'?

'Once upon a time, a very long time ago, legend has it that a lily of the valley fell madly in love with a nightingale when it heard it sing so beautifully. But it went away at the end of the summer, and so sad was the lily of the valley it withered away and went into hiding. It did not want to face the world without its nightingale'.

'But that's so sad Maman. Why did he go away? Did he not love her as she loved him?'

'I think he did my darling because he returned in the spring. But he couldn't find her. So he sang his exquisite song as beautifully as he could and as he did so the little lily of the valley popped her head up above the earth nodding her pretty tiny bell-like flowers in joyful appreciation. From that day onwards the nightingale returned every May to sing its enchanting melody, and the flower bloomed and nodded in loving approval. It is this lovely story that makes me think of you Marie.'

'Is this why you call me your little flower, Maman?'

'It certainly is. You are my lily of the valley, and as pretty as a picture and as sweet as honeysuckle on a summer's day. Now it's off to bed for you. Your sisters are already fast asleep.'

'Just give me five more minutes Maman — please'. And with that she got up, went to the door, opened it and stood there watching and thinking about the lily of the valley and her nightingale. As she did she thought she smelt the sweet smell of honeysuckle but there was none to be seen and just as it was too early to see the lily of the valley, so the honeysuckle was not in flower just yet either. She turned and went back into the house, kissed her mother and father goodnight, and made her way to her bed.

'Don't disturb your sisters now Marie. I'll be there in a couple of minutes to tuck you up and give you a big kiss.'

But Marie was so tired she fell into a deep sleep before her mother could get to her. Her dreams that night were about the lily of the valley, the nightingale and perfumed honeysuckle. All the elements of life that would make Marie a very happy five year old were in place in this idyllic rural setting.

The Duvals were very happy in Préporché. They had all they needed or ever wanted in their immediate surroundings; they were effectively self-sufficient and rarely travelled more than a few kilometres from their village. Life was a joy and the girls spent almost all of their free time outdoors in summer: walking in the woods, playing in the meadows and helping with the vegetables and soft fruits in the jardin ouvrier, or collecting eggs from the coop and occasionally even milking the cow. In the harsh winters it afforded time to be as a family, sitting around the log fire in the evening, playing and making music or reading. But as the 1930s drew to a close so a new and challenging era was about to be born, one that would test the nation's moral fibre and threaten everything families like the Duvals had held dear.

CHAPTER TWO

Every man has the right to risk his own life in order to preserve it. Has it ever been said that a man who throws himself out the window to escape from a fire is guilty of suicide?
— *Michel-Jacques Rousseau*

It was 1939, three years after the Duvals had settled in Préporché. An awareness of the mobilisation of Germany's Third Reich army and occupation of neighbouring states should have troubled the French government, but a combination of denial and poor organisation left France vulnerable to military occupation. However, though too late in the day, they woke up to the realisation that they needed a bigger and better army, and so young men throughout France were becoming fearful they may be drafted into the armed forces. Jacques was no exception, but his entrepreneurial acumen had led him to build a successful business so he did not want anything to undermine his hard work and threaten his livelihood. Accordingly, he vowed to do what it would take to avoid the call to arms. It was this that took him and his family away from Préporché and off to far away Rennes in Brittany where he had family who would help him. Leaving his village, where he was too much in the limelight, he thought he would be able to remain under the radar and therefore avoid the call-up.

Everything happened very quickly once the decision had been made. Within the month they had sold up in Préporché and bought another home in the village of Villars. Jacques did not want Rosine and the girls to remain in Préporché believing the authorities would be able to track him down by putting pressure on them from the address known to them. The home in Villars would be a place for Rosine and the children to live until they were able to join him in Rennes. He also envisaged it would be their family home to return to at some later time. It had more land than the house in Préporché, outhouses he could use as a workshop and stores for his itinerant ballroom and wine, and the house had more space for the girls now that they were growing up.

Villars was tiny but just five kilometres from the busy market town of Moulins-Engilbert, only a kilometre away from the splendid chateau of Limanton and barely three from Venitiens, where the girls would be schooled. There were woods on the outskirts of Villars and the pretty tree lined Aron flowed along the south-west corner of the village, just a stone's throw from the house. It was a lovely little village he had thought; the girls would love it. But in truth the girls were upset to be uprooted yet again.

Jacques spent a few days making the necessary arrangements and packing up what he thought he would need in Brittany, and with a wistful goodbye he was off on the road to Rennes. The plan was for him to go ahead of the family, find somewhere to stay, settle in and begin to make a living, much the same way that economic migrants from the rural regions of developing countries do today, when they journey to the big cities in their quest for something better. He promised to send for his family once settled with somewhere to live. In his absence Rosine made the arrangements for the move to Villars and within a couple of weeks they too were on their way with some uprooted vegetables, a cow and some hens all in tow. Moving all their belongings was not easy for Rosine, all the more so because in addition to their furniture, kitchen utensils and clothes she also had to arrange to move Jacques's portable ballroom, his tools for building it and the materials for his cobbling business, as well as dozens of casks of wine, all ready for bottling.

Rosine and the girls coped as best they could while he was away, but there was no income so they had to survive on the few savings they had while trying to settle into their new surroundings. Rosine knew they needed to be frugal and learn to live on very little. They had the vegetable plot and adjoining the house was a small sward where they kept the cow and some hens; they would survive. Of all three girls it was Marie who was the most resourceful; somehow she, more than the others, had appreciated their predicament and was committed to doing her utmost for the family in their time of need. It was she who did most of the daily chores and it was she who rushed back from school at midday to get the stew on the stove ready for their main meal of the day, while her mother was out tending to the vegetables or doing her household chores. Emeline, Marie's older sister, a rather plain looking girl with frizzy wheatish-brown hair and a florid, macular complexion, did very little to help around the house and seemed reluctant to sacrifice what she had become accustomed to: idling her time with friends or sitting around at home. She did little to support the family and as for Colette, she was not old enough to understand the predicament they were in, let alone toil for the family. Like Marie, Colette had pretty features but quite unlike Marie she was scrawny and had a decidedly sallow complexion.

Eight year old Marie rose early each school day and dressed herself before doing her chores. She loved the outdoors, almost whatever the weather. In winter she always wrapped up in warm clothing with several layers because the continental climate brought snow or a heavy frost most days, but in summer it was invariably very hot so she wore just a cotton dress and sabots. Every day she walked to the boulangerie to pick up a pain de campagne, unless her mother had busied herself baking the day before, and then out into the field to milk the cow, cheekily taking a few swigs of the still frothy full cream milk from the earthenware jug before presenting it to her mother.

Every morning Rosine and her three daughters ate their breakfast of milk, bread and homemade preserves together at the wooden trestle table in the stone-floored kitchen, and then the three girls walked the three or four kilometres to school in Venitiens before returning for lunch at 12 noon; the same routine almost every day.

Their school was a single story building with two adjoining classrooms, each with rows of oak double desks. Children from ages five to thirteen were taught in these classrooms, so the two teachers not only had to teach every subject but also plan a variety of programmes to suit the ages of the children. At the other end of the building was accommodation that served as the living quarters for the teachers. In each classroom was a cast iron stove that doubled up as a heat source in winter and a means of warming up the children's lunch. This was the preferred option for those children from the outlying villages whose journey was too long for them to return home for lunch. These children, including Marie and her sisters on occasions, would take their food to school in a gamelle, a metal can designed for the purpose; invariably it was the left-overs from the family meal the previous evening. Outside the building were three separate toilets, each one being merely a hole in the ground with a wooden seat above; today they are still there, exactly as they were in the 1930s. With doors that barely covered two-thirds of the opening there was little privacy.

From spring through to the end of summer, on most school days Marie left her sisters to find their own way back home at lunch-time so she could take the longer route across the meadows and down to the wood by the stream. She preferred her own company to that of her two lazy sisters, and it gave her the opportunity to pick masses of wild daffodils, and in early summer sweet smelling lily of the valley, as a token of her love for her mother, whilst always remembering to swish her wooden stick this way and that to frighten away vipers from her pathway.

*

Meanwhile, in Brittany things were tough for Jacques. Rennes seemed like a sprawling metropolis for he had only known life in a small village and this was the first time he had been away from his family. But he was a resilient and resourceful man and was not the type to succumb to pressure easily when things were tough. He spent the first week with his brother-in-law Bernard and his family, but they lived in a small house with their four children so that was far from ideal for any of them. Nonetheless they were very accommodating and made Jacques feel welcome.

'It's not been easy finding somewhere to live Bernard,' confessed Jacques. 'I had hoped to be out of your hair within a day or two.'

Bernard was a short, barrel-chested man in his early forties. He had a round weather-beaten face with close set eyes and chestnut brown bushy eyebrows. Almost every day he wore a dark blue smock and covered his balding head with a Breton beret, clothing that had become the archetypal apparel of Brittany's working classes from the 1920s. He had a large bulbous nose and always wore a wide smile, the sign of a man content and at ease with himself. The family had a small holding that provided food for all seasons and sufficient to provide a small income, selling at the local market.

'No need to fret,' replied Bernard in a very supportive and unperturbed manner. 'You're right it isn't easy just now. It seems as though all of Paris is heading our way.'

'Look,' he continued, 'I'll trawl the streets with you tomorrow and we'll see what we can find. If we have no luck you must stay on here with us; we'll manage.'

So early the next morning they set off for the centre of town. They popped into endless cafés, bars and tobacconists asking if anyone knew of any lets in the neighbourhood. There were few leads to follow up.

'Have you tried the mission?' said one. 'What about the hostels on Rue de Brest or maybe the tenements in the area around Rue de la Corderie close to the cathedral?' But Jacques did not want to take a room in an apartment block or a hostel and of course the mission was completely out of the question — he needed somewhere for his family. They tried the Mairie to see if people had left adverts there for rooms to let and they even asked stall-holders and shoppers at the market, but again without any luck. By mid afternoon, tired and dejected, Jacques contemplated abandoning his plan and returning to Villars to take pot luck that he would be able to avoid the call-up.

'Wait a minute,' said Bernard excitedly. 'We might find somewhere down by the railway yarding. There are old houses there — I've seen them from the train. Some are derelict and awaiting demolition but there are others that may be suitable. Let's take a look Jacques.'

So they made their way across town, over the river and into an uninspiring somewhat banal part of town alongside the railway. It was not long before they found a vacant property: an old building owned by an elderly couple. It was a substantial property but it backed right onto the mainline railway embankment. It had just one floor, though there were a couple of dormer windows in the roof. There was no land to speak of and the little there was had been overgrown with brambles, ivy and an abundance of the most pervasive and rampant of all weeds — bindweed. The place looked uncared for.

The lane outside the property was no better. It was not the typical verdant, tree-lined, well maintained gravel track Jacques was used to in the village back home. Here in Rennes the road was just a vacuous, barren thoroughfare whose sole purpose was to transport people from place to place. It was devoid of a soul and without any productive vegetation, just a profuseness of obnoxious weeds. Country lanes and village pathways on the other hand were organic: they helped to give a settlement personality. In Préporché at almost any time of the day people would be out on the lane chatting to their neighbours, listening to the birds singing or perhaps strolling aimlessly along it while watching the world go by. Not here in this wasteland.

The house itself had been poorly maintained and was hemmed in by other buildings of similar architectural style either side of it. There were tiles missing from the roof, the window above the door was broken and the wooden window frames seemed rotten.

They were told the old couple occupied one part of the house and in the other some rooms had been let to a family from Paris. Jacques was being offered the remaining rooms. There was a snag however — there was no toilet. The elderly couple did not want to share their only toilet with their tenants, but they did draw Jacques's attention to the toilet just a short distance down the road that, apparently, had been the only facility for all the houses in the district when they were built, probably nigh on a hundred years earlier. Jacques decided to take a look at the toilet facility before checking out the house.

'This is one hell of a shit-hole Jacques. I'm not sure Rosine will like this one bit! The stench! God almighty — it's unbearable. There's virtually no privacy, a rickety door that doesn't shut properly let alone lock, and flimsy partitions to separate the cubicles. It's no better than a cesspit; in fact it is a cesspit! You'll be needing a pretty good piss-pot under the bed Jacques, if you're going to live here!'

'Christ almighty Bernard. I didn't imagine it would be so difficult finding somewhere reasonable to live. I didn't expect to find my ideal home but this is dreadful. And there's no sink, not even a tap. And from the vile smell I can't imagine the gong-farmer's called for many a year. In fact he'd be wise to steer well clear — this pit of shit should carry a government health warning! But I'm not sure I have any choice. If I don't take this place I might as well give up and go back to the Morvan.'

Bernard agreed. Jacques was running out of options and he still had not found employment. For the time being he was living from some of the savings from shoe repairs, his ballroom business and the sale of wine, but they would not last much longer. He had left most of the small sum of money he had back home, for Rosine and the girls.

'Let's have a look inside the house, aye?'

The elderly lady let them in and left them for a few minutes to look around.

'No wonder this place hasn't been taken — its damp, poxy and poky,' exclaimed Jacques angrily. 'But I guess beggars can't be choosers, so it'll have to do. The girls will have to sleep in there. It's small, but the rickety old bed will do for two of them and we'll make a bed on the floor for the other, I guess. Rosine and I will sleep in here.'

He was standing on an uneven floor of broken flagstones in a square shaped room that doubled up as a kitchen and living room. As he looked around he tried to imagine what it would be like by the time he cleaned it up and gave the place a lick of paint. There was an old grubby cast iron wood burning range on one wall and a floor to ceiling wooden double-doored cupboard fixed to another. The walls were white-washed though no longer white; they were besmeared evidently with the grime of decades, and grease spattered the wall above the range. On an adjoining wall was the denotative sign that the room had been badly ventilated because it was covered in black mould from continual exposure to condensation and humidity, probably from drying wet clothes there in the long winter months he envisaged. In the middle of the room was an oak wooden table and a couple of chairs; he would find a couple of others he thought. There was a large ceramic sink in the corner with a single brass tap; they would have to boil water on the range. Water was dripping from the tap and presumably had done so for some time because at the bottom of the ceramic sink a brown stain had formed where the ceramic glaze had been worn away. He knew he would be able to build a simple wooden work surface alongside the sink and build shelves above it but there were no pots and pans or utensils, so he would have to get some at the hardware shop he had seen near Bernard's place. Yes, it would do. He would make it their home.

Even though Bernard said nothing his expression told Jacques he too was unimpressed, but he knew Jacques would have to take it; very clearly he was not the only 'escapee' who had moved to Brittany, the region furthest from the advancing German army.

It turned out that the house was a traditional bauge constructed building. Bauge constructions had earth walls built with a mix of water, clay and plants, not unlike the substance used in wattle and daub medieval buildings, though without the retaining wattle, and this one was no exception. The lower metre or so of the walls were built of stone but the rest had no framework at all bar simple wooden surrounds to enclose the door and windows, and the rest consisted of layer upon layer of clay stuffed with straw, plant husks and dried grasses. The Rennes basin was almost entirely of clay so as the city grew after the railways came, homes were built hurriedly and on the cheap from what was available locally.

Having agreed the rent, Jacques's next task was to find work. Fortunately this proved less arduous and through contacts of Bernard's he was offered manual work in the city's arsenal. This was ideal he thought because while he was working for the military, and therefore doing his bit for the war effort, he believed he would be left alone by the army recruitment officers. And so he was and for several weeks.

But with the Battle for France well under way, in the spring of 1940 life for the French was becoming onerous and gruelling. Over the next few weeks Jacques did what he could to make his stay as comfortable as possible and prepare for his family's arrival. He took to breeding rabbits for a reliable supply of meat, he grew what vegetables he could in the tiny garden and ate a bizarre range of unusual foods including rhubarb leaves (until the authorities warned they contained oxalic acid that could prove harmful) and chicory (though this was more normally ground down and used as a coffee substitute). Wild plants were 'cultivated' for salads and some, like nettles, were cooked to replace green vegetables like cabbage. Root vegetables such as carrots and potatoes were generally more plentiful, especially carrots which ended up being used in exceptionally creative ways including in cake. Unless people had their own goat or cow (Jacques had obviously left his back in the Morvan) it was nigh on impossible to get fresh milk, though powdered milk was available in abundance. Two things that were not rationed at all were wine and tobacco and these were even made available to children.

*

In the spring of 1940 Rosine and the girls travelled to Rennes to join Jacques. She asked a neighbour to look after the livestock while they were away which he did happily because it meant a daily supply of fresh eggs and milk. Jacques had written home a couple of times and warned Rosine things were far from ideal but she had said nothing to the girls. They were finding the thought of moving difficult enough as it was so she did not want to make things worse for them. Their journey proved to be long and arduous. They had to carry heavy bags and drag a trunk wherever they went. In the absence of a bus service from their village to Moulins Engilbert, they had to walk the four or five kilometres to get the bus to Nevers. From there they caught the train to Paris-Gare de Lyon, with a trek across the city to the Gare du Nord to catch the train to Rennes.

By the spring of 1940 the Wehrmacht were goose-stepping their way through north eastern France at an alarming rate. Parisians were leaving the city in ever increasing numbers as they had seen the writing on the wall and as the supply of food and provisions in general was becoming scarce. Paris was emptying, shops were closing and streets were becoming deserted. There were long queues at the Gare du Nord railway station and the trains were crowded beyond capacity, evacuating as many civilians as possible. The platforms were teeming with people and there were signs of distress as some were forced to leave items of luggage behind as they fought their way onto the crowded trains. The journey out of Paris to Rennes was particularly onerous, with entire families jostling for position and in a state of taciturn anxiety. Along the corridor a frail and dishevelled old man was standing hunched over his walking sticks wheezing sonorously. His hands were shaking violently causing the sticks to rattle on the boarded floor. There were crying children despairingly tugging at their mothers' coat tails whilst complaining of being tired, hungry or cold, and a hysterical woman was frantically pushing her way through the mêlée of people, calling aloud for her child before being alerted by a passenger to a young girl on the platform, hammering on the window just as the train was pulling away. The woman, with two other young children clinging on to her, screamed to her stranded daughter that she should stay where she was.

'I'll get off at the next station and return for you Emily,' she shouted, but it was unlikely the little girl heard what she was saying for she was by then out of view as the train picked up speed. Though the woman was comforted by fellow passengers there was little they could say or do to reassure her.

The journey was tediously slow because the train stopped at every station, with more people pushing their way on until it left the Parisian skyline far from view. Having to stand in carriages and along corridors with hundreds of other people the girls grew very tired and fretful, and Rosine was at her wits end trying to keep them in reasonable spirits and all together: the last thing she wanted was for them to become separated in the crowds. A feeble and ailing elderly woman was struggling to stand and yet nobody gave up their seats for her. But in truth almost every person occupying a seat appeared to be needy: heavily pregnant women, women with tiny babies in their arms and men and women who were very clearly unwell as their coughing and spluttering testified. One child was crying inconsolably as his mother chastised him for the puddle that appeared at his feet; there were no toilets on the train and people were loath to get off when it pulled into a station, mindful that they may not get on the next one. After several hours the train stopped at Rennes station. People alighted and shuffled their way along the platform to the exit.

Jacques was waiting for them. The girls were excited to meet up with their father again after such a long time away from him and pestered him for news. What was the house like? Did they each have their own bedroom? What school would they be going to? Was there a garden to play in? And was there a cinema in Rennes and a market near the house and cafés nearby? They were excited about meeting new friends for they had assumed a bigger settlement meant more friends. Rosine was less optimistic about the prospects for their new life and Jacques was decidedly pessimistic, knowing what he did about his new residential district. But he said little to dampen his daughters' enthusiasm and after a warm and loving embrace he walked the four of them to his abode. When they saw the house the children were still quite excited, but they did not know then that they had only a couple of small rooms in the house for the five of them. There was no garden to call their own, no cow to milk, no hens for fresh eggs, no sweet-smelling meadows to run across, no fast flowing brook to stroll by, no bluebell woods to play in, and a new school to get used to. Oh! And there was that foul dung heap of a toilet to look forward to.

CHAPTER THREE

Suspicion is not less an enemy to virtue than to happiness; he that is already corrupt is naturally suspicious, and he that becomes suspicious will quickly be corrupt.
— *Joseph Addison*

The Maginot Line had replaced the crude trenches in which so much of the 1914-18 war had been fought. It consisted of a series of elaborate fortifications which were confidently expected to protect France's frontier with Germany. However, given the rough terrain and dense forests of the Ardennes along the border with Belgium, it was believed that area was impenetrable and so the line was not extended along the Franco-Belgian frontier. But the French were still in the past, militarily. They had not comprehended the likelihood that a new war would be different from the slow-advancing attritional fighting of World War One. They had simply not modernised and were stuck in a time-warp. In fact Germany's plan was very different from what the French had envisaged; and so their blitzkrieg (lightning war) techniques caught them completely off-guard.

Hence the French authorities became very twitchy by the spring of 1940. By then the German army had occupied Belgium and were penetrating the apparently impenetrable Ardennes. Accordingly, the French hastily took action and accelerated mobilisation of troops in the area.

So Jacques was about to lose his battle to remain inconspicuous after all, and be forced to move away from his family to serve in the French army, leaving Rosine and the children to cope alone again, and just days after their reunion in Rennes. With the rapid advance of the German army thousands of civilians fled before it. They travelled away from the Franco-Belgian border in cars, carts, bicycles or simply on foot, grabbing what few possessions they could salvage. The roads became impassable, which slowed the advancing French army. The effort to halt the invading German army was already a lost cause anyway — a case of far too little far too late — and with a minimum of resistance, after just six weeks at the battlefront, by early May 1940 they had little choice but to begin a humiliating retreat, with some joining the British on their way to Dunkirk. This led to towns in the North like Abbeville, Amiens, Cambrai, Arras, and scores of others all but destroyed, except for their churches and cathedrals, seemingly. The loss of life at the hands of the Nazis rivalled the great slaughter of Verdun in World War One. The sudden capitulation of the army was an ignominious blow for the French, leading to surrender in June 1940 when Maréchal Philippe Pétain called on his fellow countrymen to comply fully with his signing of an armistice in Compiègne. Significantly, Hitler chose this location because it was the very one where Germany had been forced to surrender and sign an armistice to end World War One.

*

There was a surprising number of people in France who saw the *Fall of France* as an unmixed blessing. One such person was the openly fascist writer and editor of the extreme right-wing paper *Je Suis Partout*, Robert Brasillach, who stated that Germany's victory and subsequent occupation of France washed away the Third Republic that he had notoriously denounced as:

An old syphilitic whore, stinking of patchouli and yeast infection.

He had further claimed, as a consequence of the defeat, France would cleanse itself of corruption — especially, as he saw it, the Jewish predisposition[3].

He had fought in the *Battle for France* and at the fall was amongst almost two million French soldiers to be captured and imprisoned in Germany. However, unlike the vast majority of those two million, he was released after only a few months. His critics, and certainly the prosecution at his trial in 1945, argued he had been released because he was pro-German and had written prolifically about fascism while imprisoned in Germany.

He was tried immediately after the liberation of his country for advocating collaborationism, denunciation of the Resistance and incitement to murder, including of French communists and members of the Resistance. He was found guilty and condemned to death, a sentence that caused uproar along the literary corridors of France, and even amongst some of his greatest critics, because they argued he had been made a scapegoat. Brasillach was effectively executed for his opinions rather than military or political actions. And the prosecuting lawyer Marcel Reboul, somewhat ironically given Brasillach's writings that appealed to Frenchmen's suspicion of Jews, played on the likelihood of the jurors' aversion of homosexuals, by making much of his alleged sexual orientation at his trial.

His writings may have been fervently critical of the Third Republic, and even of high ranking military officers, blaming them for the *Fall of France*, but as xenophobic, vulgar and obnoxious as he may have been, many argued that his 'crimes' paled into insignificance compared with the likes of René Bousquet and Maurice Papon, who allegedly had sent thousands of Jews to the gas chambers. Despite a petition for clemency signed by many high profile writers and intellectuals including Albert Camus, Charles de Gaulle refused and so Brasillach was duly executed by firing squad on 6 February 1945, prompting Richard Corliss[4] to argue that he was the only writer of distinction to be killed for what he wrote, turning him into a martyr for the rabid right and a hero to politicians like Jean-Marie Le Pen.

There is a parallel here with the January 2015 attack by two islamic gunmen on the satirical magazine *Charlie Hebdo* in Paris. The weekly magazine represents extreme political opinion, but unlike Brasillach's theirs is from the Left. The magazine is vehemently critical of the extreme-right, and being openly secular and atheist it publishes regular cartoons mocking religion. As we have seen Brasillach too was fervidly critical, but for him it was of the Third Republic and the Resistance. After the attacks on *Charlie Hebdo* the phrase *Je suis Charlie* (I am Charlie) was adopted ubiquitously by supporters of free speech and freedom of expression. So, in 2015 Frenchmen throughout France (and people generally across the globe) gave their universal and unshaken support for *Charlie Hebdo's* writers' and cartoonists' right to express their opinions, with the French government even providing one million euros to support the magazine. And yet in 1945 Brasillach was executed by firing squad having been found guilty of expressing his extreme views. Is this hypocritical or is it just that times have changed, and some lessons have been learnt? Of course, Brasillach chose to criticise The Third Republic and side with the far-Right at a time when France was under occupation by the Nazis, which would not have endeared him to French freedom-fighters for certain.

Twelve *Charlie Hebdo* employees were murdered by the two gunmen, so those who staged a protest in support of the actions of those who lost their lives had every right to condemn the terrorist act that led to their slaughter. However, it is perhaps worth considering that if the satirical magazine's editors are at liberty to be openly critical of far-right political parties or irreverent of religious views and derisive of their deities, then Brasillach should, perhaps, have been free to express his views, however extreme they may have been.

He may have incited hostility towards France's Third Republic and the Resistance amongst his newspaper's readers, but it could be argued *Charlie Hebdo's* editors do little to promote religious and cultural harmony amongst its readers. Is it not a matter of opinion as to whether Brasillach's extreme political views and open criticism of those he thought to be corrupt and ineffective were any more unacceptable than *Charlie Hebdo's* assault on the prophet Muhammad? With freedom of speech comes responsibility; and if *Charlie Hebdo* is allowed to publish extreme views under the auspices of freedom of speech, albeit it satirically, then perhaps this may also be said for everyone else, Brasillach included.

*

Unlike Brasillach many did manage to evade capture. The chaos and commotion in the immediate aftermath of the surrender meant that some escaped and went into hiding. Jacques was one such soldier. Having laid low for a few weeks, eventually he made his way back to Rennes to be reunited with his family. However, he was aware that the German occupiers were continuing to round up French soldiers, sending them to prisoner-of-war camps in Germany as a means of reducing the size of the French army and, for some, to work in labour camps, factories and on farms as replacement for German nationals who had been sent to the western and eastern fronts. Jacques was determined he would not be one of these deportees but he found it immensely difficult avoiding detection while there in Rennes, at the address by then known to the authorities. Accordingly, he decided it would be best to return to the Morvan, but this time they would all make the journey together by road. He was relieved that he had made the decision to sell up in Préporché and move their family home to Villars because he felt it would help him to remain undetected and so avoid recapture.

The Duvals were on their way back in September 1940 in Jacques's 1931 Citroën van, originally bought to transport his itinerant ballroom from village to village. The back of the van was full to capacity with their belongings amidst which sat the three girls, while Rosine occupied the seat alongside her husband at the front. On numerous occasions the girls had to bang on the window to alert their father that something had fallen from the roof, where Jacques had piled an iron bedstead, mattresses, blankets and an array of living creatures from rabbits to hens, as well as crates of root vegetables. Leaving Rennes was not a moment too soon for Rosine and the girls who had loathed their stay there. The journey was long and onerous because they chose to travel on small roads and country lanes, and wherever possible entirely off-road, to ensure check points could be avoided, for Jacques knew his status as a soldier, albeit by then an inactive one, might prove to be his undoing.

Once back in Villars the girls were happy to return to their school and rejoiced in the knowledge they were back home as a family again. Life returned to the way it had been some years before but with some exceptions. Though Rosine had taken great trouble to store under lock and key their most prized possessions, during their protracted absence the house had been looted. The vegetable plot was overrun with weeds and those vegetables that had not been pilfered had gone to seed. The casks of wine had been emptied and the saddest thing for Jacques was that the portable ballroom he had built so exquisitely had been badly damaged and bits were missing. The wood must have proven useful to the Maquis for the construction of hideaways in the cellars of remote farmsteads or for shoring up underground ammunition and explosives stores.

He still had his shoe-making skills to fall back on but he knew he needed to establish a fresh customer base in his new surroundings. He was also aware he needed to restock his wine cellar before he could generate any income from it. He wanted to rebuild his itinerant ballroom but with playing music and dancing in public places forbidden by the occupying Germans, he knew he would have to do so surreptitiously, although there were very few occasions when soldiers visited his tiny village and so felt he was unlikely to be found out. Had he been discovered almost certainly he would have been deported for contravening the imposed restrictions. He was already a hunted man, having managed to avoid capture after the *Fall of France*, and ignoring the regulations about dancing and music would have been the final nail in the coffin.

*

With a largely non-aggressive occupation from Hitler's army, with German soldiers well-disciplined and mostly respectful, and under Hitler's direct orders to set up food depots and soup kitchens to feed the French people, their presence was very quickly tolerated by most people, even if it was partly as a result of Nazi propaganda. Some even decided that the only sensible thing to do was to become allies with the Nazis, believing that very soon they would unite Europe under their domination anyway.

So unlike in the towns and cities, in rural areas like the Morvan, in the main people did not feel the oppressive presence of the German army. The soldiers were billeted in the nearby towns like Chateau-Chinon, Saint-Honoré and Moulins Engilbert and visited the villages only very occasionally. And when they did the children in the villages sometimes played tricks on them, like the youngsters who furtively crawled under the café tables where soldiers were having a cup of coffee or glass of wine to tie their shoe laces together.

On one occasion a particularly dextrous youngster sought out a fresh-faced soldier and surreptitiously undid his gun-belt while he was sitting at a table in a crowded café so that when he got up it dropped to the floor. Surprised and somewhat flummoxed the soldier quickly grabbed it and re-buckled it hoping that nobody had noticed, whilst looking around the room accusingly at all and sundry. Of course all and sundry were entirely aware but pretended they were not by carrying on as if nothing had happened.

In another village there was a similar incident but this time as the young soldier stooped to pick up his gun-belt someone shuffled his chair and caught the soldier's fingers, with the others mocking ironically, 'Ooo, that must have been very painful.' Grimacing, the soldier made another effort to recover his belongings but as he did so an 'actor' got up from his chair as if about to leave and with some considerable skill hooked his chair leg over the gun-belt so the soldier could not retrieve it without further embarrassment. Others, in on the act, scurried around the floor as if trying to assist the poor soldier, whilst all the time hindering him by surreptitiously pushing it into a mêlée of legs or 'accidentally' spilling a glass of wine on it or arranging for a chair leg to flick the gun belt across the floor the very moment the soldier was about to pick it up. The disconcerting thing for the soldier, by then frustrated and isolated in the middle of the café, was that almost everyone totally ignored what was happening while they drank their wine and continued their conversations without batting an eyelid.

And yet another example of deriding the occupiers was when in the dead of night a couple of youngsters loosened the wheels on a soldier's bicycle he had unwittingly left outside. When the soldier got on his bike the next morning the wheels came off and inevitably he fell to the ground. And for maximum effect the two boys had arranged a congregation of the town's youngsters to be in the vicinity to witness the prank.

Most of these practical jokes were taken with good humour; the perpetrators of these incidents had learnt who amongst the soldiers was game for a laugh or, as in the case of the gun-belt incident, naive and gullible. Inevitably though, there were some practical jokes that irked the soldiers and led to sanctions to inconvenience the locals in the villages, such as when their drinks were laced with laxatives or when soldiers were harmed.

For the soldiers of course, being stationed in such rural areas was unquestionably blissful, compared with being in some of the war zones where they could have found themselves. These soldiers were conscripted; they were not Himmler's brutal Schutzstaffel (SS). The locals and their overseers tended to exist side by side in relative harmony and with a mutual respect in rural areas like this, as is evident from an incident that occurred in the Duval's own village of Villars, but this time late in the war when German soldiers were trying desperately to make a hasty exit from the advancing allied forces. Fast forward to the 1980s. A large Mercedes pulled up outside a certain house in the village. It is obvious to any onlookers that this could not be a local person's car. The owner of the vehicle had done his homework and knew exactly who was living in that house. A knock on the door brought the visitor in contact with the householder, a man in his sixties. The stranger of similar age introduced himself.

'My name is Hans. I was stationed here during the war and in my haste to get away I am ashamed to say I stole your bike. I am now making up for my very bad behaviour and ask for your forgiveness.' With that he returned to his car and took out of the boot a brand new top of the range bike and gave it to him as if on bended knee. The two families have been friends ever since and visit each other in their homes, the one is an executive for a large global corporation in Stuttgart, Germany, and the other an ouvrier from Chateau-Chinon.

This story, and untold others of similar ilk, illustrates that for many in the more isolated rural areas of France, life under occupation was not brutal, tyrannical and merciless but in the main mutually respectful, albeit notably for the one group being all powerful whilst the other being under their watchful eye. The average soldier just did his job and it was in his interests to try to understand the feelings of the local indigenous people and try to get along with them. And as far as the locals were concerned, especially in the early years of occupation, they were less concerned about the political shenanigans being played out in Berlin, London and Paris and more about their day-to-day survival. Most just wanted to get on with their lives as best they could. But as will be seen, such symbiotic mutualism was decidedly not how everyone saw the relationship between overseer and overseen.

*

During the Occupation there was only one official newspaper in circulation in France and that was published in Vichy under the watchful eye of Maréchal Pétain, the collaborator who arguably kept southern France 'free' from German intervention. Needless to say the paper was full of anti-British, anti-communist and anti-semitic propaganda. Using this publication care had been taken to praise and please the French people, demonstrating how similar the cultures of France and Germany were. 'Collaboration' was the regular theme and French businesses, banks, nightclubs and cafés were praised and admired as were French musicians, authors, artists, poets, playwrights, artisans and actors. This was all designed to show that French cultural life was buoyant under the Occupation. In some ways this ensured the French felt appreciated and valued and thus kept the masses from resisting. But as a matter of fact it also meant that French artists and intellectuals, unless they were Jewish, more often than not escaped persecution and lived to tell their tale. This was not the case in Poland, nor in Germany where potential activists had been hunted down well before the Wehrmacht were on the march.

In the countryside and small provincial towns there were some who undoubtedly benefitted from the presence of the German army, after all German soldiers needed accommodation, food, refreshment and entertainment as did the indigenous French, and so landlords, butchers, bakers and café owners gained in economic ways from the arrivals. And of course the supply was not merely to a slightly larger market as garrisons were set up in the rural towns, but also to the big cities; after all urban areas demanded and rural areas supplied. So it was inevitable that French citizens going about their 'normal' daily lives were accused of collaboration as the suppliers of produce and services. But it seemed that collaboration meant different things to different people; for some it was a matter of 'live and let live' but for others most certainly it was not.

Supplying Germans with goods and services did not come without its risks. It was a dangerous business and some saw this as a betrayal whilst others thought it just a matter of survival. In part, it depended upon whether you had the opportunity to prosper or not, but undoubtedly it was not as simple as that. It depended on the extent to which trading and supplying services was seen as black marketeering. The critical question asked was did this black marketeering make those who profited from it, collaborators? Given it was the occupying force that created the situation where profiteering was rife, led some to argue emphatically that yes it did, and of course all the more so when the sale of food and services rendered were directed at German soldiers.

There were those from the cities who actually organised 'trains des pommes de terre' and 'trains des haricots' to go to the farming districts to obtain the food direct and so avoid the 'middle man' and therefore pay less than they would have done in the urban outlets. In the sense that the suppliers profiteered from this led some to argue they were effectively collaborating with the enemy. It is a known fact of occupation that those who went hungry saved their anger for those who ate well — that is those who could not profit from the black market, or indeed chose not to, took it out on those who could and did. There was simmering distrust and suspicion throughout the entire duration of the Occupation and not infrequently it led to outbursts of violence.

Whilst there was a good deal of acceptance that the black market was necessary in order to avoid abject poverty and hunger, it was a matter of degree. There was a fine line between making a little more to survive and taking advantage of one's nation and countrymen. But hypocrisy was rife. Apparently a sizeable number would turn a blind eye to the black market goings on between French farmer and German soldier but when it came to French kitchen maid fraternising with the very same soldier, she was widely judged severely and with no attempt at understanding. There was very definitely a reluctance to recognise the similarities between close economic relations and 'collaboration horizontale'.

A further complication that heightened tension arose with the growth of the resistance movement, the most prominent of all such groups being the Maquis, that by its very nature was more widespread in rural areas and particularly so in the Morvan of Burgundy. Its relative isolation — no major trunk roads pass through the region — made it the ideal refuge for those fleeing the repression of occupied France and yet who wanted to continue the struggle for freedom. The deep wooded valleys of the Morvan countryside provided the best possible hiding places near to hamlets or remote self-sufficient farms, where information and food were easy to find.

The men and women of the Maquis were fighting a guerrilla war against the German invaders whilst living amongst those who were judged — fairly or not — to be profiteering from them. The marked rise in numbers going underground and joining the Maquis may well have been attributed to the introduction of Service du Travail Obligatoire (STO) that was first introduced by the Vichy government in September 1942 to 'encourage' able-bodied men and women to work in Germany for two years on farms, in factories and labour camps to replace those German nationals who had been sent to the western and eastern fronts. But with too few recruitments, in February 1943 the Nazis introduced a directive forcing all young men born in 1920, 1921 and 1922 to be deported to Germany.

So, not all joined the Resistance fully committed: for many it was used as a means of avoiding being sent to Germany. However, perhaps surprisingly, there were non-resistance citizens who were attracted by the offer to go to Germany believing that life there in factories and on farms was preferable to the unrelenting austerity that had become a characteristic of life in occupied France.

CHAPTER FOUR

There is no despair so absolute as that which comes with the first moments of our first great sorrow, when we have not yet known what it is to have suffered and be healed, to have despaired and have recovered hope.
— *George Eliot*

Despite having settled back into life in Villars much as it had been in the past, and with Jacques, Rosine and the girls — Emeline, Marie and Colette — as happy as they had ever been, something happened that shattered their lives and changed how they viewed things for ever. It was an unusually cold autumnal day in late October 1940. The day had started much as the day before and almost every day since they had returned from Rennes.

As was so often the case on days when the girls returned home for lunch, Marie rushed back before her sisters to give her mother a helping hand preparing the midday meal. On this particular day she left her sisters to saunter back home by way of the lane, and instead she scurried down the hill, across the meadow to the tiny brook and hence into the forest where she knew that however cold the weather, she would find wood blewits amongst the leaf litter. She thought they would make a tasty addition to whatever it was her mother was preparing for their meal.

Having collected as many mushrooms as she could carry, she

skipped up the gentle slope from the stream and broke into a run across the farmer's field, taking great care not to trample on the crop of kale, and then onto the grassland, still damp from the partial thawing of the early morning frost. After squeezing through the hedgerow she stepped between the vegetable beds and made her way to the door via her father's workshop. She was beaming because not only had she come with a basket full of mushrooms but her two sisters were still nowhere to be seen. To nine year old Marie it was much like any other school day only it was not! Taking this route she approached the house from the back and was unaware her parents had visitors. But as she approached the house she heard a disturbance from within and on opening the door she was taken aback at the sight of her mother shedding tears and tugging frantically at a man dressed in the idiosyncratic uniform of a German officer, pleading with him to let her husband go.

'Don't struggle, I tell you,' he said forcefully. 'No harm will come to you if you do as I say. If you persist in screaming at me and tugging at me you will get hurt and so will your husband.'

'Please, I beg you, don't take him away. He has three daughters and they need him so. Please, I beg you to leave. Here take this food.' She had already begun their lunch and there was bread, cheese, potatoes, carrots and fresh milk. She continued, 'And there's more out in the garden. You can help yourselves to eggs and take the hens too, and the rabbits. They'll make a good supper. But please I beg you don't take my husband.'

But each time she pleaded she was brushed aside by the petulant man. Marie was shocked and panic stricken, but instinctively she ran towards her mother, dropping the basket of mushrooms as she did, and cried out, 'Maman, Maman, what are they doing? Where are they taking Papa?'

One of the soldier's plain-clothed accomplices, a tall thin man with a long pointed nose and piercing blue eyes, intervened and seized her by her arm, and so forcefully she was swung around, banging her head on the edge of the door. She screamed

in order to prise open the oak lid but the steel tool was not long enough to get sufficient leverage. Again she took to scrabbling around in the ditch for rocks and after several seconds — by which time the cask, with Jacques still hunched up inside, had sunk even deeper into the mud, and the two men had gained so much ground she was by then able to identify them from their uniforms as border guards — she found a sufficiently heavy and sturdy rock to assist her.

Without a moment's delay she took the rock in both hands, lifted it above her head, and with all her might brought it crashing down onto the jemmy, splintering the wood and opening a size-able gap, sufficient for her to remove the jemmy and turn it head to toe so she could use the hooked end to slot into the hole and lift the lid, but before she could complete the task water flowed through the hole in the top of the cask, causing Jacques to choke as he took a hit from the muddy water.

Helga was very aware time was at a premium because not only was water gushing into the cask occupied by a terror-stricken Jacques, but the two men were getting ever closer. It took her several attempts but finally the lid came away and there before her was a manifestly relieved, if not rather bruised, shaken and decid-edly wet Jacques, staring out at her. She whispered to him that two border guards were very close by. He quickly unfurled his crum-pled body and eased his way out of his confined abode into the cold air, and without a moment's delay Jacques and Helga made their way hurriedly to the cover of pine trees a short distance from the roadside. They dropped to the ground where they lay motionless, watching nervously as the two border guards came within twenty metres or so. But the two men sauntered past the battered cask seemingly unaware it was there, just a few centime-tres below the surface of the water.

So they had not noticed the kerfuffle after all and had been unaware what had been unfolding within their sight line. They must have been so engrossed in conversation that they were oblivious to the fact that seconds earlier an escapee prisoner-of-war had emerged from a wooden cask and taken to the cover of the trees with his accomplice. The two unobservant men had even passed the cart a few minutes earlier and had either not noticed the carthorse chomping merrily amidst a veritable sea of vegetables, or had noticed but not thought of it as rather odd, and therefore worthy of investigation. Jacques and Helga remained as still as the night well after the two men, still engrossed in deep conversation, had disappeared out of sight. They could not believe their good fortune.

With considerable difficulty Jacques stretched out his limbs and straightened his back and after a brief confab they decided to make their way on foot to the border post, which meant a considerable detour. Helga was aware that given his weakened state their decision would be tough for Jacques, but she knew they had little choice. They had to get away from the sunken cask and to the border post as quickly as possible but undetected. Taking to the road in their present state would mean almost certain detection and so a trek through the forest was necessary. Helga decided she would take a chance and leave the horse and cart on the side of the road.

When within a couple of hundred metres from the border, Helga grasped Jacques by the arm and stopped him in his track. At that moment, whether simply out of a sense of utter relief or because he had an irresistible impulse to be close to Helga, quite out of the blue Jacques did something unexpected and seemingly out of character. He took Helga in his arms and kissed her ruby lips. He held on to her as if his very life depended upon it. She did not repel him but instead, the moment he withdrew a little, unashamedly she pulled him back towards her and reciprocated with a kiss that surely meant far more than her parting gesture. With that she bid Jacques farewell and turned around to head back to her horse and cart. Jacques called out to her but she did not turn back, but instead quickened her pace until she was running as fast as she could, darting between the trees with her blonde hair flowing down her back as she did so.

Jacques stood motionless looking towards Helga. He took a moment to collect his thoughts, shut his eyes tightly, clasped his hands together and drew them up to his face as if in prayer. Had he really just kissed the young Helga who, barely out of her teens, had risked everything to set him on his way to freedom? He had immeasurable respect for Helga; she was a formidable and remarkable young woman: brave to the point of foolhardiness and yet resolved to sacrifice her own well-being for the sake of those who had come under the cosh of her country's fascist rulers. He opened his eyes and she was gone from his view. A brief encounter certainly, but nevertheless one he knew would never be erased from his memory.

He waited until he had caught his breath, was sufficiently upright to be able to stride with an air of confidence up to the border crossing, and dry enough not to prompt suspicious questioning from the guards. His false papers showed he was a German national. He knew enough German from his time in the prisoner-of-war camp and on the farm to get by, or so he hoped. By the time he reached the border the sun was at its zenith in the brightening sky and he found himself in a queue of a couple of dozen people. He felt relieved by this; had he been the only one crossing the border, which would have been very likely had all gone according to plan and he had arrived at the border in the small hours, the guards may well have scrutinised his papers rather more fully. When it was his turn the border guard looked at him fixedly for what seemed an eternity, as if studying every detail of his face, before glancing down at his papers. He said nothing. He looked up and then he spoke. This was what Jacques had feared. He really did not want to get into a dialogue with a German guard but he held his nerve long enough to appear confident and at ease.

'Rather you than me Heir Keller. From what I hear things are pretty chaotic and food and beer are in very short supply. I bid you farewell.' He ushered Jacques through the check point and on his way, but not before remarking, jovially, that by the state of his

50

clothing he looked as though he had been dragged backwards through a hedge and into a quagmire.

Jacques chuckled amiably and walked away from the border control post without looking round, taking great care not to rush unduly. He could not believe his luck. He was on home soil, albeit it soil that was under the control of the occupying Germans. He was on his way to his village in the Morvan, where he would be reunited with his wife and daughters. His heart was pounding but he was excited and relieved that all had gone so well, bar the unfortunate incident of the runaway cask. He thought about Helga and how phenomenal she had been. She had taken enormous risk to help him escape and yet had asked for nothing in return.

Over the next week he crossed the southern edge of the Vosges taking refuge where he could and very slowly he made his way back towards his home across open countryside, clambering up rugged terrain one moment and striding with great purpose down steep hillsides the next. Despite taking great care to avoid towns and villages lest he be spotted, to his utter dismay, on the seventeenth day, he was recaptured while on a farm just outside Germigny, near La Guerche-sur-l'Aubois, in fact just sixty kilometres or so from his home in Villars — so near, so far! He had been spotted in the barn's hay loft by one of the farmhands who, without hesitation, alerted the authorities. Jacques was sent back to Germany and incarcerated in a prisoner-of-war camp, where he remained until his final release in October 1943. It is ironic that he escaped from the farm in Germany with very considerable help from a German national and yet he was turned in by one of his own.

*

So was the Duvals' good news about Jacques's eventual homecoming shared by all in their tiny close-knit community? It was apparent from what we now understand about the early repatriations that French soldiers imprisoned in Germany were generally treated with a mixture of suspicion and disdain by French civilians on their return to their communities. Many civilians believed they had only been allowed to return in exchange for agreeing to collaborate, though this was probably not the case, at least for the majority. It is certainly the case, however, that Vichy propaganda had implied that prisoners had lived in good conditions leading many to believe that the prisoners in Germany had suffered much less than civilians back home in France. And as veterans of the 1940 *Fall of France*, the prisoners were blamed for the French defeat and portrayed as cowards who had surrendered, rather than fight to the death. And of course Jacques had even tried to avoid the call-up by going to Rennes, something that would not have been well received by the more patriotic in his community. They were also unfavourably compared with other men of their generation who had served in the Free French Forces (the Resistance). And during Jacques's absence the Maquis had flourished in the Morvan, so this view may well have been more prominent there than almost anywhere else in occupied France. Notwithstanding this was the fact that by February 1943 the German authorities had changed the 'voluntary' arrangement of Service du Travail Obligatoire into a forced recruitment because too few had gone to Germany under the voluntary scheme. To appease the Vichy government the German government had agreed to release one French soldier imprisoned or working in German labour camps, factories or on farms for every three people sent to them via the scheme. Though he would not have necessarily been aware of it this may have been the reason for Jacques's release. Those seemingly in the know may well have been incensed to learn that Jacques may have gained his freedom at the expense of three French citizen deportees.

So could all of this have been permeating through Villars, and might members of their community, and those from nearby Moulins-Engilbert and its surrounding villages, have been venting their spleen on the Duvals, either consciously or subconsciously? If so it would not be the joyous homecoming that both Jacques and his family would have been hoping for.

It was Friday 15 October 1943. Rosine and the girls were on tenterhooks waiting for him to return. It had not been possible to contact him following the news that he was homeward bound so they did not know precisely what hour he would be home. They just had to wait. Rosine was apprehensive because she did not know what state he would be in. To minimise the worry she busied herself around the house and made a stew as a welcome-home gesture for him. Fresh meat was not easy to come by during the war, so on this very special occasion Rosine succumbed to obtaining a brace of pheasants from hunters operating illegally within the black market.

With 300,000 German troops in the country food for the French was in short supply. The government had organised food carts and tickets could be exchanged for bread, butter, meat and cooking oil and so from the day she heard Jacques was coming home the four of them had eaten little in order to save the tickets to purchase additional treats for him.

In general, throughout France there were endemic food shortages and thus malnutrition amongst the poor, the young and elderly was common. This had arisen partly from the decision to make the Reichsmark legal tender alongside the Franc, but the Reichsmark had been valued at a very favourable twenty francs so German soldiers were able to buy their food far more cheaply than the French, leading to significant shortages for them. In order to survive people had to use ingenuity and eating guinea pigs as well as pigeons found in the public parks, was not uncommon. Some even took to using cat meat in stews, even though there had been warnings that it may not be safe to eat. From 1941 people in the country had been allowed to send 'colis familiaux', or family parcels, to their city-dwelling relatives. However, many of these parcels arrived filled with maggots, or were rotten, or had been boiled in vinegar to help preserve the meat. But beggars couldn't be choosers so they had to eat what they received to survive the difficult times.

Like Rosine, the girls too were unsure what to expect from their estranged father on his return home. They had not wanted to go to school that day, hoping to see him sooner than later, but their mother had insisted. Rosine was at the open door waiting for his return, popping indoors occasionally to check the stew, to straighten her dress or to tidy things, not that any of these were necessary; it was more a cathartic response than one of necessity. She was at the door when she noticed a man making his way up the lane. It was not until he got quite close to the house that she realised it was Jacques, for he was so thin and looked cadaverous and bedraggled; she was shocked to see he was a former shadow of himself. He had lost weight and though he had always been lantern-jawed he had been handsome and upstanding; now he walked with a slight limp and looked forlorn. Nonetheless, the two greeted each other lovingly and they went into the house and sat down to catch up with news.

'The neighbours have been a bit offhand Jacques, and some of the vegetables have been stolen, goodness knows by whom, but of course always at night whilst we sleep. Oh, and fewer and fewer people are buying wine. And Jacques, I cannot remember a time when there were more German soldiers around here than at present. We had a particularly dry summer so the water level in the well has sunk and the grass in the meadow was so parched it did not yield enough for bedding in the coop. The girls are generally well and they have really missed you; they are so looking forward to seeing you again Jacques. Marie has been an absolute treasure — she helps me whenever she can and has remained so positive during these dark times. But Emeline — well, I despair at times. I love her dearly but she's been difficult these past few months and, well, quite honestly, she's done very little to help out — perhaps you'd have a word with her Jacques'.

Rosine just kept on and on and in all this time Jacques said nothing. He listened, holding her trembling hand tightly whilst he did, but said nothing. And then Rosine went on again, but this time at least her tête-à-tête was focused on Jacques.

'Oh Jacques, my darling husband, I have missed you so. And here I am blathering on and I've not even asked about you. The years have been so difficult without you Jacques. I'm so pleased you are now back here in our home so that I can look after you.'

Then out of nowhere Rosine burst into tears, weeping quite uncontrollably. Jacques tried to find the words to pacify her but found none. As the artisan that he was he may have been inventive, imaginative and innovative, traits Rosine had always admired and that had kept them financially solvent when all about them were sinking into the mire, but demonstrative he was not; words did not come at all easily to him. Had there been onlookers at that very moment as they sat there together in their scullery, they would have seen a somewhat broody idiosyncratic man, lost in deep thought and struggling to do the right thing for the woman he loved. He was transfixed as he looked deep into her tired eyes that were swollen and reddened by the tears. He saw a sorrowful, pitiful, melancholic expression that masked his pretty wife's quotidian cheerfulness and resilience, and this troubled him. As that split second of thought passed he took her in his arms and held her close in the most reassuring of ways; and for Rosine that embrace spoke more than a thousand words. And that is how they stayed until the girls arrived home, wrapped in each others' arms and sobbing acquiescently until the tension slowly faded away.

As for Rosine's initial tirade this can only be explained as a nervous reaction to the situation she faced. Subconsciously at least, she was loath to ask Jacques outright how he was because she had seen with her own eyes how liverish and haggard he looked, and so long as she was stealing the limelight she had felt, he might not lament and become overwrought and hysterical. She wanted to protect him.

Not surprisingly all three girls rushed home from school that afternoon and ran up to their father, throwing their arms around him and squeezing him so hard he thought they would crush his ribs. The hours that followed were difficult. Jacques did not want to talk and Rosine and the girls did not know what to say or do to make him feel happier and secure.

In fact it proved to be an immensely difficult time for many weeks to come. Jacques found it gruelling settling back into 'normal' life and his family were finding it difficult helping him to regain his drive and enthusiasm. But happily, with the loving care and understanding of his dear wife, over the ensuing weeks Jacques slowly took hold of his life and even began to build a new ballroom, even though a decree forbidding song and dance in public places was still firmly in place.

The days passed slowly. During most of them Jacques collected eggs from the chicken coop, milked the cow and spent some time at the vegetable garden while Rosine held the fort back at home. It was a long time before he was able to continue his work as a cobbler and shoe maker. He invariably took a stroll early in the morning into the woodlands of the Bois de Raie to collect ceps for breakfast. Sometimes he waited until later and took a longer walk just before dusk through the Bois de Raie, across the river and into Bois des Sauvés and hence to the lake, Etang du Loup. There he never ceased to be mesmerised by bats darting across the darkening sky or thunderstruck by peregrine falcons taking sparrows in mid flight. When at the edge of the wood at late dusk sometimes he saw a long-eared owl flying just a few metres above the ground with its head canted to one side listening for prey. On one occasion he saw an owl pounce, pinning its prey to the ground with its powerful talons. When out there alone in the countryside all his fears and the frightful memories of the past months evaporated and left him at peace with himself.

Sometimes he took a shorter stroll down to L'Aron where along the river banks invariably he saw the flash of colour of a kingfisher or caught sight of a dipper at work. During these walks he saw an ever changing landscape: the kaleidoscope of reds, oranges and yellows of autumn and trees stripped naked in winter, bar the interlocking ice crystals of hoar frost. As the winter set in the tree clad hills beyond the village cast their long menacing shadows. There was invariably a fine mist in the valleys at that time of the year, and as he made his way up the gently sloping bank from the flood plain and onto the grassy lane at the back of his house, his breath formed a small cloud as it condensed in the cooling air and his sabots became wet from the dew that was forming on the grassy slope. He normally saw smoke stacks from the neighbouring cottages and was conscious of just how eerily quiet it was, except for the occasional slamming of wooden shutters as families boarded up for the night. He often made his way up to the meadow leading to his house and looked back at the woodland, but quite unaware that he had taken much the same route to his house that his daughter Marie had taken that horrendous day over three years earlier when he had been captured and deported to Germany.

Jacques was a self-respecting and dignified man who loved his family dearly. He was slowly re-stocking his wine and though difficult to acquire the leather, he was once again making shoes. He had built up his businesses from nothing, gaining from the influx of clientele who needed their shoes repaired or wanted new ones, or who bought wine from him. He and some of his band of musicians had re-formed and were once again providing good entertainment for people who loved to dance as a means of escaping from their fraught lives. But given the ban on dancing and music in public places he had to be careful to arrange such events either on private premises or, very occasionally, in the village squares for those members of the community who were prepared to take the risk that they would not be visited by German soldiers. Could it be there were those from the village, or in yonder settlements he had visited, who had resented his 'illegal' earnings, in spite of the fact he had provided people with one of the few means of escapism from the harsh and hostile times they were in?

He often reflected on these thoughts but more often than not dispelled them, confident he was doing the right thing for himself, his family and the local community. But he was becoming more and more uneasy with the passage of time, because he became increasingly aware that his neighbours were indifferent to

had all but accused Jacques of collaborating with the enemy, with some highly suspicious of the reasons why he had been released from the prisoner-of-war camp in Germany. Further, many had observed him visiting the local Kommandantur on a regular basis, which led them to wonder if he was working in collusion with them. As a matter of fact he had no choice but to visit the office regularly because it was a condition of his release from the prisoner-of-war camp. Additionally, there were other people who were decidedly jealous of a man whose entrepreneurial skills had enabled him and his family to lead reasonable lives under occupation. When hatred spreads it produces 'proof' that feeds it. Suspicious feelings spread quickly in the small village, and Jacques was in no time at all treated as an outcast. In fact five men at a wine-fuelled meeting intent on 'sorting him out' after liberation, found jumped-up evidence and denounced him to the Comité in Moulins-Engilbert, who dutifully carried out an investigation. Much to the disgust of the five men the Comité found no evidence whatsoever to confirm the terrible accusations of collaboration.

Only a few days after their report in October 1944, and less than a month after liberation of the Morvan, Jacques awoke to shouting but disoriented and still half asleep he had not heard the words being shouted nor did he realise from whence they came. Mistakenly he assumed it was one of the girls having woken from a nightmare, so he left his bed and went to his daughters' room along the corridor, leaving Rosine asleep in their bed. But in a flash he realised the noise was not from his daughters' room after all but from outside the house. Instantly he made his way back to confront whoever it was that was shouting so angrily, but before he was near the room there was an almighty explosion. He was thrown backwards by the force of the blast and was aware splinters of wood and stone were hurtling through the air; he dodged some but was hit by others. He was dazed and stumbled as he fought to gain a foothold. His earlier desire for confrontation had turned in a second to one of desperation as he made his way back through the rubble and dust filled air to his beloved wife. He called out to her but there was no response. He called again, this time louder, but still nothing. By then his daughters had made their way through the fallen masonry to his side. They were numb with fright.

Jacques called again as he tore his way through the wreckage but yet again there was no response. He created a way through and as the dust began to settle he saw across the room the bed upon which he could make out Rosine. He was then face to face with her and barely a metre away. Her eyes were staring into his and her mouth was locked in a fixed position.

She uttered a few words but spoke so quietly Jacques had to strain to hear. 'Oh Jacques, I cannot move. What in God's name has happened? My arm, my arm.'

Jacques moved even closer to her. He could see she was cut on her face but what made him wince and momentarily turn away was the sight of her right arm — it had been all but severed high up on the upper arm. The humerus appeared shattered and the arm itself attached to the shoulder by little more than strands of tendons and some skin. It was hanging loose and blood was spurting out of the wound with extraordinary pressure. Jacques shouted for some towels and rags. Marie was the first to react and quickly brought them to him. He tried desperately to mop up the blood but so bad was the wound he could not stop the flow. He sent his eldest daughter to go for help. She ran out of the house and banged on doors as she went from house to house.

'Please, someone help us. My mother is badly injured and is losing a lot of blood. Please someone help us,' she screamed.

No neighbours came rushing out of their homes; the place was unnaturally still and nobody was to be seen, and whoever committed this abominable deed had certainly fled. Were these people out? She thought not because it was very late. Were they fast asleep? This was not possible either she thought, because the explosion had been sufficient to wake the dead, and she was screaming at the top of her voice. She remembered that Monsieur

Lestrange had a car so she sped down the lane, around the corner and along to the big house near the wood. She called out loudly to him and banged on his door. He appeared at his bedroom window.

'What the hell are you doing young lady? It's the middle of the night. Be away with you and let us sleep,' he retorted.

'But Monsieur Lestrange, kind sir, we desperately need your help. My mother is in a very bad way and I plead for your help. Please, please Monsieur Lestrange, you have a car and will be able to get help quickly.'

'It's well after eleven good heavens. Let the good people of Villars sleep.' And with that he closed the shutters with an ominous bang.

In disbelieve Emeline became transfixed for what must have seemed quite a few seconds. She did not know what else to do so she turned on her heel and ran back to the house to tell her father that nobody would help. The only doctor was in Moulins-Engilbert five kilometres away and they were running out of time. They had no bicycle or car and of course no telephone, and so were at the mercy of others nearby. But nobody, not one person, came to their assistance in their time of need.

In the few minutes Emeline was out of the house Jacques fought for his wife's life. He was running out of towels and could not see how he could stop the bleeding. Blood was still gushing from the wound. Then in the twinkling of an eye he had an idea. As difficult as it was to administer, all the more so because it would have caused Rosine such intense pain, he wrapped a cloth around what was left of her arm on the heart side of the wound and tied it tightly, with the hope it would stem the flow of blood. She grimaced but did not have the strength to cry out. Jacques dropped down next to her, sobbing and praying she would survive.

Marie was crouched on the floor just outside her parents' room with her younger sister nearby. She buried her head in her lap and was sobbing, though barely audibly; she was in shock.

Emeline was standing next to her. They knew their mother was in a desperate state and that their father was distraught and beside himself with fear. Jacques turned and looked back at his daughters but was unable to move to their assistance. He offered no fatherly words of comfort and did not react to their desperate need for loving reassurance, but they saw his quivering lower lip, his tears streaming down his face and his blood-stained shirt and breeches.

He increased the pressure on her wound with his hand. 'Rosine, my darling, I love you. Please, please don't leave us. We need you so much.' And then sobbing, he asked for her forgiveness. He suddenly felt pangs of guilt, believing she would not be lying there dying had he not insisted they move out of their bedroom. He did that to give the girls respite following his frequent fits and nightmares that had kept the girls awake in the next door room after his return from Germany. He should have been more resilient and less pathetic he believed.

She tried to speak but struggled to do so. Jacques could just about make out her whimpering. 'I'll miss you Jacques. I love you. Tell the girls I love them and look after them.'

He knew she was slipping away from him but he kept reassuring her that all would be well and he begged her to hang in. The bleeding will stop soon he kept saying. Though he did not know precisely what was happening he feared the worst.

In the minutes since the explosion Rosine's body mechanisms went into overdrive: her blood pressure dropped like a stone as blood drained from her body. But because Jacques applied as much pressure as he could with a tourniquet it gave a chance for the blood to begin to clot as the artery went into spasm. However, with a near amputation of the upper arm such as had happened, the brachial artery had completely severed, and without sufficient skin left intact there was not the slightest possibility of creating a haematoma with sufficient pressure to completely stem the flow. Bandaging the arm only slowed the inevitable. What was needed was specialist help but none was forth-

CHAPTER SIX

The venom clamours of a jealous woman poisons more deadly than a mad dog's tooth.
— *William Shakespeare*

Date: October 1944, less than a month after liberation of the Morvan.
Time: Around 11pm.
Place: Somewhere in Villars.
Ambiance: Dark moonless night. Calm still air.
Persons present: Two boys, one sixteen and the other seventeen years of age, dressed in dark dungarees with Basque berets pulled down low. Nobody else to be seen.
Action: Strolling through the village, both deep in conversation.

'Well, are we going to do it?' said one.

'Perhaps, but maybe not tonight,' said the other.

'C'mon, let's do it now; they've had it coming to them for ages. You know what Brigitte says about them.'

And with that they made their way stealthily and purposefully to a very particular stone cottage near the far edge of the village.

'Where's best do you think?'

'Don't know. Through that window perhaps, or why not on

the roof or maybe over there in the outhouse? Yeah, that would be enough to scare them.'

'Look, if we're going to do it then it has to be in the house. Let's frighten the living daylights out of them, eh? What about above the door, through the fanlight window? It will land in the scullery.'

And with that the older boy shouted at the top of his voice, 'You smarmy, pompous, greedy bastards; siding up alongside the bleeding Nazis one minute and what do you know you're looking all toffed up and dapper the next. Mighty suspicious if you ask me. Yeah, who the hell do you think you are?' He removed the pin from a grenade, and while shouting, 'Take this you conniving, collaborating schemers,' he launched it through the fanlight above the door. They waited a couple of seconds and sure enough it detonated. They jumped up and down with glee and with particularly smug expressions on their faces.

But a moment later they became aware that something had not gone quite to plan. There was a lot of screaming, which would not have been surprising, but there was also a lot of crying and frantic crashing about and then a girl ran out of the house and tore down the lane yelling and banging on doors. They were in the shadows so they were sure she had not seen them. This startled them and without exchanging words they shot off across the fields, through the hedgerow, up the hill and into the woods. They spent the next couple of days lying low.

On the third day they came out of hiding and put their ear to the ground. They learnt through the usual village gossip trail that the woman had died in the grenade attack.

They knocked on Brigitte's door.

'What the fuck have you done you sodding idiots?'

'It's no good you screaming at us, you're the one who told us to do it. You're the one who was insanely jealous of them, with their oh so comfortable lives.'

'Fuck you Eric, all I said was frighten them. I didn't tell you to fucking blow up the bed and kill them, you brainless imbeciles.'

'But we didn't throw it into the room where they slept. We're not that stupid.'

'So how do you account for the fact that she was killed then, smart ass?'

'I don't know, do I? They must have slept in a different room that night I suppose.'

'Yeah, Eric's right,' said Michel. 'We threw the grenade into the window above the door. That meant it would have exploded in the scullery and away from where they should have been sleeping. The grenade must have ricocheted off something I suppose and ended up detonating in the room where they were sleeping that night — bad luck I'd say.' Of course Jacques and Rosine had been sleeping in the scullery for some weeks, but Eric and Michel would not have been aware of that.

'Anyway,' persisted Michel, 'from what I heard he was enjoying himself down on the farm for month after month while we were fighting the bleeding Nazis wasn't he? On his return from Germany he could have joined the Resistance to help eradicate those fascists once and for all? But he was too busy making money seems to me. Instead of helping the cause he preferred to have a jolly good time with German soldiers did he not? Maybe he deserved what he got. And in any case why was he released? Perhaps he promised them a case of wine or two or a new pair of shoes?'

'You're right, they did make money while we all struggled to make ends meet. And he was such a bloody show-off, boasting about his earnings from his ballroom and wine racket one minute and telling everybody his fucking cow yielded more milk than any other, the next. You should have lobbed the grenade at that bleeding cow instead of them; that would have shut him up. I wanted you to frighten them, not blow them up!'

'Look Brigitte,' retorted Eric, 'nobody will know who did it, and I bet we're not the only ones to be irritated by their wheeling and dealing. They'll never trace it back to us and if they do we'll tell them they were collaborators, won't we Brigitte?'

'This better not get back to me that's all I can say. It's OK for you two — I'm sure the Maquis will protect you. But what about me? What a mess!'

*

As a matter of fact the Duvals were not making much money at all. Though Jacques made a reasonable living before the Occupation he had struggled during and immediately after it. He had been in Germany for almost three years without any income for his family and on his return he struggled to pick up where he had left off. Life was tough, very tough. However, he was more enterprising than many and found ways to survive when others did not; others in the village were jealous of him and his family, and Brigitte was one such person.

Brigitte was perceived by her community as a seductress and coquette though some were convinced she was nothing less than a strumpet. She lived alone in a small stone cottage on the edge of the forest, not far from the river. A full-bosomed woman of ample proportions with a mildly pockmarked face, well into her thirties, she had never married, but she did not deny that over the years there had been many lovers, and more than one at the same time as often as not. She did not have regular work and the gossip about her was always about how she made money to live on. It was probable that she was a schemer and black marketeer but she was canny and did not make a song and dance of it.

She was vulgar and with a reputation in the surrounding villages for befriending youngsters and leading them astray. On many occasions she was seen in bars and cafés drinking with teenagers late into the night. In fact Rosine had been sure it was she who had left a death-threat note under their door, so she warned her that if there was another she would go to the police. Rosine told her daughters not to associate with 'that obnoxious obscene woman' who 'corrupted young people'. Marie and Colette were accordingly very wary of her and obeyed their mother, but Emeline was more rebellious and latched on to her, if only to

73

spite her mother. Brigitte resented Madame Duval's inflammatory remarks and told her so in no uncertain terms.

She boasted she had contacts with the Maquis, though this was probably greatly exaggerated. It was more likely that she merely got chummy with some of the young men who claimed to be maquisards, some of whom went to her place for a drink, with invariably a little carnal entertainment included!

Eric and Michel were two boys she met in this way some weeks earlier and it was not long before she had them eating out of the palm of her hand so to speak. They told her they were communists and wanted to join the Maquis after the Germans attacked Russia, but had been told they were too young. They were idealists, members of the proletariat who despised capitalist minded people they had said. They also told her they had enormous admiration for the resistance fighters whom they saw as winners, conquering heroes, knights in shining armour; in fact their chevaliers. The boys had not realised that many maquisards had only joined the Resistance to 'go into hiding' in order to avoid the Service du Travail Obligatoire and were therefore far from heroes.

It was clear to Brigitte that as hot-headed young teenagers who glamorised the work of the Maquis she could use them for her own ends. So she groomed them, feeding them with tale after tale of heroism, patriotism and chivalry, always making sure to portray maquisards as custodians of the French Third Republic — envoys of the people that were constantly tracking down traitors, collaborators and cowards and making them pay.

So Brigitte had her boys under her control, and it was not long before they were sent on her mission to seriously scare the Duvals. She certainly achieved that, but in ways that not even this irksome, grossly unpleasant and profane woman would have wished for.

*

Though initially boastful about wanting to bring the Duvals down a peg or two, the tragic death of Madame Duval tormented Brigitte so much she was on the verge of delirium and racked with pangs of guilt. She shut herself away in her two-room hovel for days after her plan to scare the Duvals had gone disastrously wrong, emerging only to acquire the necessities for survival. She did not entertain men in her home, she did not gossip in the village and she was not seen in bars and cafés in the surrounding villages. She stayed in her own little world, suffering — as well she might — as a consequence of her dreadful deed. It did not matter that it was the boys who had thrown the grenade — she had made them do it. They were just boys wanting to show her they could act decisively, like men. They trusted Brigitte's judgement but they had been influenced by an irrationally jealous woman and went a step too far. Her insane jealousy and extreme envy for a family who had fought for nothing other than their own survival under extremely challenging circumstances, led to a terrible tragedy and now entirely of her own doing she was entering a hell-hole of eternal damnation and perdition, from which she would never emerge.

Though Brigitte appeared to others as assertive and phlegmatic, in reality she was not: she was a sufferer of chronic depression, prone to anxiety, with low self-esteem and a complete lack of confidence. In truth there was nothing more she would have wished for than for a family to love and be loved by, but because she never had a loving, supportive and indulgent family to call her own, she had not seen why other people should either, but now she regretted her actions greatly and so wished she could turn the clock back.

Of course, this was not an isolated case because all over occupied France there were countless examples of extreme jealousy and hundreds of instances where people took punitive action, having made judgements based on pure conjecture and unjustified suspicion. They may have thought they were righting a wrong but as often as not they had no evidence to back their views.

CHAPTER SEVEN

Oh, I am very weary, Though tears no longer flow; My eyes are tired of weeping, My heart is sick of woe.
— *Anne Bronte*

The morning after the tragedy Jacques sent his eldest daughter to Moulins-Engilbert to summon the undertaker and the body was taken from the house within a few hours. The next few months were to prove very difficult indeed for the four of them.

Some of the neighbours did rally round: flowers were left at Jacques's door, though they withered and died before being noticed by him or the girls. And a frail elderly neighbour had returned the kindness Jacques had shown when her husband had died suddenly in his sleep a couple of weeks earlier, by popping in on them daily to check on the girls and bring some food for them all. But for three complete days after the killing Jacques hardly spoke to his daughters. He did not know what to say to them to make things better. He had no comforting words to share, no words of wisdom to impart and no pronouncement that would reassure them that the future would bring happier times.

As he sat for hour after hour alone in the room, beside the bed where he had laid out his dead wife, he was being tormented by evil daemons: his failed effort to avoid the draft; his capture and forced relocation in Germany with the lengthy separation from his wife and children; his failed attempt to escape; the struggle to put food on the table on his return; the increasing loneliness and alienation he felt as contacts with his friends and neighbours diminished; and now the loss of his dear wife he had idolised and the terrible feelings of guilt that swamped him — all constantly churned around in his mind, taking him into a comatosed state from which he struggled to break free. How would he have the strength to survive now that she was no more? She had been a tower of strength to him. She had been the one to rally round when life's challenges got too much and it was she who always cooked for them, washed for them and looked after them when they had felt unwell. And now she was dead. It seemed there was no vessel big enough to keep Jacques from drowning in his own sea of self pity. And when on the odd occasion he did emerge from his stupefied self deprecating state, he was remorseful and guilt-ridden. But even during these instants of consciousness he did not, perhaps could not, go to his daughters in their time of need, something he later bitterly regretted and that haunted him for years to follow.

All three girls were struggling to cope. But, at just thirteen years of age, Marie had, ostensibly, an extraordinarily mature level of positivity and sensitivity that suggested to onlookers she was able to empathise with the suffering of others, even while she was stricken with grief herself. So it was she who comforted her younger sister and wiped the tears from her eyes, it was she who put food on the table and it was she who summoned the Priest, having looked in on her father periodically and been very concerned about his well being.

The girls had one bed between the three of them in those appalling, terrifying days after the loss of their mother, for their father was occupying their room while caught in his time warp; it had been to that room Jacques had carried his deceased wife. The girls used the room their parents had more usually slept in, in fact the room that doubled up as the sitting room. They either huddled together on the bed or took it in turns, with one of the girls curling up on the floor with a blanket for warmth and comfort. Of course, the bed their parents had used had been destroyed in the explosion. But they did not sleep much anyway and neither did they eat more than a few morsels, and they certainly had no recollection whatsoever of their father eating anything. They were beginning to look unkept, the house was still full of dust and debris, not that they had dared to venture into the scullery where the explosion had happened. They had not washed in three days and were still in the nightclothes they were in when the explosion occurred. They were a sorrowful sight.

Under similar circumstances today social workers would be on call to help them in their hour of need, and psychiatrists and counsellors as well as trauma and bereavement therapists available for support, but at that time there were no such services on hand and, where normally the community would rally round, this did not happen in this much transformed village. People, seemingly, had been too wrapped up in their own lives to make an effort for others, and yet how alien this is from what we know about other 'war-torn' communities, whether in London during the blitz, the response of the emergency services following 9/11 or the widespread solidarity shown after the *Charlie Hebdo* massacre in January 2015. But the difference is that in villages like Préporché and Villars during the early 1940s, people were under the heavy arm of an oppressor.

A Priest's often spoken wedding plea — *that which God hath joined together let no man put asunder* — also a deeply held affirmation between neighbours in the close-knit communities of rural France, was overlooked under occupation, and brother turned against brother and neighbour against neighbour. The Occupation had altered people's psyche causing them to behave in ways that in normal circumstances would be entirely alien to them. It made friends and neighbours suspicious of each other, and the very values that had made them the compassionate, benevolent and solicitous people they truly were, had been suppressed. That which had always been taken for granted — solidarity and fraternity — man had put asunder!

'Do you know Sylvie, according to François, that man over there is a collaborator. By the way, did you see him the other day talking with a stranger? I don't care what you say I'm sure he's wheeling and dealing on the black market, don't you think so Sylvie?'

'Now look Michel, I'm certain that slutty whore Carole is having it off with that bleeding German. And did you see that woman yesterday siding up to that Nazi bastard. She looked old enough to be his mother! It wouldn't surprise me one bit if she was up to no good with him — and while her husband is locked up in a labour camp in Germany too!'

'Have you ever wondered why it is that Henri always looks so well turned out? What's he up to? How is it he seems to have money to burn while the rest of us are living like paupers? It's that café he owns. If it were me I'd not let any German soldiers in under any circumstances. Why should we have to sit at tables an arm's length away from them?'

'Did you see that woman driven away in a military vehicle the other day, and she was heavily pregnant too. Did you notice that Giselle? I bet it's his?'

Of course there are alternative interpretations of what these people thought they had seen during the Occupation. For example, the 'stranger' could conceivably have been François's brother arriving from Paris for a few days respite. Carole may have been fraternising with a soldier true enough, but it doesn't make her a whore. Perhaps she was falling in love with the man. And just because a woman whose husband is away in Germany is seen with a soldier, it doesn't mean she must be sleeping with him. Perhaps she asked that young man — who might have reminded her of her own dear son whom she may have lost in the *Battle of France* four years previously — how he was coping away from home and whether he was missing his loved ones. And was it true Henri always looked smart? Or could it just have been that he did on the occasions when that woman saw him. She may have seen him when she visited the market every Wednesday, the very day Henri dressed as smartly as he could as a sign of respect when visiting the grave of his mother. And if he did have a café could he really have refused the German soldiers entry to his premises? And perhaps the soldier that helped the pregnant woman into his vehicle was rushing her to the infirmary for a check-up, having seen her wincing and clutching her belly just moments before — German soldiers were capable of acts of kindness!

But in their precarious situation these paysans had come to fear everything and be suspicious of everyone. And for some, the irony is that they may not have hesitated for one moment before informing on a neighbour whom they believed to be a collaborator, despite every likelihood they may have collaborated themselves — albeit it in petty ways — and perhaps even, just the day before. Or maybe they were envious of another's good fortune and did not want them to be living the life of Riley — or so they perceived — when they had to survive on next to nothing. And yet had they the resourcefulness and entrepreneurial skill to do the self same thing, to make life more bearable for their families, the chances are they would have done so. But who is anyone to judge these people? None of us really know how we would act in similar circumstances, despite knowing how we might feel about such shameful deeds. How we feel about something and the way we behave are two separate things. Circumstances can alter appreciably the way we react, even though at some later time we may look back with deep sorrow and considerable remorse because of the way we reacted at the time.

*

Meanwhile Jacques and his three daughters had to endure their considerable trauma almost completely alone. On the fourth day after the killing Jacques did emerge from his self inflicted solitary confinement, and he did take his daughters in his arms, weeping with them and trying to reassure them. He told them their mother was being watched over and that she was watching over them. He told them they would have to be very brave and would have to be there for each other. He told them they must return to school soon, though not before the funeral. He explained that times would be far from easy.

'Will there be lily of the valley and nightingales in heaven Papa?' Marie asked her father.

'Well, if there are my darling Marie, Maman will most certainly find them. Perhaps you should go and find some yourself and put them in her coffin at her funeral; she would love that. And as for the nightingale, he will find her sooner or later and then he will sing his beautiful song, to comfort her.'

These were just about the only words he spoke to his daughters over the next few days because he found it so very difficult to cope. The three girls observed him sitting in almost total silence and with a glazed expression on his face and no sign that he was about to comfort them.

The funeral took place on the fifth day after Rosine's death. The burial was at the cemetery just outside the village, a desolate place with almost no trees. There were many new grave stones in that cemetery telling the story of a country at war. The girls stood by the graveside motionless and speechless. Though they did not weep they looked forlorn and pitiful. Their father stood alongside them. The Priest spoke for an inordinate amount of time, quoting from the bible at length and almost all of the time in Latin, so nobody other than himself understood what he was saying. He finished with Psalm 23.

The Lord is my shepherd; I shall not want.
He maketh me to lie down in green pastures: he leadeth me beside the still waters.
He restoreth my soul: he leadeth me in the paths of righteousness for his name's sake.
Yea, though I walk through the valley of the shadow of death, I will

fear no evil: for thou art with me; thy rod and thy staff they comfort me.

Thou preparest a table before me in the presence of mine enemies: thou anointest my head with oil; my cup runneth over.

Surely goodness and mercy shall follow me all the days of my life: and I will dwell in the house of the Lord for ever.

But Jacques was overwhelmed by rancour. He gained no comfort from what he saw as hollow words. If the Lord was his guide and protector then why was he not meeting his needs? The Lord may have wanted him to feel at peace with himself and in a thoroughly good place, but he was not. He was desperate for someone to help him to be stronger, but he was decidedly weak and not able to cope at all well. And he most certainly was not on the path to righteousness for he still had nothing but resentment for the killer of his wife. He was also still in a very dark place and so very afraid. Nothing comforted him and nobody was there by his side when he most needed them; in fact he felt quite forsaken in his time of need. And given what had happened to his wife he simply could not imagine a time when he would relax while his enemies looked on for he knew he would want to confront them. He was also feeling far from blessed. He may have wanted to feel the love of a guiding hand but it did not exist; in fact he was quite alone in the world. And it was difficult imagining a time when he would want to share his life with the Lord, the one who had allowed such a wicked deed to happen. Jacques simply could not for one moment imagine how religion would help him face the future with optimism and hope.

Sadly, not even the suffering his daughters were experiencing helped Jacques to escape from his self loathing and self pity. He was trapped in a cocoon of torment from which seemingly there was no escape.

Jacques's brother-in-law and his family made it to the funeral all the way from Rennes, but Jacques was unable to put them up in his home because there was insufficient room. He had boarded up almost all of the scullery where Rosine had died, leaving it as it was after the bombing. He had no desire to go back in there and certainly did not want his daughters to do so. They were having to cook their food on a réchaud alcool on the floor in the living room and wash-up their utensils in a bucket. In any case the rest of the house was still an utter mess and he did not want them to assume he was not coping. Therefore, he arranged for them to stay the night at a pension in Moulins-Engilbert before having to make their way back to Rennes.

The little old lady who had been kind to the girls immediately after the tragedy was also there and she did go out of her way to speak to them.

'I am really so sorry about your loss my dears,' she said. 'If there is anything I can do to help you in your time of need then do feel you can count on me. I may be old but I am still able to cook and will do so for you if it will help. And I can be a comforting presence too if you want me to visit you of an evening.'

'Thank you Madame Perrot, we appreciate your kindness but I'm sure we shall manage,' said Jacques, before walking away.

There were a few there from the village, not that Jacques was aware — he certainly did not greet them or converse with them. But then they tended to stay well back from the Duvals, not wanting to intrude upon their grieving perhaps? Or was it because they were ashamed they had not come to his aid at the time of the explosion?

One particular bystander was dressed entirely in black. Not wanting to be noticed by anyone, she remained in the shadows of the gravediggers' hut perfectly still, so much so in fact that she appeared quite inanimate. So motionless was she that a teardrop forming on her lower eyelid remained in suspension, seemingly unable to dislodge itself onto her blemished cheek. The lady in black wore a despairing, disconsolate, mournful expression and in every sense of the word she was entirely alone.

Marie lingered for a short while and thanked their neighbour again. 'You are very kind Madame Perrot and we really did appreciate the food you brought us in the days following the death of our mother.'

Though genuinely wanting to thank her for her thoughtfulness there was another reason why Marie waited before joining her father and sisters, who were by then already making their way out of the cemetery. When everybody was out of sight she took from her shoulder bag an envelope and placed it on the coffin. Inside the envelope was a note she had written in her very best handwriting. It read:

> *I will never forget you Maman and will be thinking of you always, but especially on my birthdays, because by then — in May — all around you there will be lilies-of-the-valley popping their pretty little heads up above the ground to be reunited with their sweet-sounding nightingales. From your little flower, your loving daughter, Marie.*

With that Marie turned and left the grave to join her family.

The lady in black waited a few moments and then emerged from the shadows, and with leaden steps and heavy heart she approached the grave. She took something from beneath her shawl, and like Marie a few moments before her, placed it on Rosine's coffin. She made the sign of the cross, paused a moment — undoubtedly in mental recitation — and then slowly made her way back into the shadows. She was never to be seen in Villars or any of the other surrounding villages ever again.

*

Not terribly surprisingly, back at home life remained repressive and gruelling for them all. Emeline was her usual tiresome and difficult self, claiming she was too troubled to help around the house, and Colette was just about coping, though she relied heavily on Marie for support and needed her encouragement to get herself up in the mornings and ready for school. Marie was up with the lark every morning, preparing breakfast, washing their clothes and tidying the house as best she could before going off to school. She had been so glad she had watched and helped her mother with these chores, especially the cooking. She knew how to prepare a boeuf bourguignon, though sometimes she had to substitute the beef for rabbit, and could bake bread, not that she could do so for quite some time because the oven had been destroyed in the grenade attack. She had also learnt how to make the most of very little by substituting meat with root vegetables in stews for example. And of course the Duvals had their own vegetable plot, a cow, some hens and rabbits. Marie had also learnt how to forage in the woods, as her father had done when he was well. She picked ceps and wood or field blewits whenever she could and these became a popular food in their household, especially when added to an omelette. But whilst they were better off than many, times were still very tough for them. Queuing at the boulangerie for fresh bread could take an hour or more, but at least Marie had learnt to economise by cutting the bread into thin slices and using stale bread in soups, so she did not need to join the queues that often.

Jacques's thoughts kept drifting back to all that had happened since his incarceration in Germany and he could not leave his sense of guilt for the death of his wife behind him and in the past. He was often lost in a world of his own and like Emeline and Colette he tended to depend rather too much on Marie's apparent resilience and her good nature for his day to day existence. Jacques had taken to downing a few beers of an evening, but thankfully this never got out of hand. Perhaps he had known that using alcohol to drown one's sorrows did not work — for sorrow knows how to swim!

CHAPTER EIGHT

The dead cannot cry out for justice. It is a duty of the living to do so for them.
— *Lois McMaster Bujold*

What is of particularly grave concern is that the experience of liberation in provincial French towns and rural villages like those of the Morvan — Germany surrendered Paris on 25 August 1944 and the Morvan almost a month later — was not one of absolute joy, but moreover a period of violent retribution against petty collaborators and the intimidation of ordinary citizens, undertaken by forces of resistance who saw them as traitors to their cause for not getting involved in the fight against the occupying forces.

During the Nazi occupation, those who fought in the Resistance fell victim to bombings or endured extreme hardship, imprisonment, peremptory execution, or deportation to concentration camps such as Le Struthof in Alsace. The Nazis pursued the Resistance leaders relentlessly. In April 1944 they circulated 15,000 copies of the famous 'Red Poster' which bore the faces of ten of the 23 leaders they had assassinated in February that year.

Accordingly, some of the maquisards sought retribution after liberation, targeting families such as the Duvals, whom they suspected, rightly or not, of collaborating with the enemy. A large number of these purges were committed by boys not yet out of their teens, who had either not joined the Maquis at all or had done so very late in the day, and who wanted to cover up for their resulting subconscious guilt by singling out others they suspected of collaboration.

The enormous suffering by members of the Maquis, particularly near the end of the war, may well have reinforced the view amongst the more vociferous in the community to be openly critical of those who preferred to promote their own personal gain rather than align with, or even officially join, the resistance movement. Could this have been a further reason for their intolerance towards families like the Duvals?

So, as the Occupation came to an end, there were those from both within the Resistance as well as those from outside who suffered greatly. Those from within suffered as a result of direct German reprisals, whilst many of those outside of the Resistance were persecuted by fellow Frenchmen, and as often as not on fallacious charges.

As a matter of fact it was not at all easy living in an area where the Maquis was particularly active, as in the Morvan, even though the public perception of the organisation was one of admiration and reverence for what they aimed to do. The point is, whenever an act of sabotage by the Resistance occurred, the German army retaliated with a series of reprisals aimed to strike fear into the population and alter their opinion. They wanted local people to feel that their suffering was the direct consequence of the presence of the Maquis, and that it was best therefore not to tolerate them. For example, when Madame Lauro[5] poured hydrochloric acid and nitric acid on German food supplies in freight cars on the French railways, hundreds of railway workers were shot. However, this did not stop her from continuing her acts of sabotage, working alone and at night. She was never captured. Over the course of the occupation 30,000 French civilians were shot as hostages for acts of resistance. Was this a worthwhile sacrifice?

Corinne, a young woman working for the Resistance, lived in

a six square metre hole underground in the Morvan forests for several months. Nobody, other than a handful of prominent maquisards knew of the existence of this hideout but it was of immense importance to their work. It was Corinne who transmitted vital information about convoys and troop movements in the area and it was she who, on one particular moonlit night, guided a British air task force, charged with the responsibility of dropping supplies to the Maquis, to its target. The crew of the Stirling Bomber managed to navigate across a blacked out countryside at low altitude, zigzagging to avoid anti-aircraft fire, whilst relying entirely on the reflection of moonlight from rivers and lakes to guide them to their destination. The payload was successfully discharged, but on its return the aircraft was shot down with the loss of one member of its seven man crew. Three more were taken into hiding by the Maquis and the other three were captured by Germans and tortured by the Gestapo. Their fingers were crushed with a hammer, arms and legs broken by iron bars and teeth knocked out by wooden truncheons. Day after day, night after night they were dragged from their cells and hauled before their persecutors and punched, pummelled and bludgeoned, but as battered and bruised as they were their tormentors were unable to prise information from them as to the whereabouts of their drop.

As a direct consequence of this act of defiance there followed savage reprisals to discourage resistance. Graves can still be seen today in many cemeteries in and around the Morvan which mark the final resting places of men who were shot at the roadside. The now widely known village of Oradour-sur-Glane in the Limousin region, where 642 of its inhabitants, including women and children, were massacred by fire in the church at the hands of a Nazi Waffen-SS company, is an abhorrent example of Nazi retaliation used to discourage resistance.

This generated a wave of fury against the invaders by the general public but there was not a lot anyone could do, because any action was met with murderous reprisals. So for many — perhaps even Jacques — this was reason alone not to become a maquisard. Their acts of bravery, sabotaging German operations, may well have plagued and even subdued the occupying force but, as has been seen, at a significant cost to the passive French public.

And yet with all this suffering of ordinary French people, either at the hands of the Germans in retaliation for acts of sabotage committed by the Maquis, or by the maquisards themselves as reprisals for suspected collaboration, the inescapable truth is that there were some high ranking officials directly involved in major crimes against humanity who escaped with either minor sanctions or went unpunished altogether, as the cases of Bousquet, Touvier and Papon infamously demonstrate, as examined by Dr Simon Kitson[6].

René Bousquet was Secretary-General of the Police under the Vichy Government between April 1942 and December 1943, during which time almost eighty percent of the 75,721 Jews and communists were arrested by his police force, not by the Germans. Bousquet has therefore become the symbol of the Vichy government's involvement in the Nazis' plan for the extermination of the Jews. He was accused of organising the roundup of 13,000 Jews on 16 July 1942 and holding them in barbaric conditions at the Velodrome d'Hiver in Paris before they were deported. Many, including children, perished in the stadium from hunger, thirst and disease, no doubt due to the atrocious conditions in which they had been held, and of those who survived all but a handful perished in Germany.

However, as a result of a drop in the number of arrests, in the second half of 1943 Bousquet was removed from office and replaced by Joseph Darnand. Could it be that René Bousquet deliberately slowed the pace of the arrests because he had developed a conscience? Of course he may just have been failing in his duty to follow entirely orders received. Either way it is clear Bousquet was ordered by high command to carry out the arrest of Jews and it is conceivable he was put in a very difficult position. To have refused would have meant his own arrest. It may well be that decent citizens would refuse to carry out such an odious duty, but when placed in such a position sometimes people act in ways to save their own skin; perhaps Bousquet was one such person. And yet he may well have felt that by being at the helm and slowing the flow of deportees he would be saving some from the slaughter. He may well have thought too that, had he refused to do what he was commanded to do, there would be another to take his place who would be infinitely more ruthless, which is in fact exactly what happened. When questioned about his resolution to send children to the camps he justified his decision on the notion that children should not be separated from their mothers. In other words, given that mothers were being deported it followed from his idea of logic that their children should be deported too. Most would find his reasoning questionable given the loathsome outcome, but is it conceivable Bousquet did not know that the deportees were being sent to their death?

It is plausible that his removal from office was a factor that helped Bousquet during his trial in 1949. He was sentenced to just five years of Dégradation Nationale, a punishment involving merely the removal of one's civic rights, which seemed out of all proportion to what many saw as his complicity in crimes against humanity. What is more, soon after the court had issued this sentence it was suspended on the grounds he had supported the Resistance. Resistance fighters were heroes in post war France and it would appear that claiming Bousquet was sympathetic to the organisation was a trump card for those who worked to get him pardoned.

The one known fact linking him to the Resistance is that some time after he had been dismissed from office, Bousquet warned one Henri Queuille, a resistance fighter at the time, that he was about to be arrested. The fact that Queuille was prime minister of France at the time of Bousquet's initial arrest in 1949 may not have been just a coincidence in the rescinding of his sentence; and yet one might have imagined that with so many communists working within the Maquis, that his known anti-communist stance would hardly have endeared him to them. Clearly, this fact was ignored because it did not suit the argument made by Queuille that Bousquet was a supporter of the Resistance and was therefore hardly a conspirator against the State. The fact that his actions were anti-Semitic was almost entirely ignored at his trial. So Bousquet escaped significant punishment.

However, in the 1970s the lawyer Serge Klarsfeld demonstrated that Bousquet had not only worked alongside the Nazis in a policy to eradicate the Jews but that he had been responsible for the deportation of 194 young Jewish children. What he had uncovered led, after considerable procrastination, to Bousquet's re-arrest in 1991 but his second trial never took place. It was controversial anyway because it would have highlighted the fact that the original trials after liberation had largely failed to deal with the anti-Semitic accusations and would therefore be an embarrassment to the government, all the more so given Bousquet had become such a successful business man after the war. And additionally, some went further and argued that the government's apparent reluctance to bring this man to trial was partly due to his close friendship with the President, François Mitterrand. He was a regular guest at the Elysée Palace until the mid-1980s.

Notwithstanding all of this Klarsfeld's evidence was so strong it was decided he had to stand trial before a court of law. But before this occurred Bousquet was assassinated by Christian Didier, who shot him four times from close range on 8 June 1993. Though some have questioned on whose behalf Didier was acting, Kitson believed it seemed more likely he acted alone and that his actions were to gain publicity for the pro-trial activists, such as himself. Intriguingly, there are some still alive today who were convinced that someone in high office may well have taken out a contract on Bousquet. It has been stated that had he been put in the dock, further information may have come to light that would have incriminated others whose credentials for the status they held in society may then have become somewhat at risk. However, this notion is unproven and remains a matter of conjecture and, some would say, idle rumour and gossip.

There can be little doubt this high profile killing went part way to helping to bring other Vichy officials to trial, including Paul Touvier in 1994. He was a staunch Catholic Far-Right extremist and during the Occupation Touvier had been an active member of Vichy's black-shirted fascist militia (the Milice), first in Chambéry and then in Lyon. He had been convicted earlier in the 1940s and sentenced to death for crimes against humanity — in fact the first Frenchman to be convicted of such a crime — but he evaded captivity and then, with the apparent aid of the Catholic church, managed to persuade President Pompidou to pardon him. Following Touvier's pardon Pompidou pleaded for his compatriots 'to draw a veil over the past'.

Kitson argued that this pardon, and Pompidou's stance, led to a backlash against the long accepted Gaullist argument that France was a nation of resisters during the Occupation. Accordingly, Touvier was forced into hiding again and at the time of his final arrest in 1989 he was found taking refuge in the St François Catholic monastery that was run by the right-wing cleric Monsignor Marcel Lefebvre. But with the Government still wary of putting someone on trial who might question the norms and values of the State during WWII, it was decided that Touvier could only be found guilty if it was proved that he was a German agent and not a French one. There can be little doubt this policy was introduced to make it difficult to secure a guilty verdict, but in spite of this he was found guilty as charged, and sent to prison. However, he died just two years later in 1996.

Maurice Papon was an ardent supporter of Germany's anti-Semitic policy and in his role as technical organiser of the deportation of Jews he sent 1,560 to the death camps of Eastern Europe. But Papon's apparent wide support for the resistance movement was thought by many to be sufficient to get him off the hook and so he was not brought to trial. As previously argued, so revered was the Maquis that their support for such a man would have been taken very seriously. The fact that he did not deny that Jews were his 'bête noire' was apparently ignored by them.

In spite of Papon's war crimes accusations he still managed to hold the office of Prefect of Police in Paris from 1958 through to 1967. Kitson wrote that he was a brutal man, heavily criticised for his ruthless tactics that led to the massacre of Algerians in Paris on 17 October 1961 and also for the brutality with which his police force crushed a communist demonstration in January 1962, resulting in several deaths.

It was Serge Klarsfeld's research that uncovered the evidence of anti-Semitic and pro-Nazi activity that finally brought Papon to trial. However, it took fifteen years from the time of his initial indictment before he was convicted, which added more weight to the argument that the State was unwilling to face up to its past. Papon was imprisoned in 1998 but just two years later was released on grounds of alleged ill-health.

Further evidence that many did not want to face up to the past comes from the post war survey showing that very few French citizens supported the death penalty for Pétain, despite his being on trial for treason. This may have been something to do with his heroic deeds at Verdun in the first world war, but nonetheless seems incredulous when the evidence against him is examined. It was Pétain who induced the separation of France leaving the southern area under his control, whilst the northern zone was fully occupied by the German army. Though officially neutral in practice the regime, which was administered from Vichy, collaborated closely with Germany and brought in its own anti-Semitic legislation.

In November 1942 the allied landings in North Africa led to a change of policy in Germany and the resulting invasion of the unoccupied area of France that, whilst leaving Pétain nominally in charge, had in practice meant he was little more than a figurehead. After the allied landings in the summer of 1944 Pétain went to Germany. He returned to France after liberation but was brought to trial and condemned to death. However, this was immediately commuted to solitary confinement for life by General Charles De Gaulle. Pétain was imprisoned in relative luxury on the Île d'Yeu off the Atlantic coast where he died in 1951.

These cases demonstrate that the French State took great trouble to ensure some very high profile collaborators would not be convicted, and had it not been for the persistence of activists like Klarsfeld, the truth about their involvement in war crimes might not have surfaced and they would have escaped major punishment altogether. And yet in contrast to people like Bousquet, Touvier and Papon, all of whom committed discreditable and despicable crimes that were simply unpardonable, there were many living within their communities who were merely servile collaborators. Such people, whose trivial forms of collaboration may have provided a service to the enemy but without the ideological level of collaboration that was a deliberate espousal of cooperation, were hunted down by the mob as the extralegal purge took ahold, with the pledge to purify their lands and souls. But as the lawyer Louis Nizer observed, "When a man points a finger at someone else, he should remember that four of his fingers are pointing at himself." This purge occurred under the auspices of épuration sauvage (savage purge) that, coming well before the government's official épuration légale, lacked any form of institutional justice. Of course, Jacques was to lose his wife and the mother of his three daughters because of spurious accusations of collaboration, and it can be assumed that the Duval family was far from the only one to have suffered in this way.

Many victims of servile collaboration were women[7] who, alone during times when their husbands were in labour camps in Germany, may have accepted liaisons with, or favours from, German soldiers. However, given they had no means of support, invariably their motivation may well have been merely to put food on the table for themselves and their children. And just as neighbours had envied Jacques while publicly accusing him of collaboration, so these women were branded traitors by those who in private envied the food (and no doubt for some the entertainment) these women had received. In fact, in excess of 10,000 such women were subjected to public humiliation by having their heads shaved, sometimes tarred or daubed with black painted swastikas on their faces — les tondues (the shorn) — before being paraded through the streets of their own community. And of course at times there were occasions when such women may have fraternised with German soldiers without there being any sexual shenanigans whatsoever. And many of the tondeurs (head shavers) were not even members of the Resistance with an axe to grind but petty collaborators themselves, who wanted to divert attention away from themselves so that members of the Resistance would not single them out for punishment for their lack of resistance credentials.

Whilst the voyeur tendencies of the masses were satisfied by watching les tondeurs at their work and les tondues paraded in the streets, many French people — as well as allied troops — were sickened by the treatment meted out to these women. A large number of the victims were prostitutes who were only plying their trade but still some were kicked to death. Others were rash and reckless teenagers who had associated with German soldiers out of bravado. Even female schoolteachers living alone, as they were obliged to in those days, who had German soldiers billeted on them, were falsely condemned as 'mattresses for the boches'; and women charged with having had an abortion were assumed to have slept with German soldiers also.

*

So, as Jean-Paul Sartre declared three decades after the war ended, during the Occupation there were just two choices: collaborate or resist. And as has been demonstrated those from both camps suffered, the former at the hands of the Nazis and the latter at the hands of their own people. What has also been demonstrated is that collaboration varied from the petty, servile and unctuous to the repugnant, barbarous and inhumane and that it was those in the first group, without the protection of the authorities or the influential, who were the ones to suffer most, and sometimes at the hands of the Resistance, or at least those who claimed to be sympathetic to the resistance movement.

However, what of the vast number of people who claimed they were neither resisters nor collaborators? Sartre seemed to think they did not exist. But there were those who did not join the Resistance — perhaps because they feared reprisals to their co-patriots for the acts of sabotage performed in the name of the Resistance — but who nevertheless defiantly refused to write or perform for the occupiers under any circumstances. One such person was the celebrated essayist Jean Guéhenno[8]. Instead, he chose to use a pseudonym to publish his works via the underground newspaper *Les Lettres Françaises* and without payment, 'merely for pleasure,' he said. Commendable as it may be, unlike the itinerant ballroom entrepreneur Jacques Duval and the countless number of others who had to make a simple living or needed to put food on the table for their children, Guéhenno did have the financial security of a teaching job at the Lycée Henri IV to offset his financial losses from such a defiant act.

There were others too who were neither resisters nor collaborators, including Rose Valland who was employed by one of Paris's great museums, the Jeu de Paume. She kept a record of all art entering or leaving the building, including art destined for the Hitler or Goering collections. This was no mean feat because the Jeu de Paume had been taken over by the Nazis during the Occupation and used as their headquarters. She drew to the attention of the Resistance the trains that contained the most valuable pieces of art, so they would not attack them. After the war, Valland's notes assisted Allied officers seeking to track down the looted art, as was portrayed in the 2014 American movie *The Monuments Men*.

Sartre's claim that it was a matter of choosing one of the two extremes — resisting or collaborating — has been challenged by a number of contemporary writers and journalists, including

Alan Riding[9] who pointed out there were many that did neither. Vast numbers chose attentisme, or wait and see, he said. Jacques Duval fell into this category, and had he not been such a show-off, boasting about his entrepreneurial subjugation and relative financial successes, his family may not have been targeted in the way it was. But let us not ignore the fact that the divisions between resisting and collaborating were very blurred.

Café owners, artisans and small time entrepreneurs were in the firing line from both ends of the resistance-collaboration spectrum. If they refused to serve or produce for the Nazis when soldiers visited their cafés and dance halls, at the very least they would not have earned a living, and if they did earn they were persecuted for 'sleeping with the enemy'. Musicians, actors and writers made difficult decisions too because educated cultured Germans wanted to enjoy Parisian salons, theatres and restaurants, and foot soldiers wanted to visit the Moulin Rouge or Folies Bergeres, or shop for silk underwear to take back to Germany.

The very successful pre-war musical artist Maurice Chevalier became embroiled in such a catch-22 situation during the war. Chevalier was accused of collaboration for singing in Germany, even though it was at a prisoner-of-war camp for French nationals, and in spite of the fact that he donated over one million francs to French prisoners-of-war. He also sang at the prisoner-of-war camp where he had been interned during the first World War but he only agreed to this on condition that ten prisoners were freed. He was blackmailed by the Nazis and told that unless he played at the Casino de Paris, a venue patronised by many German officers, his refugee friends would suffer. His wife, Nita Raya, was a Romanian Jew born Raya Jerkovitch in Kishinev (now part of Moldova) and she and her parents were surviving in France on false papers, so he was very concerned about the threat from the Nazis. He succumbed to their demands but after just a few performances he refused to comply further with their wishes and so went into hiding. He was also under threat from the Maquis who knew he had sung in Germany and therefore assumed he was benefitting financially from the Occupation. Though he had performed throughout Vichy France, almost certainly their disquietude was exaggerated given that some of the London press had falsely suggested he had performed throughout Germany and not just in the two prisoner-of-war camps.

As a professional singer during the war he would have found giving up performing an unreasonable expectation. In many ways it is no different from a butcher who continued to sell meat even though some of his customers were German soldiers, or as an author who continued to write books even though some may have been purchased by Nazi officers. Are these people collaborating by plying their trade in these ways?

Shortly after liberation Chevalier was arrested and sentenced to death for collaboration. However, a *Daily Express* journalist unearthed the truth and he was set free. In his autobiography[10] Chevalier wrote:

An entertainer's profession is his whole life. If we have to fight for France or die for her, we are ready to do so. But the rest of the time we just want to be left alone. I suppose we feel that we are doing our share by giving laughter and gaiety to the nation.

In the same way Jacques Duval was doing much the same thing when he toured the villages with his itinerant ballroom. Resisting? Collaborating? Refusing to cooperate? Continuing to ply one's trade? It was a complicated business!

To a very great extent Paris lost its status as the cultural capital of the world after the war because many high profile and successful artists left for America or elsewhere in Europe. In his book, Alan Riding wrote:

French intellectuals propagated doctrines — Monarchism, Fascism, anti-Semitism, Communism, even Maoism — that offered explanations and solutions for everything.

However, he argued that given these doctrines failed to deliver the state of Utopia promised, just maybe life without them may be for the better. He pointed out that they may be less prominent in France now but perhaps they are also less dangerous. The French cultural celebutantes, idols, writers and artists don't always come out too well in Riding's hard-hitting book!

*

There is some evidence[11] that the cultural idol Gabrielle Coco Chanel worked for German military intelligence during the war. Whether this is true or not it is certain she began an affair with Baron Hans Gunther von Dincklage, an attache at the German embassy who was also a high-ranking Gestapo officer. As an accomplished opportunist Coco Chanel knew how to 'play the system' for her own ends and since the Nazis were in power, it is alleged by the historian Hal Vaughan that Chanel sided with them — but her head was never shaved or tarred! And yet some might well argue she was so heavily involved with the German secret service that she deserved a punishment significantly greater than this kind of humiliating ridicule.

Apparently, Chanel was heavily involved within the organisation as early as 1941 when she worked for General Walter Schellenberg, chief of SS intelligence. At the end of the war, Schellenberg was tried by the Nuremberg Military Tribunal and sentenced to six years imprisonment for war crimes. He was released in 1951 because of an incurable liver disease. Coco Chanel allegedly paid for Schellenberg's medical care and living expenses, financially supported his wife and family and paid for Schellenberg's funeral upon his death in 1952.

In his book *Sleeping with the Enemy* Hal Vaughan drew attention to the notion that the French public would have felt uncomfortable with his conclusions about Chanel — and no doubt many other high profile French cultural idols like her — arguing that so much loved and idolised was she, that a blind eye needed to be turned rather than her reputation destroyed. In this way retailers could go on selling, and members of the public could continue to buy, her fashion accessories and perfume without a conscience.

Stephanie Bonvicini, author of the book *Louis Vuitton, A French Saga* discovered from historical archives that there was reliable evidence to suggest Louis Vuitton had collaborated with the Vichy government and the Nazis[12]. Apparently, Vuitton's store in the Hotel du Parc in Vichy was given permission to continue trading despite all other stores, including the jewellers Van Cleef & Arpels, having been forced to shut down. Vuitton's grandson, Gaston, the wartime head of the company, had instructed his eldest son, Henry, to forge links with the Pétain regime to keep the business afloat. In fact Henry, a regular at the local cafe frequented by the Gestapo, was one of the first Frenchmen to be decorated by the Nazi-backed government for his loyalty and his efforts for the regime, presumably because the family set up a factory dedicated to producing artefacts glorifying Pétain. Bonvicini observed:

Part of the collaboration was due to the family's obsession with the survival of the company, and part down to the fact that there was a certain sympathy with the regime's rightwing views.

And Chanel and Vuitton were not the only ones to collaborate. Artists and writers aplenty have come under fire. Pierre Drieu La Rochelle and Robert Brasillach wrote for official pro-Nazi newspapers, and Jean Cocteau and Albert Camus had plays performed in occupied Paris and dined with high status Nazi officers. Were these collaborators or just opportunists? They may have been far from heroes but neither were they (necessarily) siding with the enemy.

And what about Jean-Paul Sartre himself? Was he a collaborator? Some have argued he was, given he allowed his works to be published and staged during the occupation, and even played by the rules of occupation and gave in to the censors, changing the odd word and phrase here and there. But perhaps he was merely a part of the attentisme — wait and see — brigade. Rather than tangible acts of collaboration per se he could, perhaps, have been more aptly accused of moral collaboration. But then again he did try to join the Resistance, though notably rather late in the day and when the Allied forces were gaining ground, and like Jean Guéhenno he did write for the underground newspaper *Les Lettres Françaises*. However, few would argue that he had a clean record. Both he and his life-long partner Simone de Beauvoir, also an intellectual, philosopher and writer, lived very well under occupation.

Clive James[13] is very clear which side of the resistance-collaboration line Sartre stood.

For a man whose Resistance group had done nothing but meet, he was a haughty inquisitor during l'Épuration. Memories of the French Revolution were not enough to tell him there might be something wrong with the spectacle of a philosopher sitting on a tribunal instead of standing in front of it.

James remarks that after the liberation of Paris in 1944 it was Sartre himself who called, in his capacity as a Resistance fighter, for punishment to be vented on those among his fellow literati who had collaborated with the Nazis.

But then again, was his 'moral collaboration' any different from that of the likes of Jacques Duval? Had Duval been as successful as Sartre before the war then maybe he, and many like him, would have seized the opportunity to profit as much as Sartre had done, by an occupation neither of them supported nor, seemingly, had the power (or desire?) to resist.

There are other parallels between Jean-Paul Sartre, the intellectual and writer, and Jacques Duval, the small-time entrepreneur and musician. At the start of the war they were both drafted into the French army, both captured and imprisoned in Germany and both released early. Sartre was released, allegedly, because his poor eyesight and exotropia was affecting his balance and Duval was almost certainly released because he was replaced by French nationals under the Service du Travail Obligatoire directive. Interestingly, there were those in the community who were unhappy, suspicious even, about the terms of the release of both of these men. Locals from Jacques Duval's community were unhappy that three men had been sent to labour camps in return for his release (though some even suspected a deal had been struck to allow him to return to his wine selling and shoe-making businesses for the mutual benefit of the indigenous French and German soldiers, but this is unproven).

For Sartre, there were those — though in this case from a much wider community — who thought he had been released by the Germans because of his enormous appeal as writer and playwright, on condition he continued his work in France whilst playing by their rules. Notably, in October 1941 he was given a position at Lycée Condorcet, replacing a Jewish teacher who had been forbidden to teach by Vichy law. So had he collaborated to acquire this position? Some argued that had he the desire he could have refused this position, on the basis that the reason for replacing the Jew was a racist one. The French philosopher and son of Russian Jews Vladimir Jankelevitch, criticised Sartre's lack of political commitment and interpreted his later responses to his critics' claims he was a collaborator, as attempts to redeem himself — a case of closing the stable door[14]. But according to Sartre's friend, the writer Albert Camus, he was a writer who resisted, not a resister who wrote. In the same way Edith Piaf had always maintained she was not a collaborator, arguing that — just like Maurice Chevalier — she was first and foremost a singer, but it was not going to stop her from supporting those who were working from within the Resistance.

Again, is it not a matter of degree? The perception of collaboration in occupied France during the war is not straight forward by any stretch of the imagination; in fact it is a decidedly convoluted affair, with exceedingly blurred edges. After all, the

French during the Occupation, whether they were influential intellectuals or paysan small-time entrepreneurs, found themselves in uncharted waters; they had to contend with matters that arose on a day-to-day basis without knowing the longer term consequences for themselves, their families or the wider public. Could it be that it did not matter what you did in the war so long as you did not go on trial for it afterwards? Or more significantly — you were not found guilty of it!

It might seem a case of stating the obvious but if you were wealthy, popular and influential, you stood a pretty good chance of staying under the radar when it came to retributions for alleged collaboration with the enemy. But if you were just an ordinary citizen, desperate for survival under very difficult circumstances, and as such you happened to collaborate in petty ways at the very most, then you were likely to be hunted down, trialled by the mob and publicly ridiculed and, as in the Duval's case, sometimes much, much worse. So what does all this say about how the French behaved during and immediately after the war?

*

Running parallel to the trials, purges and punishments of those accused of servile collaboration and the unjust failure to punish far more prominent war criminals who had committed momentous atrocities, was a period of joyful celebration immediately following the liberation. The Morvan villages were no different to communities all over France in this respect, and partying became a 24/7 event. But did this bring communities back together? Emphatically no, it did not. Whilst people everywhere were drinking and generally making merry there were those who were having constantly to look over their shoulders, whilst others were furtively pointing the finger of blame: people wanted revenge. Nevertheless, street parties were in abundance and people danced, drank and played music into the small hours, so much so in fact that Jacques's itinerant ballroom métier flourished again. As for the three daughters they were having a ball. They enjoyed music and dancing — it was in their blood — but their celebrations and their father's entrepreneurial good fortune were, as we have seen, very short-lived. Within the blink of an eye their ecstasy had turned to sorrow in the small hours of an autumnal night in Villars.

But of course for the majority they were not to be 'short changed'. They were in no mood to relinquish their reward for the four long years of hardship, oppression and non-stop cow-towing they had endured under the Occupation.

You would have thought the French military had liberated the French from the Nazi stranglehold by the number of tricolores on show. And from the balcony of the Hotel de Ville in Paris on 25 August 1944 General de Gaulle gave his impassioned speech before the people:

Paris! Paris outraged, Paris broken, Paris martyred, but Paris liberated! Liberated by herself, liberated by her people, with the help of the whole of France, that is to say of la France combattante, the true France, eternal France.

This must have irked the US and British liberators because the fact is the French played a very small part in liberating their country. At parades, of which there were many, not one American or British flag was flown, fly pasts were in formation in the shape of the Lorraine flag that had been the adopted symbol of the Resistance and yet the aircraft, vehicles and fuel were provided by the Allies.

Not surprisingly, the Morvan Maquis were very high profile at these celebratory events, and on view to many citizens for the very first time given their need to have operated in clandestine ways during the war. And it does not take a lot of imagination to assume that the ranks of the maquisards must have swelled enormously as young men and women aligned themselves with this much loved and honourable organisation, even though they may well have had little or nothing to do with it at the time.

Within only a few months the euphoria and jubilation of liberation turned sour for the French. Paradoxically, following liberation from occupation, in the eyes of some, France's saviours became their new occupiers, and a shadow was cast over the liberators' image. Though many GIs seemingly did not entirely trust the French before D-Day, after it the myths of French women acting in league with their Nazi lovers spread quickly and took hold. A consequence of this was that many from the liberating armies took advantage, so that by the late summer of 1944 large numbers of women were complaining about rapes by liberating soldiers. Many American GIs drove around in their military vehicles, looted, fought in the streets and generally made a nuisance of themselves. They were brash, loud and invariably drunk, so much so in fact that the French were bemused and shocked by it. The contrast with off-duty German troops during the Occupation, who had been forbidden even to smoke in the street, could hardly have been greater.

Americans, and to some extent the British, saw liberated France not just as a symbol of Europe's freedom from Nazi oppression, but as a place for merriment and reward for their valour, rescuing the French from the clutches of their occupiers. Accordingly, vast numbers of soldiers developed a preoccupation with French women. Free condoms were even issued in Paris to American GIs by their superiors and these went hand in hand with booklets telling them where to find the brothels. The Paris brothels had to cope with upwards of 10,000 men a day. GIs wanted sex: some accepting they had to pay, others refusing to do so and more still taking it by force. In her book *What Soldiers Do: Sex And The American GI In World War II France* Mary Louise Roberts[15] told the story of abuse at the hands of American soldiers.

When the brothels were full GI promiscuity took place in parks, cemeteries, streets and abandoned buildings, sexual relations became unrestricted and public; sexual intercourse was performed in daylight before the eyes of civilians, including children.

French women were regarded as commodities as portrayed in the GI newspaper *Panther Tracks*.

An especially vivacious and well-rounded harlot might demand a price of 600 francs. However the price scales downwards for fair merchandise and mediocre stock. Some fairly delicious cold cuts can be had for 150 and 200 francs.

And Roberts wrote that worse was to come. According to a report from the Supreme Headquarters Allied Expeditionary Force very young girls in their very early teens started to loiter outside the American army camps offering themselves to the GIs. The age of consent at that time was thirteen — the same age as Marie — and when the Americans suggested a solution would be to raise the age of consent to sixteen, the French government were displeased that they were trying to interfere with French laws. It is not known whether the girls were in fact prostitutes driven by hardship or just wayward youngsters seeking titillation.

If the black market had been a cause for concern during the Occupation it was much worse after it; a good deal of it was selling American goods under the counter and there were even tales of shipments of goods imported from America to fuel this illegal trade, so that GIs could profit by it before their return to the States. There were also stories of hold-ups in the city's streets by uniformed men.

The American influence was considerable. Some French cafés, bars and bistros were transformed overnight with pretty waitresses replacing waiters in their traditional black waistcoats and long white aprons. The premises were modernised and names changed to appeal more to the wealthy American liberators.

Anyone observing all that was happening could not have helped but notice there was not a black face in sight in Paris on 25 August 1944, the day the city was officially liberated, despite the fact that almost two-thirds of Free French forces were black. The

BBC's programme *Document*[16] claimed that despite fighting Nazi Germany to defeat the vicious racism that left six million Jews dead, all black soldiers were deliberately removed from the unit that led the Allied advance into the French capital. It went on to show that at the time France fell in June 1940, 17,000 of its black, mainly West African colonial troops, known as the Tirailleurs Sénégalais, lay dead.

Many of them were simply shot where they stood soon after surrendering to German troops who often regarded them as sub-human savages.

The survivors had thought their chance for revenge would come in August 1944 when troops prepared to take Paris, but despite their overwhelming numbers they were not to get it. This was because Allied Command refused to allow black soldiers to be a part of the liberating force. In fact after liberation many Tirailleurs Sénégalais were stripped of their uniforms and sent home to Senegal; and to make matters worse in 1959 their pensions were frozen. Now there's gratitude for you!

CHAPTER NINE

Love seeketh not itself to please, nor for itself hath any care, but for another gives its ease, and builds a Heaven in Hell's despair.
— *William Blake*

Jacques was not coping. He was constantly depressed and his demented state meant he was unable to discharge his duties as a good parent would. In fact he all but ignored his three daughters and seemed oblivious to their needs, at what was a dreadfully distressing time for them. They were not well looked after. Their puffy, rheumy eyes and flushed cheeks were the telltale signs that all three had been crying themselves to sleep and waking to regular nightmares. They had not changed their bed clothes for weeks and they wore the same shabby clothes every day. They were grubby and looked a sorry state. They had eaten what they could lay their hands on but none of them, Jacques included, tended to their livestock or vegetable garden and so they had not had any fresh produce in a very long time. The cow's milk had dried up and those hens that were still alive were cooped up in a shed, belly deep in their own excrement. The two children who were still of school age took themselves off to school each morning without a breakfast or even a wash. In fact it was their well-meaning teacher who raised the alarm with their father.

'I am sorry to have to say this Monsieur Duval but your children need better looking after. Have you not noticed that they are emaciated and scrawny and in need of some wholesome food. Without this, and some loving attention, I fear the worst for them. Monsieur Duval, I urge you to act swiftly, and if you are unable to cope, which given the suffering of the past few weeks would seem distinctly possible, then try to find someone who can help you and who will be able to care for your children in their hour of need.'

This remonstration had the desired effect of bringing Jacques to his senses, and over the following few days he pleaded with friends and family to help him out until he got himself back together. The outcome of these conversations was that Marie and Colette went to live with Madame Deschamps, someone who the Duvals had known for a year or two, while Emeline was taken in by distant relatives, Monsieur et Madame Charron.

'But Papa, I don't want to leave you here alone. I want to be with you. I can help around the house Papa,' said Marie.

'I know you can,' replied her father. He continued, 'but it will be for the best. I must work during the day repairing shoes and then again in the evening with the band, otherwise there would be nothing to live on. I don't want to leave you and your sisters alone all that time. It will be for the best. I know it will. Now be a good girl and let's not say any more about it.'

With that Marie began to cry, not out loud, more a whimper, but she was unable to control it. She held on to him pleading with him to let her stay.

'I want to live with you Papa, please don't send me away.'

Her father did not want to send Marie and her sisters away but he believed he had little choice. He was not discharging his fatherly duties properly and he felt the girls needed someone there for them at this distressing time in their lives. But he was confused and really did not know whether this was the right course of action or not. It must have been pitiful for him seeing his young daughter clinging on to him and begging him to stay. With a heavy heart he tried to cajole her into thinking it was all for the best, but Marie was not at all convinced. In his frustration and sense of helplessness he ended up snapping at her, which made her cry all the more. Instantly he regretted showing his impatience and so gave her a reassuring cuddle.

'Now wipe your tears sweetheart and then off to bed. Anyway, it won't be for long, just until things settle a little. Madame Deschamps is a very kind lady and she will be able to look after you.'

'Will you promise me Papa that as soon as you are better you will bring me home to be with you? Will you promise, Papa?'

'Of course Marie, I want things to be settled again too. Things will never be quite the same without Maman, but you are my flesh and blood and I will miss you, all three of you. I will think about you every day and will visit you often. Now off to bed with you.'

Marie made her way pensively to her room where her sisters were already asleep. By then they were all three sleeping in the same room while their father was occupying the tiny adjoining room. The scullery where Rosine had died was still partially boarded up. Marie took some time to fall asleep that night. She was thinking about what it would be like living with Madame Deschamps. In her funereal state of mind she felt alone and abandoned: desolate, dejected and disconsolate. As usual, when finally she drifted off to sleep, it was with tears in her eyes.

*

Within a week Marie and Colette met up with Madame Deschamps and they moved in the very next day. They took with them their clothes, books, toys, teddies and dolls but Marie, particularly, was sorry to leave behind the hens, the cow and of course her dear papa.

Madame Deschamps lived in Venitiens where the girls went to school, about three kilometres from Villars and five or so from

Préporché. She lived in a spacious one story stone built house at the corner of Venitiens Haut and Les Charmes, overlooking the rolling hills of the Morvan and with hardly another building in sight. She was a very kind lady, but this did not stop Marie worrying dreadfully about her father. After all it was she who had done almost all of the day to day chores in the house in Villars and whilst Colette helped here and there, or at least when she was asked to do so, Emeline had done nothing; she had hardly been in the house, though she still expected meals to be served to her and her clothes washed and tidied. Marie worried how her father would cope alone.

The move was not easy for either Marie or Colette, or Emeline for that matter; she had gone to her new temporary home over a week before. This was the fifth time the girls had moved home within a two year period. However, they settled in quite well all things considered. Marie and Colette shared a room and were made to feel welcome by Madame Deschamps, a tiny slender woman with an olive complexion, black hair worn up in a twist at the back, almond-shaped dark brown eyes and round face; she looked Oriental Marie had thought, which made her wonder where her roots were.

It was not until some time into her stay that she learnt more about her guardian. Madame Deschamps had been born in 1905 in Hanoi, the capital of Vietnam at the time — a part of French Indo-China — to a woman who had been 'sold' by her parents to a third party. It was a period of extreme hardship for indigenous people of the region under French colonial rule, and families found it exceptionally difficult making ends meet. Her parents had hoped she would be adopted, but as was typical for girls at the time she was not and in fact became an unpaid bonded labourer. Having served her master for a number of years she was married off to François Deschamps. He was the son of a young French woman who, with her son, had emigrated to Vietnam with a wealthy French family as their children's nanny. Madame Pascale Deschamps, Marie and Colette's new foster parent, was the child of that marriage. Pascale decided to leave the colony in 1939 to discover more about her father's homeland in the Morvan of France. At the time she left she had no reason to believe that a year later France would fall to the advancing Nazi army. However, had she remained in Hanoi her fate would not have been any better. After the fall of France in 1940, the colony was governed directly from Vichy, before being occupied by the Japanese, who were eventually overthrown by the Viet Minh, a communist army led by Ho Chi Minh. When in France Pascale Deschamps settled in Venitiens. She never married and had no children of her own.

*

Within a few days of the two girls being in Venitiens, Colette developed terrible panic fits that brought her out in cold sweats and made her shake, perhaps what today we would recognise as night-terrors. As the days passed she seemed to get worse, developing a sore throat, pain in her joints and a mild fever. She was often out of breath and felt generally fatigued. In fact there were days when she felt so bad she could not get out of bed. Madame Deschamps had also noticed a skin rash and times when she would have bouts of uncontrollable jerking so, very concerned, she called for the doctor from Saint-Honoré to visit her. He confirmed her own suspicions that Colette had developed rheumatic fever, probably because of the shock at the time of her mother's tragic death, which may well have altered her immune system, so making it difficult for her to fight bacterial infections. She missed many days of school because of her debilitating and painful condition; and to exacerbate things it was not long before she was moved on yet again, this time to her Aunt Sylvie's in Les Bourbas, no more than a kilometre in fact from where she was born, in Le Cruyot. It was thought she would better be able to nurse her back to good health.

Meanwhile, Marie made friends with Florence, a young girl of her age who had been adopted by 'la Mère Deschamps' after being orphaned with the death of her parents. Like Marie Florence was petite in stature but her face was fuller. She had a small upturned nose and cornflower blue eyes. The two girls got on very well: it was good for them both to have the company of someone of similar age. Florence also attended the same school as Marie. And at the suggestion of Madame Deschamps the two girls shared a room; they would be company for each other when they felt piteous and troubled she had said.

Madame Deschamps was a comparatively wealthy, cheerful and motherly woman. It took Marie no time at all to take to her and within a couple of weeks, like her friend, Marie too was calling her Mère Deschamps. Without the stability and kindness afforded her by Mère Deschamps, and what was to become a lifelong friendship with Florence, Marie would have struggled utterly to cope. As it was she cried a good deal, finding it impossible to leave the events of the past year or two behind her. Those terrible times made her nervous and frightened, and like her younger sister she too developed panic attacks and nightmares.

She became paranoid about the well-being of her father and kept asking Mère Deschamps if she had heard from him, if she knew how he was and when he was coming to see her again. Every night her sleep pattern was disrupted by these worries and fears.

'I couldn't sleep again last night Florence. I kept waking up terribly worried that something dreadful will happen to you or Mère Deschamps or Papa. I couldn't bear that Florence. Please never go away.' At just thirteen years of age Florence did not know how to deal with these frequent disclosures. She could only listen and sympathise.

On other occasions Marie relayed her terrible nightmares to Mère Deschamps telling her how frightening they were. On one particular occasion she had had a very vivid memory of what had happened, so kindly and patiently Mère Deschamps sat down alongside her, and while holding her hand encouraged Marie to tell her all about it.

'Well, I remember being in the middle of a meadow. It was brimming full with pretty white lily of the valley and there were nightingales. There were hundreds of them and they were all singing quite beautifully.' She paused and then continued.

'And the sky was blue, I remember it was very warm and the sun was shining. It was a lovely happy day. I could see Emeline and Colette across the meadow. They were laughing and running around playfully. Papa was there and Maman too and they were holding hands. But then …' She paused for a while and whilst she did so her facial expression changed from one with a smiling disposition to a very frightened look. She let go of Mère Deschamps's hand momentarily, tensed her arms and made fists with her hands before continuing.

'I, well I remember that all of a sudden the lilies started disappearing underground and as they did so all the nightingales flew away and that disturbed me greatly because of something Maman had said to me a long time ago. And then, I, well I remember the ground rumbling so much that I lost balance and fell and though I tried so very, very hard I couldn't get up. I tried again and again but I just couldn't get up.' Another pause as she closed her eyes for a few seconds, grimaced and then as she took Mère Deschamps's hand in hers again she said, 'I remember very clearly that there was a hand reaching out to me, but there was nobody there — just a tiny hand, and then I reached out for the hand but as try as I might I couldn't grasp it. It was as though it wasn't there at all, but I had seen it with my own eyes.' Another grimace and a shaking of her head.

'I noticed that the trees in the distance were closing in on me, as if they were coming after me and then — at first Maman, then Colette and finally Emeline — they all vanished! I was panic-stricken. I looked around but they were nowhere to be seen and so I called out to them but they didn't answer, so I called again and this time much louder but again there was no answer. Papa was still there but he was a very long way away and was holding his head and shaking it from side to side and as he tried to walk

114

towards me he seemed to stumble.' Once again Marie stopped, took a deep breath and then, after exhaling really quite forcefully, she started again.

'And although in my dream I could hear no sounds I knew Papa was calling out to me. I don't know how I knew this, but I did. But as he was 'calling' the trees seemed to close in on me even more and it got darker and darker and darker until it was as black as the darkest night I had ever seen. I was so frightened.' Another pause and this time Marie gripped her carer's hand very tightly. She then spoke again, but as she did the pace became faster and faster so that she was gabbling through the remaining recollections of her terrible nightmare.

'I remember seeing the trees turning into huge grotesque bright red monsters and they were coming after me and, well then I couldn't breathe and then I was gasping for air and I was thrashing about with my arms waving everywhere while I was desperately trying to breathe but struggling to do so. I was still on the ground and still I couldn't get up and yet they kept coming after me, getting ever closer so I called out for help but no sound came out of my mouth and nobody came to help so I tried again but still nothing and still nobody came to help me.' She stopped and then announced, 'Then I woke up. And I was screaming out loud and I was on the floor, not in my bed! I was so frightened. I really was so frightened.'

This dream became a recurrent nightmare for Marie over the months that followed and it troubled the poor girl on many occasions, so much so she was frightened to go to bed. It always involved her struggling to get up from the ground or to grasp at something or to speak out. It sometimes involved her family but by no means always, but when it did they would be there one moment and then not the next. Monsters were almost always in the dream and chasing after her while she struggled in vain to run away from them. And almost always the monsters were blood red!

These nightmares, her constant asking after the well-being of her father and her sisters, her long bouts of intense crying, and even her developing fear of monsters would today alert a psychiatrist to the likelihood that the young person was suffering from separation anxiety disorder, and given all that had happened to Marie previously it would have been a surprise indeed had she not developed this distressing psychotic condition. However, in the 1940s this infirmity had not been identified and so no professional help was forthcoming. It could even have been that Colette's diagnosis of rheumatic fever was not that at all but separation anxiety disorder, but that we will never know.

It is a known fact however, that Marie always tried to put a brave face on things and emerged, at least in the eyes of others, as a child seemingly able to cope. After all she had cooked, washed, tidied the house and collected provisions and gone to school while others seemed less able to do so, or as in Emeline's case, simply unwilling to do so. Marie had cried herself to sleep almost every night when her father was away in Germany, though she never let on about it, so it might be assumed that the foundations of this condition had already been laid then, but made a whole lot worse after the terrible death of her mother. Busying herself as she did was her way of coping. When she was doing things she was not dwelling on the traumas that had occurred, not that she would have been aware of this because doing these tasks and busying herself would have been involuntary responses — those activated by her subconscious. Nevertheless, the effect of her traumatic experiences did not go away. They were just lying dormant, waiting to surface when the providential trigger was pulled.

The insecurity characterised by separation anxiety disorder may be exacerbated by many things including a change in routine, an illness of oneself or someone close, a lack of adequate rest, a move away, a parent's response in terms of discipline or availability, or a change in family structure as a result of a death for example. Any one of these could trigger an anxious state but for Marie she had experienced all of these, and simultaneously.

In her recurring nightmares she was trapped and unable to move and yet surrounded by monsters that were chasing her, while everything that was dear to her such as her parents and sisters, the wildflowers and the nightingales, and the trees and the fields, were all disappearing and leaving her alone. And when she was awake Marie developed an obsessive fear that she would be left all alone in the world as her loved ones died or moved away. It would not be surprising if Marie were to grow up feeling insecure and desperately in need of love and affection, with constant reassurance that there will always be somebody there for her. Without this reassurance there would always be the fear that her anxiety could develop into a more serious hypochondriacal state in which she would end up in adult life feigning illness by complaining of headaches or stomach aches to attract attention and get her own way, and by so doing avoid separation.

Thankfully, Madame Deschamps and Florence were there for her and were able to keep reassuring her. So, slowly but surely, as the months went by, Marie became more secure and happier. She looked forward to her father's weekly visits enjoying their time alone together, but learnt to cope without his presence. She hardly saw Emeline during her stay with Madame Deschamps, though she visited Colette occasionally.

*

Florence and Marie went to school in the village and every Sunday Mère Deschamps took the two of them the five or six kilometres from their home in Venitiens to church in Préporché. On such occasions the two girls invariably ran ahead, hopping and skipping down the lane with Mère Deschamps in tow and calling out for them to slow down and wait for her to catch up. The walk took them the better part of an hour but sometimes on the way back much longer, for in spring and summer they loved to dawdle and look for wild flowers along the verges. Sometimes they made daisy chains, or sat while Mère Deschamps caught up with them and looked for four-leaved clovers they had been told would bring them good luck. Occasionally they pulled petals one at a time from a dandelion to see how much a friend loved them. With the first pull they proclaimed 'he loves me' and with the next 'he loves me not' and so on, hoping that the last petal removed ended up with the affirmation 'he really loves me'! When they found buttercups they held them up to their chin to test how much they liked butter, by whether or not they could see a yellow reflection.

When Mère Deschamps caught up with them she invariably told them off, warning them to wash their hands when they got home, because 'don't you know buttercups will give you diarrhoea and sickness'. However, having never experienced that themselves, invariably the girls ignored her warning and carried on regardless. She most certainly got them to keep the dandelion leaves however, because they were a nutritious additive to stews she maintained, and of course they were always on the lookout for mushrooms.

Much to the girls' particular amusement every single time they were out looking for wildflowers, herbs and fungi, dear Mère Deschamps was heard saying to them both, 'keep an eye open for hogweed and hedge woundwort won't you my dears. You know how much I adore some delicious hedge woundwort sauce on a homemade stinging nettle quiche, especially if there's a side dish of hogweed-au-gratin too.' On such occasions the girls chuckled to themselves and every few steps proclaimed, 'We've found some hogweed Mère Deschamps,' and 'Oh, quick, over here, is this hedge woundwort?' They never found any, and would not have recognised it anyway. In fact they hoped they never would find any because they did not much fancy nettle quiche, hedge woundwort sauce and cheesy hogweed! But they did like to tease Mère Deschamps and she fell for it every time, scurrying across to them all excited and calling out, 'What have you found you clever girls,' before having to 'disappoint' them with, 'Well, never mind girls, not this time, but do keep trying.'

Sometimes they avoided the lanes by going across country: through the woods, across fields, at the side of hedgerows and along by the river, then across the road, down by the farm and so on. In winter, unless icy or deep in snow, it always took much less time because they hurried back to the welcoming warmth and comfort of a crackling and flickering log fire.

When at home Marie cooked occasionally and learnt a lot from Mère Deschamps — how to make pastry, pluck a chicken and pot-roast a rabbit to add to all she had learnt from her mother, but food was still being rationed so these culinary delights were few and far between.

The girls loved to sing and Florence loved to play her harmonica which she did with remarkable savoir faire. Though Mère Deschamps was not the musical maestro that Marie's father was she still liked to listen to music. It made them all happy. The girls sometimes made up songs or mini plays which they then recited to their one person audience. A real treat for them was when Mère Deschamps allowed them to dress up in her old clothes and then act out their short plays.

As the girls got older they pestered Mère Deschamps to allow them to go to dances in the village that were staged on particular festive occasions. Initially she refused, maintaining they were too young, but after much badgering and pleading she conceded defeat. But Mère Deschamps always accompanied them and waited in a nearby café to escort them back home. Unbeknown to the girls she sneaked out surreptitiously now and again, to a suitable vantage point to keep an eye on them. Of course they had to abide by her rules: 'No bad language, no lipstick, no kissing and most certainly no canoodling,' were her strict instructions. As a matter of fact the girls were not interested in boys anyway so the idea of kissing was far from their thoughts, and as for canoodling, well they had no idea what that might be anyway! They almost always danced together and very much enjoyed the freedom of being out of the house and without a chaperone looking over their shoulders all of the time, or so they had thought. They always left these occasional soirees feeling elated and very happy. They were never home late, Mère Deschamps certainly made sure of that, but all the way home they danced and sang aloud.

Marie was very fond of Mère Deschamps and was indebted to her calm, caring and motherly approach to looking after her. However, her gentle kindness did not stop Marie from having anxiety fits and nightmares that continued to haunt her, as her mind drifted back to that fateful day when the grenade was thrown. She invariably awoke very suddenly, choking raucously on the dust that in her dream was filling the room, just as it had done the night she saw her mother bleed to death in the house in Villars. She found it immensely difficult to think about the times before her mother's death, and this troubled her greatly. She fought hard to recall the happier times they had spent as a family, walking through the bluebell woods or swimming in the lake or watching deer forage in the wildflower meadows. Whilst she knew they had happened she was unable to conjure up the sensory experiences they had generated at the time. But thankfully she did have Florence to share her worries with, and having lost both her parents in tragic circumstances, her father in the *Battle for France* and her mother to diphtheria shortly afterwards, she was not without compassion and understanding.

The girls often chatted late into the night in the bedroom they shared. They talked about school, after all their intensive studies for the up and coming Certificate d'Etudes were imminent, but also their love of the outdoors, their friendship, their interest in music and in dance, but more than anything else they spoke about their families.

Marie's father visited once a week and on those occasions Marie spent as much time alone with him as possible. As often as not, when the weather was fine, they went for long walks in the countryside but sometimes her father took her into Chateau-Chinon or Moulins-Engilbert to have lunch in a bistro as a special treat, or maybe visit the cinema to watch a film. She had seen *La Vie de Plaisir*, a story about a successful night-club owner who presents cabarets, and she enjoyed the music and dance, but she really wanted to see *Le Comte de Monte Cristo*, having enjoyed reading Alexandre Dumas's book of the same title. Her father was not at all keen given he knew it was about a man sentenced to life imprisonment for a crime he was falsely accused of committing by those jealous of his good fortune. This was too much to bear, so he always avoided it.

CHAPTER TEN

When you are offended at any man's fault, turn to yourself and study your own failings. Then you will forget your anger.
— *Epictetus*

Madame Deschamps took exceptional care of Marie and Florence and ensured they had the loving attention they needed at a time of marked upheaval, distress and heartache for them both. Not only had they undergone life changing traumas in their young lives, but these had coincided with puberty, a time when even within the most normal of family settings, chemical changes in the body can lead to disconcerting mood swings, low self-esteem and all the inconveniences associated with menstruation. These two girls, however, were having to face these challenges without the day to day care from a parent so crucial at this time in a young girl's life. Florence had lost both her parents in tragic circumstances a few years previously and Marie, whilst her father was still alive, was seeing far less of him now that, not even a year after her mother's death, there was a new woman in his life. So bringing up these teenagers and helping them to understand and cope with the biological and emotional changes they were experiencing, fell solely to Madame Deschamps.

Marie knew her father was living with another woman but he almost never spoke about her, except to say that she filled a void in his life, comforting him and caring for him. Marie wanted her father to be happy but she could not quite understand why his three daughters could not be the ones to comfort him and be there for him. She longed for the day they would be together again as a family; after all he had promised Marie that their separation would only be temporary.

Madame Deschamps cooked for the two girls, washed their clothes, attended to them when they were unwell and gave them the security of a home; and the girls repaid her kindnesses by helping around the house and working hard at school. In spite of the number of times Marie changed home and school, and with all the trials and tribulations that affected her so gravely, she sat the Certificate d'Etudes successfully. Florence struggled with her studies and despite the help given by her patient friend she was unsuccessful and therefore had to repeat a year at school.

Marie viewed her certificate as a passport to independence. She left school at fourteen and scoured the villages and towns looking for work. After a number of disappointments and false starts, she eventually secured a position as a trainee secretary in Chateau-Chinon, working in the offices of a factory making rubber shoes. She remained with her adopted mother and Florence for a few more months, enjoying the independence afforded her by her job at the office and in the company of two people she trusted and loved, and who loved her.

*

In September 1945 Jacques arranged a small family gathering at his home in Villars to celebrate Marie's success in finding a job. He surprised Marie by picking her up in a car, a new acquisition following some good business. Marie was beaming with excitement as she sat in the passenger seat of the 1920s four-door red Suére Model D, Torpedo. And with its windows wound right down and the fabric roof rolled all the way back, she sat there with her head raised skyward and backwards, her slender arms aloft and her eyes closed whilst enjoying the wind rushing past her, blowing her long hair in all directions and forming a healthy pink glow on her fair-skinned cheeks. She was in her element and loving every moment. In fact the journey ended too soon for her, so she pleaded with her papa to drive on for another few minutes before he finally turned around and came to a halt outside the house.

She had been back there a half a dozen times before that occasion, but she was never entirely happy doing so because the window above the door through which the grenade had been thrown into the house had still not been repaired, so it never ceased to bring back agonising memories. And whenever she walked into the house she had to walk past the still partially boarded up room that her father had not fully cleared.

Emeline was sixteen by then and had arrived arm in arm with what seemed to Marie like a much older boyfriend in tow. She had only seen her older sister a handful of times since the tragedy; given their very different personalities there was not a lot of love lost between them, so conversation was minimal. Colette had not changed since Marie last saw her, just a couple of months previously. She still looked anaemic and was thin and hollow-cheeked, a bit like their father in fact, but unlike her father she looked unhealthily pale and far from well-groomed and — poor Colette — she was still suffering from periodic bouts of fever and debilitating aches and pains; in fact she was continuing to spend more time out of school than in it. And of course Marie's father's new companion Claudette was also there in the house, the house where her mother had been less than a year before, a fact that Marie was decidedly uncomfortable with. It was the first time they had met and whilst she tried not to stare, Marie could not help ogle at her step-mother disapprovingly. In the few seconds she studied her she formed an image of a woman far less pretty, kind, warm-hearted and loving than her mother. Inevitably her petti-fogging, pernickety, judgemental scrutiny meant she was hardly going to see her step-mother — the woman she believed was the reason she still lived apart from her father — in a favourable light.

In actual fact Marie saw Claudette as decidedly plain and rather gangly. She thought her nose over large and unflatteringly aquiline, her chin too prominent and her bister-coloured eyes deep-set and watery. The woman wore her mop of tousled thick brown hair at shoulder length, and draped about her angular raw-boned frame, was a grubby heavy linen mid-brown shirt-style dress that she wore several centimetres below her knees. And she must have been all of ten years younger than her father. Marie could not for one moment understand what her father saw in her.

The girls sat on the floor, except Emeline who purloined one of the few seats in the room, where she sat on her boyfriend Gérard's knee, while they pawed at each other incessantly.

There was plenty to eat — Jacques had made sure of that. There was country bread with cheese and charcuterie, including saucisson and the region's speciality, cured ham. As a treat they drank red Burgundy from Irancy. After supper the three sisters, Jacques and Claudette sat outside on the small terrace that adjoined the scullery. Gérard still could not be prised from Emeline so he too joined the gathering. It was a pleasant, calm and warm late summer's evening but at a little after eight o'clock the sun was already threatening to disappear from view; it looked like an enormous yellow disc shimmering above the horizon. Jacques told them he wanted to give the three girls some news, so they sat bolt upright, and with bated breath they listened.

'Emeline, Marie, Colette — you all three know that Claudette and I have been living with each other now for a few weeks. She has been kind to me and helped me pick myself up and get me back to a degree of normality.'

He was stopped in mid-flow by Emeline who abruptly got off Gérard's lap and asked, in her not unfamiliar brusque manner, 'Oh my God, you're not telling us you're getting married are you — that's not right!'

Jacques wisely ignored this and continued. 'You will remember all too well that I did not cope well in the weeks following your mother's tragic death. But now I'm a lot better I want to settle down again. So yes, Emeline, we are getting married and we will move to another village.'

Before he continued Emeline interjected again. 'I see,' she said in a dismissive tone. 'So when is this wedding going to take place and where exactly?' Her nose was clearly out of joint, and while looking Claudette square in the face, she continued with her unpleasant tone. 'Don't expect me to be there will you, bitch.' Though gravely upset by such a comment, neither Jacques nor Claudette rose to the bait, choosing to ignore Emeline's profane utterance, with its implication that it was 'that bitch' who had been responsible for the fact that they were still living away from their father.

In line with her nature and with maturity far in excess of her years, Marie was somewhat less truculent and more conciliatory and chose her words carefully. 'I'm pleased for you both if that is what you want, but sad that in all this time Papa you've not tried to reunite us as a family. You sent us away when you were not coping after Maman's death and we understood that — just about. But all three of us had thought we would be reunited at some point, perhaps in a different house, but nonetheless be together again as a family. You promised me faithfully Papa. The last time we lived together it was a very grim time indeed, full of sadness and unhappiness for us all and I had hoped …' Marie looked at Emeline, hoping to see a nod of unity but she was having none of it and sat there sulking, with clenched teeth and nostrils flared. Marie continued. 'Papa, your decision to start afresh and in another village has confirmed in my mind that we will never again live under the same roof. I know now we will not have the opportunity to rekindle what we had in the past. This saddens me Papa because almost every night since our separation, before I went to sleep I prayed that we will be together again doing the things we enjoyed before Maman died. I have so longed to be with you again Papa, but I now know that my prayers will never be answered, but as sad as this makes me I will be at your wedding.'

And then, turning to Claudette she said, in a pleading sort of fashion, 'But please don't wear lily of the valley on your wedding day will you? For if you do, it will break my heart.' Claudette did not seem to understand why Marie had said this, and probably would not have thought of doing so anyway. But given she was a somewhat simple-minded and distinctly unsophisticated woman, without a great deal of emotional intelligence, she would not have immediately put two and two together either. Nevertheless, not wishing to inflame what had already become a fractious encounter, she chose to say nothing at all.

'But don't you think chrysanthemums would be a most appropriate choice for you on such an occasion,' retorted Emeline, contemptuously. And with that callous, sadistic remark, connecting a funeral with the new marriage, she stood up and made her way into the house. Predictably enough Gérard followed her, feeling a little awkward with the way the conversation had been going no doubt.

Marie did not know Claudette and neither did she have any desire to get to know her, but as Emeline delivered her sarcastic remark she felt somewhat sorry for her. It was not her fault that all three of them were, in each of their own ways, trying to come to terms with the finality of what their father had announced, she thought. That woman did not deserve such heartless words.

'When are you going to clear this hideous wreckage Papa?' shouted Emeline from inside the house. 'It's been a year since Maman was killed and yet still the rubble is here to remind us of that awful day. We'll all feel a little better when the place is back to the way it was Papa. And while you're at it replace the glass above the door too,' she bellowed, in a decidedly peremptory manner as she poured herself yet another glass of wine. Her father did not respond.

Colette was never one to say very much but she had nodded away in agreement with Marie when she had spoken. Now it was her turn to speak her mind, albeit somewhat timidly. 'I really do wish things had been different Papa. I wish Maman was still here, but she isn't. I also wish we were all together again, but we aren't.'

She paused before continuing. 'As Marie said, the time has now come for us to face the fact that living together again is just not going to happen — is it Papa?' She posed this question forcefully if not rather sorrowfully, but nonetheless it was asked in such a manner that a reply was expected. But their father did not say anything. He looked pensive and ill at ease. There was a long silent pause during which time everyone fidgeted uncomfortably while waiting for his response. Claudette was staring into thin air trying hard not to fix her gaze on anyone, and as the silence continued she got up and walked steadfastly into the house. Emeline brushed past her as she made her way back on to the terrace, clutching a glass and an almost full bottle of wine. She was about to hammer her point home when her father cut in.

'Yes, it is a sad fact that difficult and traumatic times separated us, but that doesn't mean we cannot be supportive of each other. I have done something that I hope you will agree is well intentioned and will be a benefit to all three of you. I've rented a house in the village La Vallée de Cours for you three girls. It's just outside Chateau-Chinon so it will be near your work Marie, and close to shops, cafés and bars, and there will be dances, fêtes and concerts in the summer too. So there'll be plenty going on for you to enjoy. I've done this for you hoping you will live there together and support each other. Claudette and I will buy our new home somewhere nearby, so we'll never be too far away and we will be able to visit you regularly. I do so hope you approve of what I've done.'

After a brief period when nobody uttered a word, Marie spoke in a hesitant almost stifled manner. 'Papa, I hope I speak for all three of us when I say I know how difficult things have been for you these past few years. But we've struggled too Papa.' She paused to wipe a tear from her eye. 'We have had trauma after trauma, followed by move after move, and now you are proposing yet another move Papa. I must assume from this you are saying it would be impossible for all of us to pick up where we left off.' She turned to Claudette who was by then standing in the doorway.

'And I cannot imagine what you must be making of all of this? You would surely find it very difficult too if we all lived in one house.'

Marie took a moment to think about what to say next. 'The decision you have made to rent this property Papa seems a curious one. You say your intention is to provide us with somewhere secure to live and where we can support each other, but we live in supportive homes now. Isn't it rather the case that you are feeling that Madame Deschamps, aunt Sylvie and Monsieur and Madame Charron would begin to question why they still need to be looking after us now that you are 'back on your feet' and about to re-marry? And given this and, presumably, believing that your marriage may be threatened if your three daughters reinvade your space, you have been left with little alternative but to find this accommodation for us. Put bluntly Papa we seem to have become something of a liability. But, just maybe this will prove to be a new chapter in our lives? Maybe we three sisters will support each other and perhaps we will enjoy the independence this new home will afford us. Only time will tell. Anyway, there's no point in discussing this further so let's change the subject.' But the moment she said that she realised there was no way anyone was going to change the subject and engage in some form of social chit-chat. That was jut not going to happen.

Their father had the last word. 'Yes, there is a certain finality in all of this. Yes, I did come to the conclusion we would never live together under the same roof again. Yes, I am remarrying and yes I do want a new start in life and with my wife to be, and further it is true that your guardians can't be expected to go on looking after you for very much longer. Being all together in the same house after all that has happened since Maman died just would not work out, and I believe you three girls would not be at all happy. Somehow I wanted to find a way of enabling the three of you to live together again. I know that at eleven, fourteen and sixteen years of age living together in the same house, without parents there to guide and care for you, seems unorthodox but what else could I do? You will have to make your own way in life sooner or later so why not now at a time when I am able to provide for you? If you live in this new house together you will be safe and secure, and you will be there for each other, and you will have some independence. It will offer you a practical transition from being cared for to being fully independent. I only want what is best. The problem is I don't know for certain what is for the best.'

He turned to his eldest daughter. 'Emeline, I know this has been difficult for you to comprehend and I know you are angry, but I urge you to believe me when I say all I want is what is best for you, Marie and Colette. There is no ideal solution. We cannot resurrect the past. Whatever I do I know inevitably it will be a compromise. Give my idea a chance Emeline, please.' He was trembling, tears were trickling down his cheeks, his voice was shaky and his eyes looked full of remorse. In fact he looked a sad figure, and it reminded Marie of the way he looked when he glanced back at her and her sisters at the moment immediately before her mother died. She knew her father was pleading with his hot-headed and confrontational eldest daughter. She also knew that he would be hoping she would not respond with her usual belligerence, but would instead begin to understand that he was thinking of her and wanting to do the best for her.

How Emeline responded took them all aback, even Gérard! She sidled up to her father, lent forward, gave him a gentle — though hardly emotionally charged — kiss on his cheek and with a rueful simper, proclaimed she would try to make it work. She did not openly apologise to Claudette for the cruel words she had spoken, but there was something contrite in the manner in which she was behaving then that suggested she regretted her earlier rebuke. Having listened to Marie, perhaps she had thought there may be some gain by reuniting in the same house. She was sixteen after all and was tiring of living with the Charrons who, well into their fifties, were hardly familiar with the needs and desires of teenage girls. On a more cynical note she may also have remembered just how domesticated her sister had been when they lived together years before when their father had been in the prisoner-of-war camp. And of course she now had a boyfriend so being independent would be useful too, she mused.

Marie was instantly relieved by Emeline's reaction as was her father of course. She strode across to her sister and cuddled her in a most loving embrace. Emeline did not push her away, but then neither did she reciprocate. Marie turned to Colette to give her a reassuring look, and then announced to her father that it was time for them all to go. With that her uncharacteristically diffident father escorted all four of them to his car. He drove them to their respective homes, pledging to make sure the new house would be made available to them early in the new year.

With the night air by then cool they drove along with the windows and roof closed. Very little was said as they made their way through the Morvan countryside for each was deep in thought, wondering what the future would hold for them. Marie, particularly, was apprehensive, wondering how she would be able to tolerate her older sister and, given her frailty and ongoing ill-health, imagining that caring for her younger one would prove challenging. Was her father abdicating his responsibility or had he found a way out of a difficult situation that would be beneficial to them all? One thing was for sure the three sisters were very young to be setting up home together.

CHAPTER ELEVEN

You don't love someone for their looks, or their clothes, or for their fancy car, but because they sing a song only you can hear.
— *Oscar Wilde*

By the early spring of 1946 the three girls had said their final goodbyes to their guardians and had made their way to their new home in La Vallée de Cours. All three were excited though Marie was sad to be leaving Madame Deschamps and Florence. They agreed they would keep in touch and visit regularly.

The house was basic but suitable. They had the luxury of two bedrooms (Marie and Colette agreed to share), a kitchen with a wood-burning range and an adjoining living room. There was very little land but Marie was sure there was room for some hens and a small vegetable plot.

The village was just five kilometres from Chateau-Chinon and less than half a kilometre north east of the River Yonne. It was tucked between a series of tiny lakes and surrounded by dense forests. There were scores of small fields in the surrounding countryside all well stocked with Charolais cattle and pigs. Being so close to Chateau-Chinon was a real bonus, not only because Marie's place of employment was in the town but also because it offered everything they needed from shops and cafés to a library and a dance hall, and there was a bus service to their village in the morning and afternoon every third day.

For the three young girls settling in was far from straightforward. They squabbled and bickered over who would shop, cook, clean and wash the clothes. Colette played the 'oh I'm too weak to do very much' card and though Emeline pledged to do her bit, inevitably most of the chores fell to Marie. At first it was a novelty for her so she did not seem to mind but she soon tired of running around for her two sisters whilst still being reprimanded by them when food was late getting to the table, or the girls had run out of clean clothes to wear. They really took advantage of Marie's good nature.

Marie had never taken to her older sister and found her lazy inimical attitude and malevolent manner very upsetting. To outsiders it was plain to see Emeline was jealous of Marie's prettiness and her confident and unflappable manner. Marie did not like arguing and therefore tended to back down when her sisters challenged, with the result that she became a prime target for exploitation. And yet Marie was the only wage earner of the three; Colette was still at school, and forever badgering Marie to do her homework for her, and Emeline had not managed to get a job, not that she had made much of an effort, Marie had thought.

Emeline was still dating Gérard, but he seemed to be tiring of her and becoming irritated by her ill-tempered and confrontational attitude to almost everything. But now she had her own room in a house — and without adult supervision — he was prepared to tolerate her unsavoury qualities in the hope she would let him stay the night with her. She was not an overly attractive young woman; as she had grown older she had become rather pear-shaped and a little heavy featured, and her frizzy brown hair was never well coiffured, but she would do for nineteen year old Gérard who had not managed to persuade any girl to let him kiss her, let alone fondle or have sex with her. But Gérard was no oil painting himself. He looked gaunt and gawky and struggled to keep acne at bay. He had a better side to his nature than his girl-friend, but he was far from the brightest pin in the box and so too often upset people with his bumbling lack of tact.

The girls saw their father once every week or so, at which time he came laden with goodies from the épicerie as well as with eggs and fresh milk from his own livestock. He paid the rent but only occasionally chipped in with money to help out with the house-keeping. This tended to fall to Marie, which meant she had very little left over for herself once all the weekly bills had been paid. It was far from easy holding down a job, and particularly at a time when there were plenty of men without work and wanting jobs, having only recently returned from the farms, factories and labour camps in Germany. And she had to do her job whilst also doing most of the household chores. She was constantly tired and had little time to socialise so finding a boyfriend would be an im-possibility, she thought.

Marie always looked forward to Florence coming to see her. Florence was a very good friend, cycling the twenty kilometres or so from her home in Venitiens to La Vallée de Cours almost every weekend. When together the two girls chatted until late and shared jokes but their greatest joy was to visit the dance hall in Chateau-Chinon. They tried to do this every fortnight. When there they danced together, often singing along to the songs Marie remembered from the days when accompanying her father to his dance evenings.

On one such occasion in late autumn 1946 they were sitting at a table in the dance hall sipping their drinks while resting after a particularly energetic series of dances, when Florence gently poked her friend and encouraged her to get on to the dance floor again.

'C'mon Marie, let's have another dance.'

'Not just now Florence, I'm a little jaded. Let's sit down for a little while more.'

Florence did not question this knowing Marie tended to tire more easily than she because she worked so hard to keep her sisters in food and clothing, whilst holding down her job at the office. In fact this was not the first time Marie had chosen to sit out a dance that evening but Florence had not been aware of it. Unbeknown to Florence at the time, Marie actually had an ulterior motive for making a point of sitting out the dances. She had taken a shine to one of the boys whom she had seen the last three or four times they had been to the dance hall. Boys never danced together so they always had to look out for a potential dance partner from the girls not already on the floor. Marie thought that if she was not dancing she might get asked by him. She had an inkling the boys were looking across at her. She sat with fingers crossed in nervous anticipation. Marie had never been with a boy before so would not know what to say or do, but she was willing to learn!

It took some time for the penny to drop. 'I think I know what you're up to you cunning minx,' Florence said. 'It's not that you're tired is it? You've got your eye on that rather good looking boy sitting at the table over there, haven't you?'

Marie was not a brazen girl; in fact she was really quite reserved and modest. In spite of her good looks and her apparent confident air she would not have wanted to draw attention to herself. She tried to play it down but Florence would have none of it.

'I'll go and tell him you haven't anyone to dance with, shall I?'

'Oh God no Florence. Don't do that — I'd die if you did that.'

But the boys had heard the girls speaking. Raymond had already told his friends how lovely he thought the slim girl in the red dress was. And he was right. Marie was gracile and alluring. She wore a simple red dress tightly wrapped at the hips but otherwise flowing down below her knees. She had a wide belt at her slim waist and wore ankle-strap black shoes. She was as pretty as a picture with an unblemished complexion, big hazel eyes and long, flowing brown hair. Her face was slender with high cheek bones.

Goaded by his friends, the handsome, well-groomed, broad-chested young man, who was sporting a narrow black moustache that made him appear really quite distinguished, sauntered over, sat down at the table the girls were occupying and introduced himself. 'I'm Raymond and I live here in Chateau-Chinon.' And looking at Marie he asked what her name was and where she was from. She told him and then sat waiting for his next move.

After a short pause during which nothing was said, a little nervously he blurted out, 'Would you like to dance with me Marie?'

They danced once, twice, three times and then a fourth without sitting down in between time. They chatted on the dance floor and Marie giggled at Raymond's jokes and quips. They got just a little closer to each other with each new dance.

As the evening drew to a close they left the dance floor, grabbed their coats, went out of the building and walked aimlessly for a good few minutes, chatting freely until they came to a quiet sheltered spot beside the big plane tree. It was a particularly cold day for early November and the frost that had already formed on the grass made a crunching noise as the two innocent young lovers passed over it. They paused and somewhat hesitantly turned to face each other; and then Raymond boldly stole a kiss. It was a very tender kiss that touched her silken lips. For Marie it was most beguiling, and she closed her eyes to savour the moment. This was the very first time she had been kissed on her lips and so intoxicating was it that it sent a tingling sensation down her spine. She felt radiant and as they uncoupled a moment later, she was aware she was blushing. She wanted to put her arms around Raymond and thank him for that beautiful moment but she was not at all sure how he would respond so, reluctantly, she did not. She smiled at him though, albeit a little bashfully, but the message it conveyed was sufficiently clear for Raymond to smile back and then take her gloved hand in his and walk her back to where Marie's friend was waiting.

When Marie caught sight of Florence she saw that her friend was beaming all over her face. She was very happy for Marie and she was not going to hide the fact. On their walk back to the village Marie kept talking about Raymond. 'Isn't he handsome?' she said. 'He's so kind and so funny and he kissed me Florence. He really did kiss me and it was so lovely. I was floating on air. It made me feel so, so happy. It was a very short kiss but still exquisite. He said he would go to the dance hall the same time next week. Do you think we could afford to go again then too Florence? Please say yes.'

Florence was far from sure how her finances would be the very next day let alone a week from then, but being the good friend she was she reassured Marie that they would find a way of getting the money.

Marie had a boyfriend! She felt unassailable and at peace with herself for the first time in a very long time. She was enveloped in a magical state of serenity and yet she had only just met Raymond. Naturally, logic might suggest he was not yet her boyfriend but she believed he was. He must be fond of her she thought, after all he had looked into her eyes and kissed her, he had held her hand and he had smiled at her — they were boyfriend and girlfriend! She could not wait for the next dance evening.

She chose not to share her exciting news with either of her sisters lest they spoil her sublime feeling, a feeling like no other she had ever experienced, a feeling that had been so all consuming she had been unable to think about anything else but him. Of course she wanted to share her news, but given their jealous nature she felt it inevitable that one or both of her sisters would tease and ridicule her, so saying nothing seemed the best option. When alone in the house Marie danced her way across the room twirling and gyrating whilst singing her heart out. Marie was undoubtedly a very, very happy fifteen year old.

The next weekend she and Florence did go to the dance hall and Raymond was there. She was not at all sure how he would respond when he saw her, but she need not have worried for he made a beeline for her the moment she entered the room. She had put on her best dress and applied a little make-up this time, including rouge on her lips.

Raymond had a friend with him who partnered Florence on the dance floor while Marie and her boyfriend — yes he really was her boyfriend for this was their second date — danced continuously throughout the evening.

Just like the previous Saturday the two youngsters took a stroll in the cool night air pausing at the same plane tree. Marie stood quite still waiting with bated breath, hoping he would lower his head and kiss her. She was not disappointed. He kissed her diaphanous mouth passionately this time, and whilst he did so he held her close in a reassuring and loving embrace. Marie did not want that moment to end; she felt safe, loved and needed.

Marie and Raymond continued to meet at the dance hall over the next four or five months and almost always her good friend Florence was there too. In fact Florence seemed to be enjoying the company of Raymond's friend Pierre, which Marie found most satisfying. Raymond came to the house quite a few times too but sadly never when they could be entirely alone. Marie was convinced she was in love with Raymond and wanted to tell him so, but felt that making such a move was perhaps a tad too soon. He was almost two years older than her, but he was still at school preparing for the Concours de l'Ecole des Arts et Metiers, specialising in natural sciences, physical sciences and mathematics. He was intelligent and hoped to become an engineer. Raymond was kind and patient and listened when she told him about the difficult times she had experienced in the months following her mother's death. Thankfully, he had not witnessed her dreadful nightmares and so was still unaware just how insecure she felt at times. Given Marie's chronic state of anxiety it was not at all surprising that she latched on to the first person of the opposite sex to come into her life, believing he would bring her a welcome feeling of security and a sense of belonging, but, by chance, Raymond really was the perfect match for her. He was everything she wanted in a companion and lover. He had been sent from heaven. He was her strength and her soulmate.

They enjoyed each other's company so much they did not need to plan specific outings. They were both just as happy strolling through the countryside hand in hand while talking about this and that and pausing every now and then to kiss. But it was winter and so they rarely lingered out of doors, and yet the alternative was being at home with her two sisters as often as not. Out in the countryside was their only real chance of spending quality time together, alone.

Marie wanted to see more and more of Raymond and felt she was ready for something more intimate. She knew her sisters would be away the last Saturday in March so she asked Raymond to come to the house rather than go dancing with her, hoping they would have a romantic evening together.

Raymond arrived earlier than Marie had anticipated. She saw this as a good sign. She let him in and excused herself for a few moments while she finished preparing the meal she had planned.

'There's a flagon of wine on the table,' Marie called out. 'I'll be with you in just a minute Raymond. Make yourself comfortable.'

'Fine. Where are your sisters Marie? Are they in?'

Marie popped her head around the door from the kitchen and with her chin up a little, her eyes wide open and eyebrows raised she gave him a sardonic grin. She did not need to say anything.

Raymond poured two glasses of wine and sat at the rustic oak drop-leaf table waiting for Marie. He noticed a distinct smell of cigarette smoke and knowing Marie was not a smoker he assumed it must be one of her sisters who did. Sipping his wine he looked around the room. It was small and a little drab he had always thought, but homely none-the-less. Everything was in its place and spotlessly clean and the telltale sign that the place was regularly swept and mopped was in the corner of the room, where up against the wall stood a long-handled broom, a mop and a zinc bucket. There was just one window which he noticed was already shuttered, even though it was not yet dark outside. Floor-length heavy print drapes hung either side of the window. The walls were clad in a mustard-coloured paper festooned with red marguerites repeated every few centimetres. The same paper also embellished the ceiling and the floor was covered in small rectangular brown mottled glazed tiles. There were three communicating doors leading from the room and they were all stained in brown lacquer. There was very little furniture. Besides the table and four chairs there was a small walnut sideboard and against one of the walls was a grandfather clock cased in stained pine. As Raymond waited patiently for Marie to join him, the clock chimed on the quarter hour. It was a quarter past seven.

Marie entered the room, sat down and beckoned her boyfriend over to join her. In almost all company Marie was self-effacing and modest but in her boyfriend's she was self-assured and relaxed. She wore a mid-calf, midnight blue cotton dress that buttoned from top to bottom at the front. Unashamedly Marie had undone the top buttons to reveal a little of her burgeoning breasts, and a few at the bottom so that when seated her dress would part a little to show a modicum of bare thigh. She wore a pretty necklace and had spent nigh on an hour earlier that afternoon fixing her hair in rolls, both at the fringe and along the sides, all held in place with pins, discretely placed. She looked stunning and certainly older than her fifteen years.

'It's so lovely being alone with you at last Raymond. I cherish the times we spend together but almost always it has been in the company of others. Tonight will be different. I'm not expecting Emeline and Colette back until much later. Isn't that wonderful?'

Raymond nodded but said nothing. He seemed a little distant. He had not kissed Marie since he arrived and neither had he complimented her on her seductive appearance.

'Kiss me Raymond. It exhilarates me. Kiss me.'

Raymond kissed her, but not the long lingering kiss she had hoped for.

'Are you all right Raymond? You seem a little distracted. Do I look nice? Do you like my hair? I've done it this way especially for you; it's all the rage in Paris you know.'

'Marie, you know I think the world of you and you know I really enjoy dancing with you and — well — just being with you.' He paused and took a sip of his wine.

Before he continued Marie chipped in, 'And yes, what are you saying? You do want to be alone with me, don't you Raymond?'

'Yes, I do want to be with you Marie but ...' he hesitated, not knowing quite how he should continue.

'But what? What are you trying to say Raymond?'

'I'm trying to say I think the world of you. But I don't think we should get too serious just now. I have my exams coming up very soon and I need to concentrate on preparing for them. I'm sorry if this upsets you. Please understand.'

This was earth shattering news for Marie. She had felt so close to him and since she had known him she had been happier and more content and secure than at almost any time in her young life. But at that precise moment all that was plunged into the abyss — his sentiments had transported her to the brink of oblivion in a trice. She was stunned and knocked senseless. She began to cry, something she was prone to do whenever she felt troubled and ill at ease.

'But I thought you loved me Raymond,' she said between sobs. 'Those kisses, those cuddles and your reassuring words. Were you deceiving me? Didn't you mean them? I can't ....' She stopped: upset, confused and unable to find the words to express how she felt. She was beginning to panic.

'I'm so very sorry Marie. It's not that I don't like you. Quite the reverse. There's nobody else I would prefer to be with. It is just that I don't want to get too serious at this particular time.

Telling you this is painful and the last thing I want is to upset you.'

Marie said absolutely nothing. She shifted a little away from Raymond, dropped her head and held her hands against her temples pressing her fingers deep into her flesh.

Raymond continued. 'Who knows what the future will hold Marie. I think I do love you, but this has come too soon. I have to finish my studies. Please understand. Please don't be mad with me.'

Marie was not mad with him. She was just shocked. It was a bolt from the blue! In the absence of anything else she could say or do she merely gesticulated in such a way that Raymond was in no doubt what she wanted him to do. He stood up, paused as if to touch her, thought better of it and instead made his way across the room and out of the door, closing it quietly behind him.

Outside the house standing there in the drizzle, Raymond wondered if he should go back inside. He hated the thought that he had upset Marie. She was so lovely. She deserved better. Had he done the right thing? Would he regret making this move? He pulled up the collar on his jacket and solemnly walked down the gravel path, across the field and onto the lane that led to the bus shelter.

Marie remained in the seat where Raymond had left her a few moments before. She was still sobbing. Her eyes were swollen. Her make-up was running and her face puffy and red. She sniffed vigorously and hugged her knees tightly, rocking slowly backwards and forwards one moment and burying her head in her hands the next. She was ashamed. She had been too bold, she pondered. And with that thought, and with quivering fingers, she fumbled at the buttons on her dress until they were fully fastened to the collar. Gingerly, with trembling hands she wiped away her tears, whilst sniffing in short rapid inspirations as she tried in vain to stop herself from crying.

Perhaps that is what he meant when he said it was all a bit too soon. She felt she had messed things up and now he was gone. She was alone again. She had not eaten any of the food she had prepared; she had no appetite for it. Marie remained where she was for a very long time, so long in fact that she was still there when her younger sister opened the door. Marie was dreading this moment, fearing her siblings would gloat when they found out she had been jilted. But Colette's response surprised Marie. She was really quite understanding and sat beside her sister wiping away her tears with her kerchief and trying to reassure her by suggesting there were plenty of other boys she would be able to pick from, not that Marie wanted anyone other than Raymond of course. Colette had remembered the numerous occasions back in Villars in the hours and days after the loss of their mother when Marie had consoled her and wiped away her tears. She did not say a great deal but then Marie would not have wanted that.

Not long after, her older sister arrived. Had she been the first to appear Marie was sure she would have relished the moment, teasing her incessantly. However, Emeline saw Colette being reassuringly sympathetic, and so in spite of her more usual bolshy and insensitive nature, on that occasion, no doubt partly because she had been stood up by Gérard only the week before, she was more benevolent; so she said nothing and went to bed!

Not for the first time Marie did not sleep at all well and what with her tossing and turning and constant sobbing, Colette did not sleep well either. The next day, and for many days afterwards, Marie moped about the house keeping herself to herself, doing her chores as best she could and going to work as usual. She needed the comforting presence of her best friend Florence, but she would not be arriving until the following weekend.

CHAPTER TWELVE

Storms make the oak grow deeper roots.
— *George Herbert*

'You told me Raymond hinted that there may be a chance you will get together again sometime, perhaps after he's finished his studies Marie,' announced Florence trying to console her friend. 'You must be optimistic; if that's what he said I'm sure he meant it. In the meantime you have to try to put this down to experience. Who knows what the future may hold.'

'I suppose so,' Marie said with a sigh. 'But I had no idea he was about to leave me. I had thought we were so well suited. He was my saviour and now he's gone.'

'Let's plan what we're going to do today,' said Florence cheerfully. 'I can stay over tonight if you would like. I'll make up a bed on the floor in here. Let's go for a walk and clear our heads.'

So that is precisely what they did. Florence was wearing a cream-coloured culotte dress; she almost always did when she cycled over to see Marie. Marie wore nutmeg-brown trousers and a grubby-cream cotton shirt with rolled up sleeves and a brindled cardigan across her shoulders. She looked a little dishevelled. She did not look as though she had had a decent wash in days and her complexion had lost its flawless appearance, and given she had not been eating well she had lost weight, and rather than the slim, elegant and attractive young woman she had been, she now looked haggard and hollow-cheeked. Florence had tried to encourage her friend to take more care of herself but Marie had simply responded, 'What's the point?'

It was a pleasant day, dry and mostly sunny for the time of year. The cirrus clouds that were high in the sky did not veil the sun much at all as they travelled slowly on a gentle breeze across the pellucid-blue sky. The trees were in leaf. Blackthorn in the hedgerows, and clusters of broom here and there on the hillsides, were already in blossom. There was a profusion of golden-yellow daffodils fringing the farmers' fields and flocks of goldfinches were flittering by, stopping only to feed before moving on.

The two girls set off via the tiny neighbouring hamlet of Les Diolots for the Forêt de Poisson via the tree-lined winding lane. They entered the dense woodland and made their way to the two tiny fishing lakes from which, presumably, the forest had derived its name. They rested for a while, watching swallows swoop low across the rippling water.

They had done this walk many times before so did not need a compass or map. From the lakes they walked northward and on into Forêt Jacob before joining the sinuous but shallow rivulet, Le Touron. They turned west downstream towards its confluence with the Yonne until the road bridge. They crossed the river and traversed the field heading into the pretty nucleated village of Vouchon that sat in a clearing in the vast forested area.

There they rested for a while drinking freshly pressed apple juice on the terrace of the village's Café la Nuit. They had chatted but only very occasionally along the way. Florence respected her friend's apparent need to remain silent at times, though she found it unnerving that her more usually bubbly and vociferous friend remained in deep thought for so much of the time.

As they sat at the wooden trestle table they became very aware the sky was darkening as heavy cumulus clouds rolled in from the west. A storm was brewing for the wind had picked up and it had suddenly turned cool. Marie put on her cardigan and

Florence buttoned her light jacket and with much haste they set off. They took a path almost directly south but the two intrepid travellers became a little less adventurous on entering what had become a very dark and scary forest. They scuttled across the ferny floor frequently stopping in their tracks as birds squawked and flew out in front of them, scattering tiny embryonic leaves in all directions. A rabbit scurried across their path heading no doubt to the safety of its burrow and a roe deer, reacting to an alarm call, barked and flashed out its white rump patch before springing into action and prancing to the protection of the herd. The girls kept hearing eerie sounds and feeling compelled to look around to be sure they were not being followed, often became disorientated. And without the sun to guide them, and in the absence of any familiar landscape features to navigate by, they struggled to escape the forest that had taken on such a spooky, spine-chilling aura. Gusts of wind that periodically whistled through the trees alarmed them. No longer nature's haven the forest had become a frightening inferno and they most certainly did not want to be there when the first bolt of lightning struck.

Eventually, and with a sense of relief, they emerged out onto the meadow. By contrast the light was dazzling, even though the sky was overcast. The clouds had thickened and the sky had turned a dun iron-grey leaving them no choice but to quicken their pace and head for home before the rain set in. They saw a bolt of fork-lightning illuminate the sky and heard the deafening clap of thunder that followed a second or two later. The sky looked ominous. The high-level wispy cirrus clouds had given way to billowing dark anvil-shaped cumulonimbus clouds, but those that developed that day were marked out by the monochromatic pouch-like appearance of mammatocumulus at their base, giving fair warning that a severe storm was about to break. Home was in sight but then suddenly the heavens opened and the rain came down in stair-rods. Another flash of lightning was instantly followed by the ear-splitting, cannonading crash of thunder that by its enormity brought the girls to a halt and yielded an involuntary scream of unmitigated fright. They quickened their pace but the unrelenting driving rain that was hammering the titanium hard ground soaked them through, and as they were so wet the strengthening wind was chilling their bones to the core. The bucolic idyll that the girls had stepped out into a couple of hours before had changed dramatically. The daffodils had been beaten to the ground and the blackthorn blossom lay carpeting the earth.

Arriving at the door of the house they shook themselves to get rid of as much water from their hair and clothes as possible and then entered. Marie knew Colette was out because she had gone away for the weekend to stay with a friend, but Emeline was in the house somewhere. She did not emerge though, not even to greet them let alone to come to their aid with towels so they could dry themselves. Marie made her way to her bedroom where she took from the tall walnut linen cupboard two large towels, one for each of them. The two girls took off their clothes and towelled themselves down. Had there been an observer close by he, or she, would have been mesmerised by the curvaceous olive skinned attractiveness of the one and the sylphlike peaches and cream skinned elegance of the other. Both, in their different ways, would have turned any potential suitor's head, not that the girls knew it: they were modest, unassuming and virtuous, both of them. Perhaps this is why they got on so well; they were not the kind of girls to score points off each other.

'God, that was scary Marie. I thought we'd never get out of that forest.'

Feeling a little less uncommunicative by then, Marie agreed but then added, 'Invigorating though. In a strange kind of way I quite enjoyed it. I think the birds, rabbits and the deer — flying, running and bolting this way and that — took the edge off the scary, eerie side to it all. I love being out there Florence, with all those creatures.'

'That's good. I'm glad you have somewhere to go when you feel sad; somewhere to lift your spirits. We all need that. For me, it's being close to Mère Deschamps.'

Marie was a little thrown by what her friend had just said. It did not surprise her that Mère Deschamps was her comforter and confidante, but listening to her made her realise that she had nobody she could turn to when in despair. The person who had always been there for her was dead, now that Claudette was on the scene she hardly saw her father, she did not live with Mère Deschamps any more, her sisters were almost always ghastly to her and she did not have Raymond's shoulder to cry on. But that very thought generated another: she realised that when she was courting Raymond she almost never needed a shoulder to cry on. The love she felt for him and the happiness and contentment he brought her, lifted the oppressive lid from her cauldron of intense anxiety, generated from her fear of being left all alone. All she had in the world just then was her good friend Florence — thank heaven — but she was twenty kilometres away most of the time. No, only Mother Nature was always there for her when she felt disconsolate and depressed. She said nothing more and continued to dry herself, as did her friend.

Emeline appeared at her bedroom door. She was dressed in a house coat as though she had just got out of bed. She was leaning against the door jamb with a Gauloise between her lips. She stood there staring at the two of them seemingly deep in thought. She looked away momentarily, perhaps a little embarrassed to be staring at the two naked girls maybe, or was it because she was envious of how striking and seductive they both looked? She took a drag on her cigarette and then, in her characteristically demeaning manner she said, 'Oi, am I going to get any food or what? And while you're at it there's no firewood in the house, we've no milk and the mice have been at the bread again.' She turned and walked back into her room but not before calling out, 'And get some clothes on the two of you. Cavorting around the room like that you're nothing better than a couple of whores!' As she disappeared from view the girls could just about make out her muttering. 'I wouldn't mind but who wants to look at what they've got, anyway!' The door slammed and she was not seen again until her

148

meal was on the table.

Florence did stay the night and Marie was grateful for that; she simply could not bear the thought of being in the same house alone with her obnoxious bully of a sister. In fact, with Colette away overnight, Florence slept in Marie's room with her. As always they chatted until late. Florence dropped a few hints that perhaps they should go dancing again.

'It's Labour Day soon Marie; we should plan something. I think there'll be a fête in the village and there's bound to be all kinds of celebrations in Chateau-Chinon. I wonder what the dances are like at the hall these days — we've not been for a while have we?'

Marie did not say yes, but then neither did she say no, which gave Florence hope that she may come round. She would approach the subject again in the morning she thought.

The only reason Marie had not responded was because as soon as her friend had mentioned Labour Day she ceased listening to her and instead thought about her mother and the lily of the valley that would be out in bloom on that day. Marie was making a mental note to collect some and take it to her grave next weekend. She remembered her mother telling her about the love story of the lily of the valley and the nightingale that came back to the woods in May, to entice the flower from of its slumber with its beautiful song. She wondered if her nightingale would return in May; just maybe he was having second thoughts, and was about to return to her and love her.

She remembered the other tales her mother had told her about her favourite wild flower. She recalled being told it was also known as 'Our Lady's tears' or 'Mary's tears', from the Christian legend that it sprang from the weeping of the Virgin Mary during the crucifixion of Jesus. She was called Mary and her life had been tinged with sadness that on numerous occasions had made her weep.

And she remembered that her mother had also told her that the lily of the valley had been considered the symbol of Christ's second coming, which led to its association with the power of people to envision a better world, effectively signalling a return of happiness. As she thought about it she wondered if it was an omen suggesting she and Raymond would find each other again one day. She knew that was the reason why the flower was always sold in France on Labour Day, as the symbol of the beginning of spring which itself conjured up the notion of a new and joyful start. As she lay there in her bed thinking about her life past and present, she remembered too that her mother had told her the lily of the valley was also sometimes called 'the ladder to heaven' due to its bell shaped flowers hanging down from the stem. Was Marie's mother in heaven? Marie was sure she was, and no doubt with lily of the valley all around her.

Marie suddenly became aware that Florence was bidding her 'good night' and realised she had not taken in a word of what Florence had been saying before that. It was time for sleep so she thought she would make a point of asking her what she had said in the morning. She went to sleep thinking about the walk in the forest, Emeline's cutting remarks and Florence's reaction to the storm. Life is not about waiting for the storm to pass, she thought; it is about learning to dance in the rain and by doing so, grasp the essence of survival.

CHAPTER THIRTEEN

To be, or not to be: that is the question:
Whether 'tis nobler in the mind to suffer
The slings and arrows of outrageous fortune,
Or to take arms against a sea of troubles.
    — *William Shakespeare*

Sitting beside her mother's grave Marie remembered writing a note and placing it on her coffin at her funeral. Would her mother be reunited with her nightingale? And would hers return? She prayed every night that Raymond would come knocking on her door, but as time went by — it was six weeks since he walked away and out of her life — slowly she was coming to terms with the thought she may never see him again.

For the rest of the weekend she stayed at home: cleaning, cooking, washing the clothes and the bedding, and generally busying herself. In all previous weeks she had been in the house she had lived in hope that her sisters would rally round and help with the domestic chores, but for the time being she was pleased they were nowhere to be seen. She had the house to herself for much of each weekend and she had learnt that being occupied was a sure way of keeping her 'black dog' at bay. When she did have time to relax she invariably retired to her room and curled up on the bed with a good book.

Her latest, borrowed from the library in Chateau-Chinon, was *The Little Prince* by Antoine de Saint-Exupéry. She was discovering that it was a lovely story. It had been recommended to her by a colleague at the office, but of course her co-worker was quite unaware that her choice of book was so profoundly apt for Marie. Though it paralleled the author's life, being a compassionate tale of loneliness, friendship, love and loss it could have been written as an allegory of Marie's life too. He wrote the book in 1943, the year before Marie's mother was killed so tragically and at a time of enormous turmoil in occupied France. The book is a search for childhood certainties and inner peace, that Marie had craved as a child but had so rarely experienced. But it is also an allusion to the tortured nature of some relationships; for Marie this was indubitably the wretched entanglement she experienced daily with her elder sister.

The Little Prince makes several observations about life and human nature, many of which may have been beyond her understanding but one or two almost certainly touched a nerve and helped her on her way through life. From the book she learnt that it was important to remain true to oneself, never to give up hope and that much can be achieved when following one's dreams, however difficult they may be to acquire and however long they may take.

In the book Saint-Exupéry told the tale of a fox meeting a young prince. The crux of the story is found in some of the lines spoken by the fox, such as when he says:

One sees clearly only with the heart. What is essential is invisible to the eyes.

This line relates to a part of the story where the Prince found a rose that he came to cherish and love as his most prized possession. But he became separated from his rose and on his travels he discovered, much to his disappointment, dozens of roses all looking like the one he had cherished and had thought unique. He became disillusioned and disheartened believing he had been deceived into thinking his rose was special and unique when it was not. But the astute fox told him that whilst the other roses may look similar they were not; his rose was the object of love from his heart and not as seen through his eyes. Therefore, his rose was very special, beautiful and unique.

So Marie was coming to terms with her separation from Raymond and was trying to live a life without him. She may have assumed that one day she would find another soulmate and partner, but she knew she would never stop loving Raymond. It was he who was truly unique and very special to her. Dreams may be made in heaven but they can be realised on earth. Would her dream be realised on earth or would she have to wait until she was in heaven?

*

Florence next met up with her friend on the weekend of Marie's birthday, 19 May. She was determined to take her dancing in Chateau-Chinon and this time would not take no for an answer. Marie liked to dance but she had been apprehensive, wondering if she might see Raymond there, perhaps even dancing with another girl. However, she had believed him when he said he needed to study for his exams and so felt the likelihood of bumping into him at a social event very unlikely.

Being the good friend she was, and aware how miserable Marie had been the past few weeks, Florence wanted to give her a birthday celebration to remember. She had planned a walk in the forest, a simple meal in a bistro in town and then onto the dance hall. Their afternoon stroll passed without incident: no storm or scary forest and no confrontation with her elder sister! Many of the meadows they crossed clearly had not been ploughed for decades and so they were an abundance of colour with wildflowers aplenty; and they did not have to search too far before they found some lily of the valley either. They had taken a different route this time, heading west from the village, through Les Mouilleferts to the woodland on the banks of the Yonne where they sat in the sunshine for the better part of two hours.

'Oh, I nearly forgot — Mère Deschamps insisted on making one of her specials Marie.'

'Oh no Florence — not stinging nettle quiche with hedge woundwort sauce and a side dish of hogweed-au-gratin!' said Marie, sarcastically.

'No, don't be stupid. She's made a lovely apple tart. Do you want some?'

'Phew! Thank goodness for that. You know Florence, it's lovely sitting here isn't it? I really do feel so peaceful when outside sharing Mother Nature's home with all her plants and wildlife. The sound of birds singing and crickets chirping is delightful. Let's just hope the vipers are not about,' she said warily, whilst wiggling her arm along the grass to show how a snake might creep up on them. It was not the first time Florence had heard Marie say how at ease she felt when out and about in the countryside.

'I was bitten by a viper a year ago, when walking along the path in the woods near Venitiens,' said Florence.

Marie gasped with trepidation. 'So what did you do? Did you take the anti-serum?'

'No,' Florence retorted, but then she explained. 'It's important you take the anti-serum within a couple of hours otherwise you may die. For us the nearest pharmacy was more than ten kilometres away in Saint-Honoré. Mère Deschamps thought this would be too far, so she had little option but to cut the venom from my leg with the folding knife she was carrying with her. It was fortunate she had it with her that day; she had been using it to cut wild flowers to take home. It was a lucky escape.' And pointing to her ankle she said, 'There, see, I've still got the scar to prove it.'

The two girls swished their sticks this way and that just to be sure there were none around, and once satisfied their little haven was viper-free they lay out on the grass, occasionally staring up at the azure sky.

Marie lay very still on her back observing a solitary sky-lark beginning its flight song while climbing steeply into the sky, until it appeared to hang almost above her head. The bird's long, liquid warble was exquisite and remarkably resonant, so much so she thought it must have been heard from quite a distance. She closed her eyes to concentrate on what was to Marie the quintessential sound of summer. Suddenly there was silence. She opened her eyes and squinting against the bright sunlight, just made out the sky-lark parachuting back down to the meadow where it dropped out of sight, presumably to feed on a profusion of seeds and insects. Marie rolled onto her side to face her friend and as she did so she called out to her.

'Look! Florence, there are rabbits over there. One, two, three, oh there's a whole family of them, playing in the meadow.'

Florence sat up and looked in the direction where Marie had been pointing and sure enough there were six or seven rabbits darting this way and that, playfully.

'And over there Marie — there's a red deer on the edge of the wood.'

'And down here on the steep river bank amongst the roots of that huge tree I noticed earlier the characteristic signs of a badger set. And can you smell the fox Florence? It can't be far away.'

It was impossible to venture out into the Morvan countryside at any time of the day or year without seeing an abundance of wildlife, and the day they sat there on the banks of the Yonne was certainly no exception. The girls felt privileged to be sharing nature's home with such a rich and diverse flora and fauna. And to top it all there was nobody else in sight!

They looked up at the sun and thinking it must be fast approaching five o'clock agreed they ought to be on their way. They still had two or three kilometres to go before reaching Chateau-Chinon, so feeling happy and relaxed, though decidedly soporific after their snooze in the warm sunlight, they slowly sauntered along the path leading to the little footbridge across the river, into the Forêt de Rafigny and hence to the road that would take them across town to the little restaurant Florence had selected. The girls were astonished to see how busy the town was. The cafés and bars were bustling with people, spilling out onto the terraces. Another glorious spring-time without the watchful eye of the Nazis, and people were making the most of it.

The restaurant was a simple bistro set out with wooden tables each with either two or four chairs. The tables were very close together; it was not a restaurant of choice for a couple hoping for some privacy and a romantic meal. In fact along one wall was what today prestigious restaurateurs call 'the chef's table'. It was a large refectory style table alongside the kitchen door to seat close to a dozen people. Customers were either served the chef's dish of the day with no other choices or expected to try out his new creations.

Marie and Florence chose a table for two near a window looking over the busy thoroughfare. Eating out was a rare treat for the girls and they took a while looking through the menu that included a host of traditional Burgundian specialities such as Escargot, Coq au Vin, Boeuf Bourguignon, Cuisses de Grenouille, Jambon Persillé and Lapin au Cidre. Having mulled over the mind-boggling choices for what seemed an age Marie chose Andouillette, a very stinky sausage made from pig's colon — amongst other things — and to finish she chose her favourite, Ile Flottante, that consisted of fluffy egg whites floating on crème anglaise. Florence had a plate of Tête de Veau, calf's head enriched in ox blood and red wine, with Tarte Tatin to finish. They audaciously washed it all down with a glass of red Burgundy. They were ready to party!

By eight thirty the dance hall was packed and couples were competing for a place 'centre stage' as the band struck up. The sound of an accordion reminded Marie of the times when she was at home with her family listening to her father playing and singing. They were something of a dysfunctional family these days and this saddened her. However, she was very much looking forward to the evening with Florence; Marie had quite forgotten how therapeutic dancing could be. She scrutinised the room rigorously to be sure Raymond was not lurking somewhere in the darkened corners with an admirer by his side, and when entirely satisfied he was nowhere to be seen, she took to the dance floor with her good friend. They danced until they dropped, hardly stopping for a breather or refreshment. They found the noisy, crowded party atmosphere enthralling and sang along with the music as they cavorted across the dance floor. They had not had so much fun in weeks.

While they were dancing Florence spotted a couple of boys looking their way, but she did not tell Marie thinking it would faze her. Being sensitive to Marie's wishes, thinking another relationship was too soon after Raymond, she thought it best the boys did not have the opportunity to approach them that night, so she made an excuse to Marie that she was not feeling too well and therefore perhaps ought to return home.

'I'm so sorry Marie, but I think I must have had a little too much sun earlier. I feel a little sick and have a headache. Could we go home? I know it's early and I know you are having such a lovely time too.'

'Oh! Well, if you are ill then of course we'll have to go, but you're right I was having a lovely time. Perhaps if you were to sit down for a while and have a drink of water then maybe you'd feel better.' Marie was clearly hoping her friend would stay. She continued, 'Look, there's a table over there. Let's sit down for a while and see if you will feel better.'

'No!' said Florence emphatically, noticing that the table Marie was pointing to was next to the one occupied by the boys who had shown such an interest in them earlier. 'I'd rather just get out into the night air if that's okay and make our way home. We can return in a week or two if you wish. We'll wait for a bus.'

'Okay, okay. If that's what's best for you, then let's go' Marie said, if not a little harshly.

And so with Marie none the wiser as to the true reason they were leaving, they walked across the road to the bus shelter and waited. It was rare for buses to be operating at night in this part of the world but with the town enjoying a holiday atmosphere they guessed one or two would be running that particular Saturday. They waited thirty minutes or so before one pulled in by the bus shelter. Along with a dozen others they boarded, paid their fares and sat down while the bus made its way along the bumpy road out of town. Though only a five kilometres walk to Marie's home the bus journey took nigh on an hour, criss-crossing the countryside to drop off partygoers en-route to Vallée de Cours and beyond. Marie sat pensively, staring out of the window into the darkness. She had enjoyed her night out but wished it had not ended so abruptly, and just because her friend had been in the sun too long! Florence stayed with Marie that night, and yet again in her room because Colette was out over night.

*

The next day Florence left early, leaving Marie alone with her elder sister; Colette was not back from her overnight stay with friends. Emeline got up out of bed at around ten and somehow expected that her breakfast would be on the table for her. It was not. Marie was outside putting out the washing.

'Where's breakfast?' she called aloud. Marie heard but ignored her.

Emeline went to the door. 'Oi, where's my breakfast? The table's normally laid by this time. I want my breakfast.' Her tone was getting more aggressive and louder with each syllable uttered.

'I ate my breakfast with Florence. She had to go early. I cleared the table thinking you might not be up until lunch-time, your more usual time for getting out of bed on Sundays I do believe.' Marie spoke slowly and precisely.

'Well, not this one,' Emeline said forcefully. And walking

across to her she prodded Marie in the ribs, shouting, 'Now'.

'Get it yourself Emeline. I'm busy with the washing.'

'For Christ's sake Marie, you can bloody well put the washing out later. Coffee, bread and jam.'

She could have cow-towed to her sister; in fact that is what she had nearly always done when on the receiving end of her abhorrent sister's demands, if only to prevent a row. But this particular day was different. Marie was no longer prepared to be used and treated as a slave to her sister's every command.

To hold her nerve, Marie took a deep breath and as calmly but as firmly as possible she spoke directly to Emeline. 'Well, you may be surprised to learn this Emeline, but I'm not your slave. I seem to do almost all the chores round here and I'm the only wage earner too. Have you been out lately looking for work? No! Why? Because you're too damn lazy to get off your ass and out of the house. You insult, malign and revile me and yet still expect your meals on the table, your clothes washed and the house cleaned, and all at my expense at that. There's absolutely no reason whatsoever why I should be your servant Emeline. For once sort out your own breakfast.'

This went down like a lead balloon. As was so often the case when Emeline was put in her place she clenched her teeth, flared her nostrils and thumped her fist on the table. She was red with rage but did not know quite what to say. She was not used to Marie arguing back: she had the wind taken out of her sails and was startled. She muttered a few incomprehensible words, some of which were almost certainly expletives, turned on her heel, strode across the room and disappeared back into her lair, where she stayed for the rest of the day, sulking. Marie had been shaking like a leaf whilst speaking to Emeline, fearful that her sister would become violent and abusive. As her sister disappeared from view Marie dropped down on a chair, wearing the smile of someone who was relieved to have completed a difficult task with aplomb.

It was several weeks before Marie and Florence went back to Chateau-Chinon and in the meantime things continued as per usual at the house. Colette was as surly as ever and as for Emeline, she had not amended her ways since the stand-off, but Marie had; she no longer felt threatened and was now more inclined to stand her ground.

CHAPTER FOURTEEN

Respect was invented to cover the empty place where love should be.
— *Leo Tolstoy*

'Oh my word, Florence, I do believe we're being watched. Don't look around now, but there are two boys over there and they keep looking at us and muttering things behind their hands. Oh Florence! I said DON'T look around!'

'Sorry Marie. When you say don't, it's inevitable I will, isn't it?'

'I don't know. Is it Florence? Anyway it's too late now. They know we know they've been looking at us and because you turned round they also think we're interested!'

'Let's just ignore them, carry on dancing and see what happens,' said Florence furtively. When she had turned around she had realised that the boys were the same ones she saw looking at them the last time they were at the dance hall, a few weeks back. She had not told Marie about that then, so said nothing.

'Well, I'm not going over there to plead on bended knee for them to dance with us Florence, even if I am interested, which of course I am not. Hmm … at least I don't think I am. But now that I think about it, I suppose it would be quite nice to be dancing in the arms of a handsome young man.' As she spoke she was gently swaying to the music, with her eyes closed, her chin up and arms extended, as if one hand was gently clasping the hand of an admirer, and the other resting lightly on his opposite shoulder. 'Anyway, if they're interested they'll come to us; let's not make them too cocky,' retorted Marie assertively.

But unbeknown to the two girls, the two boys were standing immediately behind them as they were speaking. One of them coughed and the girls spun round in disbelief.

'So eh, you two girls might like to dance in the arms of a handsome young man then? Well, it's your lucky day ladies,' he said confidently, and then while looking directly at Marie, 'I guess I'm prepared to provide you with such a service, and my friend here will do likewise for your friend I feel sure. Isn't that right Alain?'

'Well, given they both look so fetching, how could we refuse Arnaud,' said Alain, trying with some difficulty to appear aloof.

'So you heard everything then did you?' Marie uttered, irritatingly. 'Now look boys, there's no hanky-panky you know. We're not push-overs even if my comment did suggest we were a tad desperate,' retorted Marie with mock disdain. And she added with unflinching boldness, 'Now behave yourselves and come on, let's dance!'

Marie was a far more assured and assertive person these days Florence had thought. She said nothing but her exuberance, slightly raised chin and pursed lips, with wide-eyed facial expression and raised eyebrows, suggested unequivocal approval.

Marie danced with Arnaud and enjoyed his robust and confident but respectful manner. They chatted, at least as far as was possible given the big-band sound that was in full throttle that evening. They swung each other around one moment and got just a little close to each other the next. Marie liked Arnaud. She was happy to spend the rest of the evening with him. At the end of the evening they declared they had enjoyed themselves but there was to be no hand in hand stroll along the road or a kiss. Would they see each other again? Marie was not sure, or at least if she was, she was not letting on to Arnaud.

'Let's wait and see shall we? Come on Florence,' and then in earshot of Alain, 'unless you've got other plans of course'. It was Marie's time to embarrass Florence. Like Marie she had enjoyed her evening and had rather hoped Alain may have wanted to arrange another date right there and then, but though he appeared to be about to say something, before he could, Marie grasped Florence's arm and ushered her toward the door, and with some haste.

Turning away from the boys Marie spoke softly to her friend. 'We mustn't look too keen Florence. Absence makes the heart grow fonder you know, so let's wait and see what happens shall we.' This was not so much a question, as an instruction. And as they left the room Marie turned, waved at Arnaud, and while lifting her voice so he would hear her, she said, 'The return makes one love the farewell.' And with that they left without turning again.

'That will get them thinking Florence. Do you know Alfred De Musset said that a hundred years ago! But it's true isn't it? There's no need to fret when saying a goodbye because a farewell is necessary before you can meet again, and meeting again if you're fond of someone is such a glorious thing to do. So until then?'

'Who's Alfred De Musset?' asked Florence, sheepishly.

'He was a famous Romantic poet, author and playwright Florence. Don't you remember learning about him at school? Oh well, not to worry. Anyway that's what he said. Food for thought isn't it?'

Florence nodded in agreement, but not only did she not remember learning about Alfred De Musset at school but she was not really sure what her friend meant with all her 'goodbyes', 'farewells', 'meetings' and 'glorious things to do', so she quickly changed the subject. 'Anyway, where have you got all this newly acquired confidence and self-assurance from Marie?'

'Well, as a matter of fact Florence I can thank my bone-idle, callous, inconsiderate and self-centred sister Emeline for that. But that's another story,' she said, skipping joyfully down the road with Florence at her side.

Of course, Marie did not always manage to remain oblivious in the face of the constant chiding, importunity and general unpleasantness at the hands of her nasty sisters: panic fits, nightmares and shaking still haunted her from time to time. However, anyone observing Marie's behaviour that evening would have seen a sixteen year old who had very much enjoyed the company of a young man, but who was prepared to walk away and take a chance as to whether they would meet again. She would not have been that way with Raymond. The question is why? Was it because she was wiser and more mature or was it because she had been hurt before and did not want to experience that again? Perhaps it was neither or maybe both. Some might suggest she behaved as she did because she simply did not feel the same about Arnaud as she did about Raymond, and that was that. Raymond was special and unique and she knew that from their very first meeting. Arnaud on the other hand was just one more rose in the garden of a dozen or more: charming, colourful, impressive and eye-catching yes, but not special in a unique kind of way.

A couple of weeks later they did meet again but this time at L'Oustalet, a restaurant come dance venue on the edge of the town looking out over the Morvan hills. But Marie was not quite ready for the next step and therefore continued to keep Arnaud at a distance. He was tall, slender, clean-shaven and decidedly handsome, and she liked his company, thought a lot of him and respected his direct but genial manner, but did that mean she wanted him to kiss her passionately? Not yet anyway. As well as the dance hall they met in cafés, bars and once at the cinema. She did not invite him to her house but he was a good reason for Marie to escape the clutches of her irritatingly dependent sisters.

In between dates with Arnaud she continued to keep the house clean and tidy and she still worked at the office in Chateau-Chinon, and as the only wage earner of the three sisters. She saw her father less and less given that Claudette was about to have a baby. She was still very friendly with Florence and they met up frequently but as often as not Marie preferred to visit her, than the other way around; another excuse to get out of the house. On those visits she was delighted to see Mère Deschamps and the three of them chatted about earlier times when Marie had lived there. The girls joked with her about their forays into the 'cauldron of buttercup hell', but appearing confused they had to remind her that she always warned them to wash their hands when they got home after handling buttercups because 'don't you know buttercups give you diarrhoea and sickness'!

Unbelievably, it was not until mid September, almost three months after they had met, that Marie and Arnaud had their first serious embrace and a passionate kiss. For Marie this was fair evidence Arnaud was pretty serious about her, since at no time before that had he tried to take advantage of her. He was content to be with her and to wait for the right moment. That moment happened to be in the back of the cinema, but whether it was because they were eager to get close, or because the film was so dreary, remains a mystery. However, they did get more serious after that kiss and in fact Marie met his parents a week or two later. Marie found them very kind and they seemed to like her. They lived a couple of kilometres from the centre of Chateau-Chinon in the tiny hamlet of Précy.

The house where Arnaud lived was a large end-terrace stone-built property at the far end of the road looking out onto open countryside. The house had a garden on three sides and a small field adjoining it well-stocked with vegetables and soft fruits and with a goat, a donkey, some hens and a very noisy old cockerel. The house was of the same construction as so many in the villages of the Morvan. The steep-angled slate roof was supported by substantial oak beams and red terracotta tiles covered the floor. The walls were nigh on a metre thick, whitewashed throughout on the inside and with small windows and a wood-burning range. The living rooms were not on the ground floor but above the hay store where, in days gone by, a small-holder's livestock would take cover in particularly bleak winter conditions. The hay and live-stock would insulate the living space above, helping to keep the occupants warm.

Marie's first memory of the house was the absence of running water: so no flushing toilet and water for washing and cooking was from a well a short distance away. In fact the toilet was not dissimilar to the one she remembered using in Rennes, the difference being the hole in the ground was in their own garden, and unlike the one in Rennes theirs had a simple wooden seat above it. The bizarre fact, at least judged by today's code of behaviour, was that it was positioned in the front garden just back from the low level wall that separated the plot from the road. And of course, as is so for some public toilets in France even today, the door was merely a half door so offering little more than a smidgen of privacy to the occupant.

*

As the weeks passed it became abundantly clear that Arnaud and Marie got on very well. Arnaud was very keen on Marie and nothing was too much trouble for him when it came to providing for her. As a matter of fact Marie enjoyed the solace afforded her by being a part of Arnaud's family; she had missed the family life she remembered from her pre-teen years. Arnaud's parents lived simply and were very largely self-sufficient. They had all the vegetables and fruits they desired, hens to yield a daily supply of fresh eggs and the occasional meal or two when the cockerels were fat enough for slaughter. They got fresh milk directly from the farmer only a couple of hundred metres from their home or from their own goat, and the house was always full of the redolent aroma of freshly baked bread, pies and tarts. The shelves in the kitchen were stacked high with preserves of every type from jams and compotes to jars of green beans, chutneys and pickles. There were no shops and no market so Arnaud's mother walked the couple of kilometres into Chateau-Chinon every two or three days to buy the produce they could not provide for themselves. Life in Précy after the war may have been physically demanding but it was rewarding nonetheless.

As the weeks rolled by Marie saw more and more of Arnaud and though still just sixteen years of age she did not hesitate when he asked for her hand in marriage. Arnaud was to Marie the epitome of thoughtfulness and compassion, providing her with security and stability and the bonus of congenial company. But did she love him? Well, is not love having someone finally at your side long after fate dealt you a bad hand? And isn't it about security and stability when all about you had seemed uncertain and ephemeral? And also isn't it about thoughtfulness and benevolence when for so long the daily reality had meant being at the beck and call of self-centred rancorous tyrants? Well then, she must have loved him.

She moved in with Arnaud's family almost immediately she was betrothed to him. Monsieur and Madame Rousseau had known from their son how distressed Marie got at the hands of her bully sisters, but even had they not known from him they would have seen the unmistakable signs of someone troubled, tired and weary from her daily grind; they genuinely wanted to help provide respite. She did not lose touch with Florence, the one person in her life that had always been there for her in times of great need, but she did not see so much of her, though this was in part because Florence too was in a relationship; in fact with Arnaud's friend, Alain.

They were married in the town shortly after her seventeenth birthday and continued to live in the house in Précy for a few more months. She helped around the house but Arnaud's parents were insistent that she did very little, to make up for the hardship of catering for her sisters for so long. She resigned from her job and left her sisters to cope at home without her income or relentless hard work. Their inconceivable selfishness meant they had always expected their sister to cook, wash and clean for them, and her leaving them to cope alone was something they never forgave her for, and found every opportunity to present her in the worst possible light when talking about her to friends and relatives. Marie of course was over the moon that they were no longer her responsibility.

The two newly-weds moved to Paris just after Christmas 1948, having chosen first to spend the Christmas period with Arnaud's parents and his brother and sister. Arnaud's siblings were more than twenty years older because, rather astonishingly, Arnaud had been born when Madame Rousseau was forty-five years old. Marie's family had not really celebrated the festive season since her mother had died, preferring to have a simple quiet Christmas Eve meal with her father, Claudette and her sisters and little else. And over the past four years Christmas Day itself had been spent quietly at home reading or taking a stroll in the countryside. However, Christmas 1948 was different. It was her first as a newly-wed and cuddling up with her husband in front of a wood-burning range in what was to become the coldest winter for a century, whilst playing games and chatting freely with his family, was very comforting.

In Paris they lived in a family run hotel come hostel on Rue Cardinet in the seventeenth Arrondissement, in fact within walking distance of the artists' quarter in Montmartre and the Basilique du Sacré-Cœur. Their hotel room was adequate and simply furnished. They shared with four other families a toilet, bathroom and small area where they prepared food and cooked their meals, and whilst far from ideal at least they had the convenience of not having to maintain a home. The rent was very low, being heavily controlled by the authorities so that for the average family, and Arnaud and Marie were pretty average, the rent took only about four percent of the budget. The downside was that hoteliers and landlords had little money to spend on repairs and safety. The cramped and sometimes unhygienic conditions did little for the government's drive to repopulate France. With too little space to swing a cat in, let alone bring up children, the birth rate dropped as many women resorted to back-street abortions as their contraceptive.

Finding an apartment had been impossible in post war Paris, given that thousands had been flocking back to the city after their war-time transient migration to the countryside. And though many French intellectuals, artists, writers and actors had left for good in the wake of reprisals after the war, many foreigners of similar worth, including the likes of Ernest Hemingway, Orson Welles, John Huston, James Baldwin, Samuel Beckett and Audrey Hepburn, had arrived in Paris to make it their home.

Parisians had become retrospective, trying to comprehend the past whilst waiting for the tide to turn. Though Parisians may not have suffered the consequences of a wide-scale London type blitz that is not to say they had not suffered. For Parisians there may not have been the tangible signs of the Nazi footprint like fallen masonry and burning buildings but their jack-boots had left their imprint nonetheless, but on the minds of the people rather than their bricks and mortar. Theirs was an insidious 'blitz' that left minds in turmoil rather than their streets. Whilst it would be untrue to suggest Londoners escaped entirely from the mental scarring caused by the bombing of their homes, nevertheless it would be fair to say that having something tangible to see from the bombardment of the Luftwaffe's blitzkrieg, they had something visible to get angry about. This had the effect of uniting Londoners in a common cause: the defeat of the enemy during the war and the rebuilding of communities after it, and all the more so given there was a strong and articulate leader in Winston Churchill, who was able to unify people with his patriotic rallying cry. But Parisians had neither the physical signs nor the stirring leadership to unite them in a common cause. The old Third Republic had collapsed and the newly constituted Fourth Republic was in chaos. In Paris, and throughout most of urban France, individuals were left to fight for their own cause rather than unite with others in a common one.

A new wave of Parisians was rising to the fore, however. In 1947 Christian Dior launched his fashion house's first collection.

The war was over and women stereotyped as 'soldiers in boiler-suits with Basque berets' from the days of the Resistance had gone and in their place had come Dior's 'woman-flower', with prominent bust, wide shoulders, belted waist, flat stomach, very full skirt and flamboyantly large hats. Others followed: Pierre Balmain, Jacques Griffe, Hubert de Givenchy and Pierre Cardin. The old Paris with a culture based on intellectuals of the pen and easel had given way to those of fashion and couture. But Haute Couture was for the well-heeled and not the likes of Arnaud and Marie. However, they too were soon to benefit for, as the decade neared its end, these celebratory couturiers introduced the world to Haute Couture's ready-to-wear clothing. This was heaven sent for Marie, giving her a new lease of life. Her time in Paris transformed her into a woman with a desire for quality and affordable fashion; looking good made her feel good and that was a real fillip.

Arnaud and Marie made friends in their neighbourhood and liked to visit the nightclubs and riverside guinguettes, where they danced to American swing bands or jived until they dropped. But they were just as happy strolling into Parc Monceau, or watching the artists at work in Montmartre or taking a longer walk along the Seine, where occasionally an accordion player could be heard, coaxing the two of them into a frivolous impromptu dance, much to the enjoyment of passers-by. Marie particularly loved dancing; it was a pleasure that had been forged years earlier by her father and reinforced time and again by her life-long friend Florence.

Life in Paris was very different from the Morvan. Food was hard to come-by and queues in shops and in the market were horrendous. Incomes had dropped by a fifth from before the war and the recommended calorie intake for children was never met by the majority. For many the cash economy had given way to bartering and exchanging goods and services. Inevitably this caused problems for the government since it was difficult collecting taxes, and without taxes infrastructural improvements could not be made. Bizarrely it was butchers who seemed to gain most from all of this. With meat in demand many chose to hold back supply so they could increase prices and benefit from the more wealthy. Many adopted a dog eat dog mentality in post war Paris. Marie and Arnaud were not wealthy and found it difficult making ends meet, eating meat was a luxury for them.

But despite the hardships, on 28 September 1949 Marie gave birth to a lovely baby boy Daniel and two years later on 25 November 1951 a beautiful daughter Nathalie, but not before they had moved out of the hotel and into a small apartment in Rue de Levis, just a few streets away. Life was changing and changing very much for the better.

*

Nevertheless, as the weeks passed Arnaud became more aware that Marie was not able to leave behind the panic attacks and occasional nightmares that brought her out in a cold sweat. It was not unusual for him to awake in the night to find Marie in her nightdress sitting in the chair shaking, while staring into space and rocking backwards and forwards mindlessly. He was immensely sympathetic and genuinely wanted to help but, mistakenly, he believed she was best left alone to recover when these occurrences struck, thinking she needed her own space without him constantly checking how she was feeling. He often saw her in tears for which there appeared no obvious reason. He found her crying difficult to handle.

Though Marie was unable fully to comprehend what was happening to her, she knew she needed a more tactile response from her husband. She was insecure and felt dependent and very much in need of physical warmth and constant verbal reassurances that she was loved. Arnaud knew the difficult times she had experienced but had hoped their marriage would be the panacea. However, the simple fact was that it was not so. Her psychological equilibrium had been thrown out of kilter following her mother's death and the subsequent forced separation from her remaining family by her distraught father, leaving her a sufferer of chronic depression and anxiety. She had never received the medical support needed to rid her of the 'black dog' that snapped at her heels, following her like a hound after a wounded fawn.

CHAPTER FIFTEEN

When sorrows come, they come not single spies, but in battalions.
— *William Shakespeare*

Early in 1952 Arnaud and Marie moved again, this time to one of the most densely populated municipalities in Europe, the Paris suburb of Vincennes, seven or eight kilometres from the city centre. This was a far cry from the bustling inner city Rue de Levis of the seventeenth Arrondissement. In the suburbs people were more insular and self-effacing and there you walked to the shops rather than have them on your doorstep, but at least it was nearer to Arnaud's work. The two room apartment still meant all four sleeping in the same room, but the splendid park of Bois de Vincennes was nearby, so during the days Marie was able to escape the confined space of the apartment and visit the park with the children. At almost a year old, Nathalie was just walking and three year old Daniel was into anything and everything. He was a cheerful little boy and for his age fiercely independent. He often ran off quite happily to play with the other children, but he always came scampering back soon after to enjoy a loving cuddle with his mother.

The Bois de Vincennes was and still is the largest public park in Paris: three times the size of New York's Central Park and about the same size as London's Regent's Park. The park of the

Bois de Vincennes was created in the mid nineteenth century by the Emperor Napoleon III and is still a major destination for Parisians escaping the hustle and bustle of city life. Marie and the children often visited Lac de Saint-Mandé (the closest of the four lakes in the park to their apartment) to feed the ducks; and the children played on the swings and roundabout, visited the Paris zoo and watched puppet shows at the Théâtre de Guignol.

The imposing Château de Vincennes, a former residence of the Kings of France, is also in the park. In fact in 1422 it is where England's Henry V died suddenly from dysentery, a little short of his 36th birthday. Henry had been victorious in a number of battles in France between 1415 (the Battle of Agincourt, where he was victorious against all the odds) and 1422. In 1419 he took Rouen and the following year the Treaty of Troyes recognised Henry as the heir and regent of France, leading to his marriage to Katherine of Valois, the French King's daughter. Had he lived two more months he would have outlived Charles VI of France and therefore would have been crowned King of France. Towards the end of 1422 — the year Henry died — his last battle led to the capture of Melun and the castle of Montereau, a short distance from the walls of Paris. Later in her life Marie got to know these places very well indeed, having chosen to live for thirty years until her death in the village of Saint-Agnan, barely ten kilometres as the crow flies from Montereau.

The Bois de Vincennes was part of the ancient forest that surrounded the Roman town of Vilcena, from which the park has been named. A hunting lodge was built by Louis VII in the 12th century, in the thirteenth century Philippe-Auguste built the castle and in the fourteenth century a chapel was added by Charles V to house religious relics, just like its sister chapel, Sainte-Chapelle, that had been built a little earlier in central Paris.

The park was laid out to provide green space and recreation for the large working-class population of eastern Paris, similar to the Bois de Boulogne, which Napoleon III had begun building in 1852 for the more affluent population of the west side of Paris.

Most of the events for the 1900 Paris Olympic Games took place in the Bois de Vincennes. The velodrome built at the end of the nineteenth century was used to stage cycling, rugby, football, gymnastics and of all things, cricket. In fact the park hosted the first — and no doubt the last — international cricket match between England and France; England won!

Also of significance, even more so given it was Marie's birth month and year, for six months from May 1931 the Paris Colonial Exposition took place in the Bois de Vincennes to showcase the culture, products and resources of the French empire. There were cafés and restaurants, and even a zoo that became the inspiration for the permanent Paris zoo that opened in 1934.

The point of the exhibition was for the French government to show the world that it was assimilating the French colonies. To facilitate this, above the facade of Vincennes's colonial museum, now the Cité Nationale de l'Histoire de l'Immigration, was the inscription:

To her sons who have extended the empire of her genius and made dear her name across the seas, France extends her gratitude.

But in spite of this, and a range of exhibits that included pavilions from each of its colonies, it did little to appease the critics who accused the French government of exploiting the people from its colonies. In fact the French Left staged a smaller alternative exhibition to highlight the abuses committed during the colonial conquests, including that of forced labour. They suggested that visiting the exposition was no different from going to a zoo to stare at the strange animals there. Just fourteen years later such an accusation was repeated in an even more fervent manner when Senegalese troops, who had done so much to help liberate Paris, were banned from joining in the celebrations; instead, their job done, they were sent back to Senegal.

*

The apartment block was typical of those in the Parisian suburbs. A tiny entrance hall with high-gloss cream coloured walls led to the concierge's lodge, and a staircase with wrought iron railings and highly polished mahogany hand rail. The floors and stairs were covered in brown linoleum, which greatly exacerbated the noise made by tenants making their way to and from their apartments. Invariably the lift was out of order, and out of bounds too for those with an inkling of claustrophobia, given the enclosed space was barely enough for two people, and, it might be said, two who knew each other very well at that. You certainly would not have wanted to be in the confined space with a total stranger.

Their apartment was on the fifth floor. It was small with just one bedroom and a living room with a stove, sink and table for food preparation tucked away in the corner, shut off behind folding doors. However, whilst a step-up from their two previous lodgings, they still had to share a single toilet with three other families.

Arnaud and Marie bought a wireless and a second-hand gramophone soon after moving to Vincennes. Their favourite music was of course dance music, including small time French accordion music as well as American swing bands. They listened to these sounds seemingly night and day.

One piece that Marie was all but obsessed with, though nothing to do with her passion for dance, was Gustav Mahler's hour long symphony number three in D-minor that he had written about the story of creation. Marie knew the story from the record's sleeve notes. The first movement tells the story of a new beginning as winter gives way to summer via spring. Inevitably she thought of her mother and the lily of the valley when she heard this movement. The second (Mahler called it "What the flowers in the meadow tell me") also struck a chord with her. It begins with a lovely graceful Minuet, interspersed with stormier episodes later in the movement. Listening to this Marie remembered with joy her ventures into the countryside and recalled the battle against the tempest in the dark wood with Florence six years earlier, when she was fifteen years old. She found the third movement invigorating ("What the animals in the forest tell me"). However, she particularly liked to listen to the fourth ("What humanity tells me"), though it is difficult to rationalise why this was so because as a young woman prone to chronic depression and anxiety one might have thought that the sparsely instrumented movement, with its eerie and funereally haunting contralto solo, would be all too much for her. The soloist sings the "Midnight Song" from Friedrich Nietzsche's *Also Sprach Zarathustra* and tells of the deep pains of the world.

> *O man, take heed!*
> *What does the deep midnight declare?*
> *"I was asleep*
> *From a deep dream I woke and swear*
> *The world is deep,*
> *Deeper than day had been aware.*
> *Deep is its woe*
> *Deeper yet than agony."*

And Nietzsche, who ended his life a psychotic, also tells of the deep pains for mankind, warning that the worst enemy will always be yourself[17].

> *You lie in wait for yourself in caverns and forests…. You will be a heretic to yourself and witch and soothsayer and fool and doubter and unholy one and villain. You must be ready to burn yourself in your own flame: how could you become new, if you had not first become ashes?*

He warns that to escape the prison of a tormented mind and begin anew we must first exonerate ourselves and not make the mistake of playing the victim. Only then will we overcome the painful effects of life's traumas and move forward. But Marie never managed to lay her 'black dog' to rest. She could not step aside from the misery that engulfed her, but instead it was though she was involuntarily embracing it, accepting, with some grave pessimism, that her destiny was to live out her life with constantly recurring painful ordeals, without light or hope. Of course she was blameless for the traumas she experienced in her early life, and in times of rational thought would doubtless have known this, but in her moments of deep depression she became both victim and creator of sorrow and grief. And as often as not it was in the dead of night that they came back to haunt her, in her dreams.

As for the music it was, perhaps, the absence of the tactile loving comfort she craved that enabled her to gain a kind of perverse comfort from the words sung by the contralto soloist, wallowing in her sins, as well as the intensely spectral and contemplative music that accompanied them.

*

Marie made every effort to escape the confines of their tiny apartment on a daily basis, walking the streets or visiting the nearby park with her three year old son Daniel in tow and Nathalie, her eleven months old daughter, in a push chair. However, the cold, damp late autumn weather of 1952 had left Daniel with a persistent cold that made him uncharacteristically miserable and tearful. His swollen, reddened eyes and never ending runny nose led Marie to put him to bed for a good night's sleep. It was barely four in the afternoon but given Daniel did not object to being sent to bed early, Marie concluded that he really was not well. She kissed him on his forehead and noticed he seemed feverish. The next day he was no better.

'I'm concerned about Daniel, Arnaud. He's had a cold for several days and now he's developed a fever.'

'I'll take a look,' Arnaud said calmly.

They both went to his bedside. He was hot and red-faced and cried he had a sore throat. Arnaud examined him and noticed whitish-grey spots on his tongue.

'Do you think these spots is a reaction to something he may have eaten?' asked Arnaud.

'I don't think so. He doesn't seem to be in pain so maybe it's not such a problem after all. Maybe he'll be fine by tomorrow.'

He did not want to eat anything more than a consommé that day, and the following day Daniel was no better and had developed a rash around his neck and ears. He also said that his eyes hurt.

'You know it may well be something he's eaten and could even be a wild plant he may have been playing with in the Park. Perhaps he put it in his mouth,' said Arnaud, kind of reassuringly. 'Of course he may have developed a heat rash from the fever and with his face against the linen pillow-case that may not have helped.'

'Yes, maybe, but I think we should ask the doctor to call nonetheless,' retorted a concerned Marie.

So while Arnaud looked after the two children Marie went down to ask the concierge to use her telephone. She rang the doctor and described the symptoms. He agreed to pay a visit first thing the next morning. She returned to the apartment and spent the rest of the day playing with Nathalie, while both she and Arnaud looked in on Daniel from time to time. Though he slept almost all through the evening the rash had turned browny-red and was by then widespread across his face and even on his chest.

Arnaud and Marie finished their day with a light supper and then sat near each other listening to the wireless. Arnaud took himself off to bed early but Marie stayed up until very late thinking about the past and wondering what the future would hold. Suddenly she felt crestfallen and doleful; for Marie such all-consuming emotions were never far from surfacing. She switched off the wireless and turned to the gramophone and not for the first time listened to the inordinately powerful and emotive Mahler symphony number three, the fourth movement of course. Though this always but always touched a nerve, making her feel more desolate, more mournful and more woeful, it was as though someone was forcing her to listen to it. Mulishly she all but wallowed in the haunting, melancholic sound that resonated around the room and filled her emptiness. She was obsessed. She closed her eyes and was transported to another world, a world where she was alone and utterly absorbed in her own thoughts. When in that dark, deep place — the midnight of her soul — she re-lived the past years: the time when she was desperately unhappy knowing her father was incarcerated in a prisoner-of-war camp; the time when her mother was so tragically killed; the time when she was told by her father she would have to leave her home because he was unable to cope; and the time her soulmate and beloved told her he did not want to see her any more. Why she listened to this particular piece of music knowing it would only deepen her lugubrious state she did not know, but somehow she felt compelled to do so.

As the English horn, bass clarinet and contrabassoon began the movement with alternating notes, Marie rocked gently back and forth to the tempo, but tears soon welled-up and leached through her eye-lashes when she heard the contralto soloist's voice, weeping for the sins she had committed. Did Marie feel more cheerful and optimistic about her own future as the Angels then offered the woman absolution and forgiveness in the fifth movement, with the notion that joy always transcends death and worldly suffering? Probably not, for, by then, she was in a trance drifting through a seemingly never ending fog of spiritual darkness and despair.

*

The doctor did call early the next morning as promised and diagnosed measles. Neither Marie nor Arnaud had suspected that, but they were reassured that whilst not to be taken lightly there was every reason Daniel will be fine.

'This is not unusual in young children. Daniel will continue to have a high fever for a few more days, the rash may spread over his entire body and he may complain of bright lights hurting his eyes. If he does keep the shutters closed, at least partially.'

'Is this something to worry about?' Marie asked, a little uneasily.

'You must keep him in bed, warm and rested. If he is like most children he will recover in a few days. Oh, and make sure he has plenty of fluids.'

Marie and Arnaud felt somewhat reassured knowing other children had contracted the condition but had been none the worse for it ultimately. They were not going to fret and were resolved to let nature take its course. In a few days' time it would be Nathalie's first birthday and they were determined to ensure nothing would stop them from celebrating this joyous milestone.

But Daniel was no better four days after the doctor's visit. His rash had by then spread, covering much of his body. He was sweating profusely with a high fever and at times was almost delirious. They comforted him as best they could and encouraged him to drink a lot but he did not want to drink or eat. Arnaud went down to the ground floor to telephone the doctor from the concierge's office but the phone was out of order. He went back upstairs to tell Marie he would call in on the doctor on his way home from work the very next day. This did not reassure Marie. She was worried things were deteriorating rapidly and so spent the night worrying. Thankfully, Nathalie was no trouble at all. She played by herself for much of each day as if she somehow sensed her parents needed to devote their time to her brother. Her birthday came and went, almost without cognisance; in fact it proved to be a most uneventful day. Marie was concerned Nathalie might contract measles given the doctor had told her it was highly contagious, so they made sure she kept as far away from Daniel as possible, but this was not so easy in their small two-roomed apartment.

The next day Daniel had taken a turn for the worse. He was very poorly. His fever had worsened and he was by then incoherent. Arnaud went straight to the doctor rather than wait until later in the day, and within a couple of hours he was alongside Daniel examining him.

'I think he's developed a lung infection; it is most probably pneumonia. He should now be in hospital where the doctors and nurses can keep a close eye on him.' The doctor left to make the necessary arrangements. Daniel was soon on his way by ambulance the three or four kilometre journey to the Hôpital pour enfants Armand-Trousseau with his mother by his side. Arnaud stayed at home to look after Nathalie.

For Marie it was a decidedly unpleasant experience entering through the great oak doors of the hospital knowing at some time that day she would have to leave Daniel in the care of strangers. As she stepped across the threshold she was struck by the unmistakably pervasive smell of disinfectant that, with some irony, told a story of sickness and malaise. Her shoes made a resonant clanking sound that echoed along the corridor as she walked across the perfectly clean and varnished oak parquet flooring. The walls were totally bare — no pictures, no posters and no notices, bar those that hung above each doorway she passed through, spelling out in bold capital letters the word SILENCE. The yellowing white high-glossed lofty walls seemed to go on for ever. The lights hanging from the featureless ceiling were large plain white opaque glass spheres that seemed to add to the forbidding austerity of the building. This was not a welcoming place to enter, she thought. They opened more oak doors, and turned this way and that as they made their way to the ward. Marie tightened her grip on Daniel's hand as they entered. The room was simply a much wider version of the endless corridors they had passed through enroute, except that iron bedsteads were lined-up perpendicular from both walls like so many soldiers on parade, and with only a modicum of space between each one.

Daniel remained silent staring up at the ceiling as he lay on the trolley that wheeled him to his bedside. Uniformed nurses, complete with white heavily starched hats and aprons, black stockings and black flat-soled laced-up shoes, were busying themselves at bedsides. In the near corner of the room was a large square wooden table around which were children drawing, reading, colouring and playing with wooden bricks and puppets; seemingly not all the children were so ill they needed to be bed-ridden. In the middle of the room was a small rectangular desk with a large carver chair where sat a nurse in what appeared to be a markedly different uniform. Beneath her somewhat flamboyant hat Marie noticed that her grey hair had been pinned in a bun at the back of her head. Aware they had entered, the middle-aged woman rose unhurriedly from her chair, turned and made her way towards them. She looked stern and imperious. Her face was long and narrow and her deep-set eyes, up-turned nose and narrow mouth, with noticeably thin lips, suggested a rather reserved and perhaps even unfriendly disposition: the head nurse, Marie assumed.

'Madame Rousseau, given your son is likely to be suffering from a contagious illness his home for the foreseeable future will be over there in that small room.' She pointed to the far end of the ward where Marie saw that there was a glass-walled room. 'He will be able to see what is going on in the ward but forbidden to leave the room, except under medical supervision. I trust you understand why this is necessary.'

Marie did not respond immediately; she was deep in thought, imagining how her ailing son would cope while confined to that tiny room for every hour of each day. But a minute or two later she did start to challenge what she had been told, only to be interrupted by her family's doctor, trying to reassure her that all would be well.

'Madame Rousseau, Daniel will be prescribed penicillin, a relatively new drug. The idea will be to stem the pneumonia and allow the measles to take its normal course. He should be out of hospital within a week at the very most. He is in very good hands;

after all this is a specialist hospital for children's diseases[18].'

Marie was of course distinctly worried, but nevertheless pleased the doctor was confident all would be well. She stayed with Daniel for the rest of the day and at lights out she reassured him he would soon be home and that she would return to his bedside the very next morning. Daniel was not at all happy. He pleaded with his maman, begging her to take him with her. It was painful for Marie to walk away with her little boy in tears while being only tentatively consoled by a rather po-faced nurse. Neither Marie nor Arnaud slept at all well that night. It was the first time they had spent a night without both of their children by their sides.

The next day Arnaud again remained at home to look after Nathalie while Marie set off early for the hospital. She greeted Daniel with a kiss and a smile. He seemed comfortable enough, though still feverish and largely uncommunicative. Marie stayed at the hospital most of the day though had to leave his bedside on countless occasions as nurses performed their routine tasks: scrubbing the floor, tidying his bed, taking his temperature, washing him from head to toe, giving him his medication, making him take sips of water, and then, much to his displeasure, also making him swallow his daily dose of cod-liver oil — the ubiquitous remedy for all childhood ailments the world over, or so it seemed. When beside him Marie held his hand, mopped his brow and made him as comfortable as possible, but she found it extremely upsetting seeing her son lying there in a hospital bed, suffering as he was. Marie read story after story from his favourite collection *Le Journal de Tintin*, but she was very choosy about those she read because she thought some a little racist. But Daniel had always loved hearing about the adventures of the young Belgium reporter Tintin and his fox-terrier Snowy and best friend Captain Haddock, and whilst he seemed to listen, on this occasion he said nothing. This was unusual because Daniel was normally a very talkative little boy, forever asking questions.

With the inevitable worry, given the tension that had built up during the day, that night Marie was exhausted and when she dropped the casserole she had prepared on the parquet floor, shattering it and spreading its contents across the room, Arnaud snapped angrily at her. This caused a flood of tears from both Marie and young Nathalie. One might have thought Arnaud could have been the one to prepare the meal that evening while he was at home with Nathalie; but men simply did not perform such domestic chores in those days, so cooking, cleaning and washing the clothes fell solely to Marie.

For the next two days she repeated the same routine as the previous day and again Arnaud remained at home. On the fourth evening Marie caught a glimpse of how Arnaud was feeling. Over the previous few days she had been so absorbed in her own feelings that until that moment it had not really dawned on her that he too was desperately worried and anxious. They agreed that with Daniel still in hospital for a fifth day Arnaud would have to return to work for they desperately needed the money, and Arnaud was being paid nothing while he was at home. Prices were rising for by then rationing was over and the cost of living in Paris was extortionate, and to cap it all they were having to pay hospital fees they could ill-afford.

So on the sixth day Marie had Nathalie in tow on her way to the hospital while Arnaud returned to work. She had hoped her father would have been able to help out but by then Claudette had just given birth to another child and so he needed to be with her in the Morvan. Catering for one year old Nathalie's needs and three year old Daniel's while he lay ill in a hospital bed was far from easy. Periodically she had to leave Daniel while she took Nathalie out to play in the park or when she needed changing or feeding, and each time she did he became fretful. The nurses were tolerant but clearly would have preferred it had Nathalie not been there, especially given the contagious nature of the illnesses on the ward, but what else could Marie do? She was so thankful the hospital allowed her to be with Daniel almost any time of the day for this was not normal practice in other hospitals at the time. For certain had they lived in a town without a specialist children's hospital nearby, Marie would have had to keep strictly to visiting times so that Daniel would have been alone without his parents for most of each day.

By the time Marie got home she was overly uptight and fractious which did not bode well for the time when she would be alone with Arnaud. He had been busy at work and without direct knowledge of how his son had been he depended on Marie to tell him, but she was so tense she did not handle the situation at all well.

'Look Marie, I've been at work all day and have thought about little else other than how Daniel is. The least you can do is tell me about him when I get home.'

'He's ill Arnaud. He's very ill and it's not easy you know. With you at work I'm the one there for him, and I have to look after Nathalie too.'

'Good God Marie, I'm only concerned. And we agreed I needed to be back at work because …'

Before he could finish his sentence Marie cut in. 'Yes, exactly, but if you'd been earning more we wouldn't be in so much debt would we Arnaud? You'd be able to be at home with Nathalie, things would be less stressful for me and you never know, you might even think about having the evening meal ready for me when I return from the hospital.'

'You really can be so bloody nasty can't you? I earn what I do. My time will come. I will earn more, but …' He stopped, not really knowing quite what to add.

Marie got up from her chair, grabbed Nathalie under her arms and lifted her out of her high-chair, perhaps rather more roughly than normal so that Nathalie started to cry. 'Now look what you've done. Clear the table and wash up while I bathe her and get her ready for bed.'

This was the pattern for the next few days. Tension, anxiety and worry had got to them both and in such a small apartment, and with their financial difficulties getting worse by the day, perhaps the arguments were inevitable. Night after night they seemed to hurl abuse at each other and as often as not while Arnaud was sitting with his head in his hands and Marie was cooking, tidying, washing up, or getting Nathalie ready for bed. She was worn out and ready to drop, and Arnaud was at his wits' end.

By the middle of the second week Daniel seemed no better. The doctor asked to see both parents, so that meant more time off work and without pay.

'Has Daniel been unwell a lot over the past year?' asked the doctor.

Marie explained that he seemed to have a persistently runny nose and the odd tummy upset but little else. He had been reasonably healthy and never complained of being unwell.

'Has he had flu? Has he complained at any time of neck pain? Has he seemed disorientated? Did he find it difficult speaking during the days before he was in hospital? For example, did he slur his words?'

'I don't think he's had flu at any time. As I said he's had a runny nose and occasionally with a little fever maybe, but I didn't think it was flu. He has hardly spoken while he has been so unwell so I'm not sure if his speech has been slurred in any way. And no he hasn't complained of neck pain, but he did say his head hurts. Why do you ask?'

'Because very sickly children are at risk from complications. But from what you say there seems no obvious sign that he is a sickly child and apart from what we see there's little else to worry about. We'll keep him here under our watchful eye. He has had a difficult time and with the pneumonia it is inevitable that it would take longer for him to recover. He should soon respond to the penicillin so things will be a good deal better by the weekend. Make sure he drinks plenty of fluids while you are here with him.'

None of this made Marie feel any better. What was he so concerned about? If Daniel was responding to the penicillin surely he would be home soon, she felt.

Daniel was still in hospital after two weeks but thankfully, by then, Marie's sister-in-law, Adrienne, had come to their rescue. She took Nathalie back with her for a few days while Marie and Arnaud coped as best they could. She shopped for them, tidied their apartment and did what ever else she could to ease their distress. She was a good bit older than her brother, married with four children of her own, all of whom were in their early teens. Her slight build and seemingly demure nature belied her true self: a woman highly organised, decisive and authoritative. She was both generous with her time and money, not that she had much money to be generous with, but she was happy to share whatever she had with those in need. Marie and Arnaud could not have coped without her, though in truth so wrapped up in their own problems were they that they tended to take what she did for granted.

Things at home were tense, so much so you could cut the atmosphere in their room with a knife. They were beginning to blame each other for their son's illness and they were finding it immensely difficult paying the hospital bills. They were given numerous reminders but simply could not pay. Arnold even had to negotiate a lower fee on the grounds that he was a low wage-earner, but even then they had to take a loan to pay up in full. They were surviving on very little food and what they did eat was little better than scraps, the apartment was not being properly cleaned — something that really irritated Marie — and both she and Arnaud were struggling to get more than four or five hours sleep at night. They knew almost nobody in their district; it was simply not the neighbourly atmosphere of the seventeenth Arrondissement. They felt as isolated as they would have been had they lived in a remote wilderness.

However, much to Marie's delight, as she entered the ward on the seventeenth day she saw that Daniel was out of bed and playing at the table with some of the other children. He was a good deal better. He had eaten well and for the first time in two weeks was taking drinks without having to be forced to do so. He seemed more communicative and even asked when he would be able to go to the park. He was getting better and soon he would be home in time for Christmas.

That evening the atmosphere was markedly different, with both Arnaud and Marie feeling that the strain of the past couple of weeks had been lifted.

'Arnaud, I'm so sorry I've been so tetchy and argumentative. It's been a worrying time for us both and we shouldn't have let things affect us in the way they have.'

'We've said some unpleasant things but we've turned a corner. Daniel is getting better and soon he'll be back here with us and Nathalie.'

'I promised Daniel we will make things special this Christmas and was thinking we should buy him a bicycle. He saw one he liked a few weeks ago. Perhaps a red one Arnaud — his favourite colour. I know things are very tight but we'll manage won't we?'

'Of course. You're right. We must do something special and for Nathalie too — she's suffered this past couple of weeks or so.'

And so the next day before setting off to the hospital Marie bought a brand new red bicycle. She took it back to the apartment before going on to see Daniel. Again he seemed a good deal better, though he was still complaining of headaches. She told the nurse but she was not unduly concerned.

'He's probably getting too excited knowing he'll be home with you soon,' she remarked.

'Yes, I'm sure you're right. When will he be able to leave?'

'Well, tomorrow. Why not? I'll check with his doctor.'

So that night Marie and Arnaud were ecstatic and for the first time for three weeks they relaxed together listening to the wireless.

On her way to the hospital the following morning Marie bought a couple of packets of pipe-cleaners thinking they would be able to make something with them while waiting for Daniel to be discharged. On her arrival Daniel was sitting up at the table with some other children. He was excited and gave his maman a hug and a big kiss. She was over the moon. She sat down with him and started to play with the pipe-cleaners.

'Here Daniel let's make a little dog.' So she bent and twisted one pipe cleaner for the body and head, added another bent around the tail end of the body for the hind legs and another behind the head for the front legs.

'Let-let's call him Snowy Ma-Mam-Maman. Can we make Ca-captain Haddock now?'

'Are you all right Daniel?'

He did not answer. Marie shaped a couple of pipe cleaners for the body and legs and then encouraged Daniel to try to add a head and another suitably bent for the arms, but when he started to crumple a pipe cleaner to make a head and then bend one for the arms she noticed that his fingers and mind were not properly coordinated. She was not particularly worried because he had not been at all well for weeks and was probably very weak. But nonetheless it struck her as a bit odd that given he was normally such a dextrous little boy he simply could not do with his hands what she assumed his brain was telling him to do. It was very odd to observe.

'Daniel, are you all right?' she asked.

He struggled to speak but just about managed to tell his mother his head hurt and that he was very tired. The nurse put him back to bed and Marie was astonished to see him fall asleep almost immediately. The doctor came within the hour accompanied by a colleague. He was introduced to Marie as a Consultant Paediatric Neurologist. She was by then frantic with worry and insisted that she was told what was wrong with her little boy. She had turned a ghostly white and her hands were visibly shaking. Marie had lost a great deal of weight over the past weeks and looked skeletal and exhausted.

'He was better and coming home,' she said. 'Why is he suddenly so tired and why couldn't he use his hands properly? His speech was slurred. Oh! I remember that you asked me some days ago if he had slurred his words. What on earth is happening? I'm so very worried.'

'I don't know for certain Madame Rousseau,' said the consultant, an exceedingly tall man with a wide pencil thin moustache and round black-framed glasses. He had a kindly manner. 'Bear with me for just one moment please,' he said, in a distinctly calm fashion. He examined Daniel, shaking him gently to awaken him from his sleep. He asked him questions and like Marie earlier he too noticed that his speech was distinctly slurred. Perhaps it was because he was still half asleep Marie suggested. The doctor said nothing. He tried to get him to perform the most simple tasks like picking up a tumbler and moving his teddy from one side of the bed to the other, but to his shock the little boy could not do either task. He fumbled with his fingers and kept missing the items he was asked to touch, as though he had no coordination. Marie was utterly confused and looked at the nurse as if to say what next? What is happening to my boy? The consultant told Marie he needed to perform a lumbar puncture so he could sample Daniel's cerebrospinal fluid surrounding his brain and spinal cord.

'What!' she said abruptly. 'What are you telling me? What are you so concerned about? What is a lumber puncture? What will it do? Why was my son so much better and yet now, just hours later, you seem to be implying he's very ill again? I'm confused and terribly, terribly worried.'

The doctor responded in an unruffled and considered way. 'A lumbar puncture involves passing a needle, under local anaesthetic, between two of the back bones at the base of the spine. This will enable me to collect a small amount of fluid very safely. I'll also take blood samples and examining both these and the cerebrospinal fluid I'll be able to compare them and make an accurate diagnosis. Are you happy for me to go ahead with these tests Madame Rousseau? The reason I ask is because it's a procedure that has only become standard practice in the last year or so and performing it on children of Daniel's age can be tricky, especially if he is frightened and restless.'

Marie did not know what to say. She wanted answers to all her questions and said so. The consultant interrupted her and as before he very calmly proceeded.

'It's very important we act quickly Madame Rousseau. Do I have your permission to go ahead with these tests?'

Through quivering lips and with tears welling up in her eyes, she agreed. Without delay the doctor summoned the porter to take Daniel to the theatre. Marie was asked to remain in the waiting room. She was in a terrible state. She could not just sit and wait. She strode up and down the corridor, this time completely oblivious to the constant clattering noise she was making with her heels on the floor. She asked the receptionist if she could contact her husband.

On receiving the message Arnaud was perplexed and desperately worried in equal measure. He left work, ran to the bus shelter and took the bus to the hospital. He was there well within the hour and met Marie at the door. She explained as best she could what had happened to Daniel and what the doctors had planned to do. They remained restless, pacing up and down whilst waiting for the doctors to return.

After the longest hour they had ever experienced the consultant entered. 'The procedure we have just undertaken takes only a short while but obtaining the results from the test requires several hours. We will not know the results until the morning. I am very sorry. Daniel is back in his room. We think it best for you to go home and get some sleep, and return early tomorrow morning.'

Arnaud and Marie started to speak simultaneously. Marie paused and Arnaud continued. 'We're going nowhere until we know our little boy is safe and well. We'll stay the night if that is what it takes. Now please take us to his bedside.'

Within a few minutes they were sitting beside Daniel's bed. He had once again drifted off into a deep sleep. Marie held his hand but he did not respond. He was as still as a church mouse. The room had fallen strangely silent. She could not even hear him breathing. But whilst worryingly ill, as he lay there motionless, she saw in him her angelic dear little boy, and knew in her heart of hearts that he would emerge from his sleep and very soon would be cuddling up to her and asking if he could go to the park.

However, Daniel never came out of his sleep; by mid morning the very next day he was pronounced dead.

*

The results of the tests showed that Daniel had been suffering from encephalitis, a rare complication of childhood illnesses like measles. The consultant expressed his condolences and then explained.

'Encephalitis is an inflammation of the brain; the brain swells and presses against the inside of the skull and in time the pressure becomes so great it induces a coma and then death. In most cases the condition is chronic so that when it develops it does so very slowly over a number of years. But in Daniel's case it struck far more quickly and no doubt his pneumonia had both masked the symptoms and weakened his immune system, making him more prone to contracting the condition. There was nothing we could do. I am so very sorry.'

Arnaud and Marie heard the words but had not taken in what the doctor was telling them. They were heartbroken and in state of abject despair. Daniel was just three years old. It was just before Christmas 1952. He would never ride the red bicycle they had bought him for his Christmas present. Their little boy was dead. Marie and Arnaud remained in a state of absolute shock. Nobody could console them. Over the next few days neighbours and relatives called by, even Emeline and Colette turned up, but nobody could comfort them in their state of unmitigated hopelessness. Marie's father stayed with them for a couple of days in spite of the very recent birth of his third child, but his presence was of little consolation. He too was utterly grief-stricken and was yet again tormented by the memory of that fateful night when his wife had been killed. He went back to Claudette on the third day, the day of the funeral.

Nathalie was still staying with her aunt; thankfully she was too young to comprehend precisely what was happening. Soon they would need to tell her that her brother had died but first they needed to drag themselves out of their purgatory. Should they have acted sooner? Was Daniel's cold really flu? Should they have made him drink more rather than give in when he said he did not want to drink? These and so many other questions circulated in their heads.

'Perhaps you should have got the doctor earlier Arnaud,' Marie said after she had exhausted thinking through every possible mistake she may have made.

'But I did so as soon as we were concerned.'

'What about the colds he'd had earlier? Were these early symptoms of what was to come?' And so it went on for days and days. And as time passed Marie blamed Arnaud, and likewise he retaliated with comments like, 'Well you were by his side every minute of every day. Didn't you realise he was so ill?'

At a time when you might imagine Arnaud and Marie would be comforting each other they were in fact back-biting and blaming each other. Marie would scream at Arnaud and Arnaud would hurl a book across the room in her general direction.

On the first night of the day they lost Daniel, Marie did an odd thing: she turned on the gramophone. Nothing particularly odd about that given music was in her blood and could have been a comfort to her. What was odd was her choice of music for yet again she listened to Mahler's third symphony's fourth movement and as she did so tears streamed down her rubescent cheeks. Had she chosen something more uplifting then maybe it would have raised her spirits but instead, as if punishing herself, yet again she chose one of the most sombre and doleful pieces of music known to mankind. And once again it was as though she did not want to be dragged out of her suffering. How could she be anything but distraught when her little boy was lying dead in his coffin? She could have done more. She went through all the different scenarios time and time again.

It was an extraordinarily turbulent time for both of them. There were periods of relative calm but they were always followed by periods of intense emotion, which then faded before returning. There was confusion and it became difficult for either of them to make decisions or concentrate for any length of time. They had little sleep and seemed constantly exhausted. Marie frequently drifted into a virtual hypnotic state. She thought she was going mad. Daniel was always on her mind. In fact she even experienced aching arms and she swore she could hear him cry out for her.

*

Marie and Arnaud grieved for the rest of their lives. Grief is a parent's link to their child and therefore they did not want to let go of it. It touched every aspect of their lives and was triggered by countless incidental experiences. Nathalie ignited their grief every time she cried or felt unwell or was out of sight, even if only for a moment. Of course Marie suffered most. She was already emotionally insecure given the sequence of events between her eighth and sixteenth birthdays: the detachment from her father when he was in Rennes; his arrest by the Nazis and the resulting three years away from him; her family's struggle to survive during the Occupation; the death of her mother in such tragic circumstances; her all but forced move away from her father when he failed to cope; and Raymond's departure. All these separations, and having to live with her fiendish bully of an elder sister, had combined to stoke Marie's fire of damnation; and now there was another even more terrible separation for her to endure: the loss of her own very, very dear son. No wonder she became hermetic in hell. She needed some very special loving to pull her out of her pit of darkness and ocean of unquenchable fire and brimstone, but Arnaud was not that person. As the weeks passed she grew further and further adrift from him.

The funeral was on 23 December at the Cimetière Nouveau de Vincennes, three kilometres or so from their apartment. Neither Marie nor Arnaud wanted a funeral with lots of people. They accepted family and close friends expected to be there but they wanted the funeral to be simple and short. They could not imagine what it would be like to stand around a grave dug for any small child let alone their own, but they were about to find out. It was a most sombre affair even though the Priest did his best to celebrate Daniel's short life, referring to his sense of fun, his good nature, his love of playing in the park with his sister, parents and friends, and his infectious smile. But for Marie and Arnaud it was all a bit surreal, like being an observer at another family's funeral; they did not feel emotionally involved. It was as though it was all a dream and the next day they would wake up to a normal day with the children again.

They left the graveyard barely twenty minutes after they had arrived but Marie revisited it every day for the next seven years with her daughter, bar a few isolated days when she was away from home. And even when she moved home hundreds of kilometres away she returned on his birthday. She did this for 63 consecutive years until she died in 2014. She never played Mahler's third symphony ever again.

*

Arnaud was back at work after three weeks at home with Marie, during which time the relationship remained strained. By then they were in significant debt with hospital and funeral bills to pay. Arnaud's most treasured possession, a Napoleon Bonaparte gold coin, his father had given him, was sold to help settle some of the expenses for the funeral.

Arnaud wanted to do the right thing for Marie but he struggled to discover what that might be. He thought it would do them both good to go out into the city for a walk or a meal, but every time he broached the subject he was rebuffed.

'Do you really think I could dress up, stroll down the Avenue des Champs-Élysées, pop in to a smart shop, buy a Christian Dior outfit and then off to Maxim's for a slap up meal. Our son is dead Arnaud; has that not sunk in? And we have no money!'

'I was thinking it would be good to get out of the apartment that's all. Nothing grand, just a short walk and into a simple café, that's all. Look Marie, when people express their condolences you are treated as having lost the child you loved but me, well I'm treated as having lost someone I was responsible for. I loved him too, you know!'

'Yes, yes, okay Arnaud, but I can't relax. I can't go out to enjoy myself. I feel guilty, seriously guilty. He died in my arms. I should have seen the signs much sooner. And the bloody doctor failed to diagnose his condition when Daniel ....' She broke off at the mention of his name. She held back the tears as her eyes moistened. She swallowed, took a deep breath and continued, '... after Daniel was hospitalised. Had he diagnosed the condition sooner he may still be alive. All you want to do Arnaud is go out and enjoy yourself! Well, go on then, but don't think I'm coming with you.'

Shouting, Arnaud retorted 'That's unfair. I don't want to go out thinking it'll be all fun and games. I just want different scenery and something to lift us out of this insanely depressed state that's all.'

'Sometimes I feel I'm facing this terrible loss alone Arnaud. I feel so lonely. It's as though I'm shouldering the burden alone.'

Of course she was not alone and if only she realised it Arnaud was suffering greatly too, but perhaps differently from Marie. They seemed unable to understand each other's grief and could not find the words or deeds to make each other feel better. Marie drove herself into a dark world of her own, shutting out everyone around her, but alone it was easier to fall apart. All she really wanted was a husband to comfort her during the sleepless nights, to hug her and dry away the tears, to share memories. But whenever she took a metaphorical step closer to Arnaud he seemed to misinterpret it as a green light to undress her and make love to her. Marie still could not give herself to her husband in an intimate way. She did not feel good in body or mind and the thought of discarding her clothes and brazenly flaunting her naked body at such a distressing time filled her with dread and made her cringe. The pain of losing her son was gnawing into her and the misery and despair she felt was all consuming. Normally she was a tactile person who loved physical contact with passionate lovemaking, but nothing was further from her mind at that moment in her life.

Arnaud was suffering but his way of dealing with it was different: he wanted to take his wife in a fiery, lustful embrace and touch her intimately. For him such a libidinous act would dissipate his pent up frustration and accumulated tension of the past weeks in an instant. He could not understand why Marie felt differently, which only served to fuel the edginess between them, causing a strain like a dangerously stretched elastic band that threatened to snap at any moment. But women generally do not feel this same intense testosterone fuelled surge at the best of times, and for Marie at such a traumatic time in her life her hormones were in complete disarray.

Christmas came and went and the red bicycle remained where it had been placed, out of Daniel's sight, to ensure he had a lovely surprise on Christmas Eve. They did their best for Nathalie but at just one year old, fortunately, she was not old enough to get excited about the mystery of Christmas, so they were spared the pain of having to pretend there were 'good tidings' and a 'cup of good cheer'.

CHAPTER SIXTEEN

Life and death are balanced on the edge of a razor.
— Homer, *Iliad*

With a wife and three young children to care for Marie's father, Jacques, was finding his dwindling itinerant ballroom and shoe-making businesses insufficient to make ends meet. The car was long gone and he was again living in a small two-roomed house. Accordingly, he took to helping out a friend who had a licence to fell trees in the area around Lac des Settons, thirty kilometres or so from Chateau-Chinon. This was and still is a particularly lovely area with many waterfalls, including Saut de Gouloux and the rapids of Saut de la Truite along the Caillot, a tributary of the Cure. For many generations these have been the stomping grounds of trekkers and artists alike.

Jacques's long-standing friend Laurent, a short, stocky man in his late thirties with a mop of fiery red hair fringing his ruddy weather-beaten face, and his fresh-faced teenage apprentice, were two of only a handful of woodcutters with a licence to fell trees in the Morvan during the post war years. In its hey-day at the turn of the century, there would have been hundreds of woodcutters felling oak, beech, hornbeam and elm and transporting the logs out of the Morvan via the River Cure, after the river was suffi-ciently swollen by the snow melt in March or April. Woodcutters used massive hooks to steer the logs on the river creating one hundred metres long rafts in the process. The wood, destined for Paris, was transported out of the Morvan in such vast quantities that it was sufficient to heat the whole of Paris for an entire winter. However, with the increased use of coal, wood was no longer in such great demand for the Parisian power stations and so the Morvan timber industry declined significantly between the wars; the last floating raft was in 1924. Thereafter the much smaller quantities of wood required for the construction and furniture industries could be facilitated by road transport alone and by far fewer loggers.

The three men felled trees according to a strict plan laid out by Laurent. As an experienced woodcutter he felled a tree in such a way that it fell within a five degree error of margin either side. This was very important because the licence did not allow the men to strip an entire area but rather take out trees here and there so as to preserve the general appearance of the forest, and therefore trees needed to fall within a very narrow corridor. It was a highly skilled job. Laurent and his apprentice Christophe used axes or a two-man saw, depending on the girth of the tree. Normally, Laurent first used an axe to cut a seventy degree notch on the side of intended fall to not more than twenty percent of the diameter of the tree. He calculated the precise position of the notch according to the relative symmetry of the tree crown and the angle of inclination of the trunk. When ready, the two men used their two-man saw to cut towards the notch on the other side of the tree, taking care to leave a little more than ten percent of the diameter of the trunk to act as a hinge. At the appropriate time Laurent drove an iron wedge into the saw-cut in a precise position having once again taken account of the shape of the crown and the angle of inclination of the trunk. When he was cutting a tree with a small girth he also made adjustments according to the wind speed and direction. When ready, he drove the wedge further towards the hinge and as the tree creaked and was about to fall the workers vacated the site according to a predetermined escape plan. Felling a tree was not a simple task and certainly not one for the faint-hearted. Laurent and Christophe felled the trees and Jacques's job was to use an axe to strip the tree of its branches once it had been felled.

*

One particular Saturday in late February 1953 Marie was at home with Arnaud and Nathalie when they heard a knock on the door. Since visitors to their apartment were extremely rare, Marie was a little surprised but she rose from her chair and went to the door.

'Telegram for Madame Rousseau? Is that you? Please sign.'

Marie was perplexed but signed nevertheless. 'It's a telegram Arnaud. What on earth could this be?'

'Well, the only way to find out is to open it,' said Arnaud.

So Marie tore at the envelope and revealed a flimsy slip of paper on which were typed the words:

REGRET TO INFORM PAPA IS DEAD.

ACCIDENT FELLING A TREE.

COME AS SOON AS POSSIBLE.

EMELINE.

Marie dropped the telegram, went suddenly very pale and before she was able to say a word she fainted. Arnaud grabbed the telegram and read it. For a split second he was frozen to the spot, but in a trice he crouched to take Marie in his arms and coax her back to consciousness. As she came round she burst into tears. Meanwhile, Nathalie, who just moments before had been playing cheerfully on the floor, wondered what was happening. She called out to her mother and father but neither responded. She called again and with that Arnaud approached her and lifted her onto his lap as he sat down on a chair.

'My darling Nathalie, I'm guessing you'll not really understand but Maman is very sad because her papa — your grand-père — has just died. We have had a telegram to tell us he is now in heaven with his wife — your grand-mère — who died before you were born, and their grandson — your brother, Daniel.' Nathalie looked thoroughly perplexed as though she had not understood what she had been told, but somehow it satisfied her and so she returned to her playing on the floor.

Marie still had not said a word. She picked up the telegram and read it again, as though to check that what she had read was in fact true. She was struck dumb. Tragedy and turmoil had followed her wherever she had gone. What would she do? She was just twenty-two years of age and she had lost both her parents in tragic circumstances as well as her dear son Daniel. What on earth would come next she thought. Arnaud tried to console her but his words seemed hollow. Marie was shaking like a leaf and tears were trickling down her cheeks. Still she said nothing. She just stared across the room at the wall opposite.

The hours passed. Arnaud did his best to occupy their confused daughter and Marie just sat where she was, trembling continuously and saying nothing. Tears were still welling up in her eyes. Arnaud told her he would make the arrangements for the three of them to journey to the Morvan to see Marie's sisters, step-mother and paternal half sisters the very next morning.

The journey to the Morvan was painfully slow and gruelling. Marie sat in absolute silence in the seat opposite her husband and daughter. She seemed totally oblivious to the passage of time and unaware her daughter was sobbing, almost throughout the long journey. Marie just stared out of the window. After an inordinate amount of time on the train and buses, eventually they arrived. It was late afternoon. On entering the house Marie found it exceptionally difficult fighting back the tears. Claudette and the young children were clearly distraught. Marie said nothing. She had never been close to Claudette but hugged her nevertheless. Emeline and Colette were present and were already making arrangements with the undertaker.

Before saying anything at all to Claudette, or to her children, and before commiserating with her sisters, Marie went alone into the room where her father had been laid out to rest. There were no visible signs to suggest he had been crushed by a fallen tree for he was mostly covered with a white sheet. She sat down beside him and with tears welling up in her eyes she spoke to him.

'Papa, I love you dearly and always have, even when you told me I could no longer live with you in the house in Villars. I just wish I had told you this when you were still alive. I am sorry I was not more understanding. I will miss you terribly — we all will. You have had such a sorrowful and agonising few years Papa, but now it is all over and you can rest in peace, and be with Maman in the kingdom of heaven.' She took a hold of his ashen hand and bent down to kiss it. As she did so her tears fell one by one onto his waxen skin, where they gathered for a moment or two before slowly trickling down his fingers and onto the floor. She wiped her eyes with the palm of each hand and rose to leave the room. 'You have been a good man Papa and despite what some might believe you have always done your best for us all, that I know.' And with those her parting words she made her way to the door and out into the scullery where she was greeted by a very sombre family gathering.

She embraced each one in turn, including her own daughter, who at just fifteen months was unable to comprehend fully what was happening. She had lived the past three months knowing her brother was no longer with them and now she had been told the same was true for her grandfather.

Marie was shaking uncontrollably. She spoke with a trembling voice. 'What did happen out there in the forest Emeline? How did Papa die?'

'Papa had been stripping the branches from the trees the two woodcutters had felled. Apparently they had worked in such a way that with Laurent's careful calculations there should have been no way father would have been anywhere near a falling tree; evidently he was always several metres to one side of its trajectory.'

'Then how did he get trapped under the tree?' asked Marie, anxiously.

'Well, we don't really know,' she said. 'But trapped is what he became. Laurent told me that after a tree had been felled father would proceed to the fallen tree to begin stripping it of its branches while he and his apprentice moved several trees (and therefore several metres) to the left in order to fell another tree. In this way Laurent had thought there was no conceivable way he could have been trapped under a falling tree.'

Turning to Laurent, Arnaud asked, 'Is it possible you made a mistake in your calculations and the tree fell further to the right and therefore in his direct path?'

'No, certainly not. I have been cutting trees for twenty years. There's no way the tree fell in completely the wrong direction, which would have had to have occurred to fall on Jacques. No, this was not possible.'

'But I don't understand' snapped Marie. 'Then is it possible our father had erroneously wandered too far to your left and come under the direct line of the falling tree?'

'This too is very unlikely. Your father had been helping me for weeks and knew the protocol. He appreciated the dangers and what is more every time I planned how to fell a tree I calculated the route of escape and made sure your father knew precisely what to do.'

Claudette was listening in and although she had already been told what had happened she too was perturbed. She still could not come to terms with her loss and would not, she thought, until she knew precisely what happened out there in the forest. 'Could Jacques have tripped on a branch and fallen at the precise time the tree had been felled?' she asked.

'No, I don't believe that either,' said Laurent. 'The tree would have fallen several metres away from where Jacques would have been standing. If he had tripped he still wouldn't have been close to the falling tree.'

This left all of them totally flummoxed. They had all assumed it was an accident, but none of the scenarios described seemed plausible explanations.

'Wasn't it possible to remove the fallen tree and somehow get him to hospital? Was he in pain? Did he say anything?' enquired Marie.

Poor Laurent. He was himself still in shock, and given he had asked Jacques to help him in the forest he somehow felt responsible for Jacques's death. He was then being asked awkward questions he did not really know how to answer. He simply did not know how the accident had occurred. However, he understood why Jacques's family wanted to know exactly what had happened.

'What I do know is that the tree fell on him and crushed his chest. He was alive when I got to him but he was obviously in dire pain. I tried desperately to remove the tree but couldn't, not even with my assistant's help. I cut away many branches to lighten the load but with just one hand saw it took a long time. We couldn't use either the two-man handsaw or the axe for fear that vibrations would cause more distress and further injury. Your father did not say anything as we frantically worked to strip away the branches; perhaps he simply couldn't, I don't know. Eventually we managed to lighten the load sufficiently to lift the trunk from his body. I'm afraid we were confronted with an unpleasant sight. His chest was badly compressed with fractured ribs and sternum.'

'Arrr, how awful! I know things have been difficult for you too Laurent. I'm so sorry to have hounded you like this but it's all very baffling,' said Marie, fretfully.

'Yes, Marie, it has been a dreadful time. We go back a long way your father and I. In fact I remember you when you were a babe in arms. I'm so sorry Marie. If there is ever anything I can do then call on me. You know where I live.'

'Thank you. When I'm next in Chateau-Chinon I'll call by.'

*

Not that Laurent knew it at the time but Jacques actually died from multiple wounds caused by what medics refer to as a blunt force trauma. The force and weight of the falling tree had created a transient surface reaction leading to a flail chest, whereby multiple rib fractures had caused a segment of the rib cage to give way and become detached from the rest of the chest wall. This not only caused severe pain when trying to breathe but irreversible damage to some of his major organs, partly because, simultaneously, the manubrium and sternum had also been fractured, leading to the perforation of both lungs, as well as rupturing his liver, kidneys and spleen and damaging the valvular mechanism of the heart. The back of his cranium was fractured too, though given the tree had straddled his torso, more from the impact with the ground than from the tree itself. None of these injuries was sufficient to cause instant death, hence the reason why Jacques remained semi-conscious and in extreme pain for a number of minutes while the two men tried to remove the tree trunk. It was a freak accident.

But was it an accident? The coroner had certified the cause of death but had not asked for an investigation, assuming it had been a genuine accident. However, in his own mind Laurent was certain such an accident could not have happened, but did not want to press the point further, fearful he may cause more distress to the family who were already tormented and heartbroken. It was common knowledge that Jacques had been chronically depressed from the moment he was captured by the Nazis, and the traumatic events that followed that distressing time further intensified his depression. And yet being a proud rather narcissistic person he hid his inner feeling, believing others might see it as a weakness.

To add to his already worrying state of depression, just two months before his death and while grieving the loss of his grandson, Jacques re-lived the harrowing minutes when he had sat beside his dying wife, remembering how helpless he felt then as he watched her die in such horrific circumstances. And he remembered that she died in her bed from a grenade that was destined for him, or at least thrown into the room by someone angry and irritated by his actions, not his wife's. His feeling of intense guilt had never waned. To cap it all he knew he was innocent of the accusations of collaboration levelled at him and had a very good idea who committed the crime, as well as the name of the woman who orchestrated it, despite the fact that they were never brought to justice. And inevitably the death of his grandson brought to the fore of his mind the fact that he had hardly been a model father at that time, choosing to foster out his three children just weeks after the death of their mother in 1944. As if losing their mother had not been bad enough for them, he sent them away to be brought up by virtual strangers. And of course he had rescinded on his promise to Marie to reunite them as a family, and instead rented a house for the three sisters to live in while he fathered three more children. Furthermore, in the weeks following his grandson's death it was a case of déjà-vu for him; for once again he failed to be the emotional support his daughter craved, she having to somehow cope with the loss of her dear son without his fatherly succour.

So could he have taken his own life? If he did then he left behind a grieving wife and six children, three of whom were under five years of age, the youngest being barely ten weeks old. We shall never know the truth, but for Marie, her sisters and her stepmother, another funeral had to be planned. As for Marie's state of mind she was once again dogged by tragedy. Just as she was making headway taming her 'black dog' so he slipped his noose, snarled at her angrily, and attacked ferociously.

CHAPTER SEVENTEEN

Love never dies a natural death. It dies because we don't know how to replenish its source. It dies of blindness and errors and betrayals. It dies of illness and wounds; it dies of weariness, of witherings, of tarnishings.
— *Anaïs Nin*

It was January 1954, a little over a year since their son's death and just ten months after Marie's father was killed. Marie was still shrouded in grief and almost always as tense as a coiled spring. By then her hair was short, she had lost a lot of weight and chose to apply no make-up to ameliorate what had become a flawed complexion. She wore the same clothes almost every day, changing them only when they were so soiled they had to be washed, and almost always she carried a despairing look on her thinning face. She did not want to turn on the wireless or put on a gramophone record and neither did she want to go out with friends or even with Arnaud. She busied herself as she always had when tense and troubled: she mopped the floor every day, sometimes twice or three times a day, and in a day she would dust the shelves, clean the oven, polish the copper pans, wash some clothes, clean the sink and tidy the apartment and then she would do it all again the very next day. She went out to get food or clothes for Nathalie and that was about all. Nathalie was by then two years of age and constantly growing out of her clothes but Marie liked to buy clothes for her. She wanted her to look well-dressed and looked after, even though she felt she was not being a particularly good mother to her just then. She still went to the Bois de Vincennes but only very occasionally, and whenever she did she saw Daniel running here and there, feeding the ducks and laughing. She never lingered in the Park. Nathalie was allowed to play on the swings for a few minutes and then it was back to the apartment. Every time she was with Nathalie she saw her little boy. This made her over protective of her daughter but also caused her enormous grief.

It was not until the spring that Marie felt able to be with other people without bursting into tears. She really wanted to get out of the apartment as much as possible; it had too many bad memories and in any case time spent with Arnaud was becoming strained. Without her own father to go to for a shoulder to cry on, during holidays she took up the offer from Arnaud's parents to stay with them in Précy. Marie had always liked them and enjoyed the tranquility of the country setting, and she had even grown fond of the noisy old cockerel!

For all the years Marie desperately craved Arnaud's hugs and kisses and intimate caresses, but too infrequently got them, now she was hoping he would not get too close for it made her feel strangely claustrophobic and prickly. Arnaud was very aware of this and so more often than not he kept his distance. In fact he went out almost every evening, supposedly to the café for a drink with friends. He felt that Marie had simply not appreciated just how much he was suffering from the loss of their son. But in spite of Marie's insular frame of mind she was still insecure and therefore still needed Arnaud's presence, albeit without intimacy and lovemaking. She needed time but Arnaud was running out of patience.

Marie and Arnaud still had not made love in all the months since the day Daniel died in Marie's arms, though the atmosphere had eased a little. At least they were not arguing as much. But on one occasion when Arnaud was out and she was tidying up she found his wedding ring under some clothing in his drawer and wondered why on earth he would do that. All kinds of thoughts went through her mind. Why had he taken it off? Perhaps it was simply to wash. But if so then why put it in his drawer and particularly under his clothes? She became suspicious that he was with another woman. Perhaps there was good reason to wait and see if it happened again she thought, but as the grossly insecure woman that she was there was no way she was going to ignore it and carry on as if she had not discovered it. Waiting for him to return she became paranoid, wondering if she had driven him away and fearful he did not care for her anymore. Her nerves had already been as taut as piano wire but by then she was also growing intensely jealous of another woman. Of course there was no proof, but to Marie it all added up. She knew he had been intolerant of her for weeks and had been going out more frequently and for longer periods of time, and without his wedding ring on!

Arnaud came home shortly after eleven o'clock. He did not expect to see Marie still up.

'You look flushed Arnaud and dishevelled. Where have you been since six o'clock?'

'What do you mean? You know where I've been.'

'All I know is what you told me. You said you were going to see Fernand.'

'And so I did. What's this all about Marie?'

'Arnaud, why did you take your ring off to see Fernand?'

'I didn't take it off because I was seeing Fernand.' He looked down at his finger. 'I took it off because Fernand wanted me to help him with the bikes he was preparing for the race.'

'I don't believe you. If so, then why put it under your clothes in your drawer?'

'Did I? I've no idea why. Are you sure?'

'You've been with another woman Arnaud, I know you have. It's gone eleven. You couldn't have been helping Fernand all that time? I can't bear the thought ...' She was interrupted by Arnaud.

'What the hell are you on about? We went to the café for a

beer after we finished working on the bikes. You mope about all day long, you push me away when I come close, you don't want to go out with me and now you're jealous of a woman who doesn't exist. What next?' He was agitated, angry even. He went to bed without so much as a 'goodnight'.

Everything Arnaud had said was true. She did mope about the house, she did rebuff his advances and she did not want to go out with him. However, her sense of insecurity was so great that she desperately needed an endorsement of his love and devotion, even though the physical acts necessary to consummate the love were not welcomed. Without his declaration of unbridled fidelity she was liable to re-enter one of her bouts of acute manic depression and irrational anxiety; she simply could not bear the thought of him being unfaithful to her.

Marie stayed up late that night sitting in her chair mulling over everything that had happened in the past few months. She was not a happy woman but she did not listen to Mahler's symphony number three!

The altercation did not change things. Arnaud still went out and far too often for Marie's liking. She kept an eye on the drawer but she did not find his ring in there again. Every time he went out she searched high and low to see if he had left it elsewhere in the house but she never found it. She remained very suspicious and wondered if he had put it in his pocket or maybe hidden it somewhere in the apartment that so far she had not discovered. When Arnaud returned home she studied him carefully to see if he looked guilty or flushed and to see if there was a trace of lipstick on his face or shirt. She even checked to see if he had missed a button on his shirt, and when she washed his clothes she examined the items to see if she could detect the aroma of a woman's scent. She did not find anything but then he was aware she was suspicious and so took great care to hide the truth, she thought.

When they did spend time together it was normally at meal times but she grew suspicious at the table whenever he requested food she did not normally cook. That woman must have prepared it for him she thought, and he had liked it! When they walked to the park together with Nathalie she questioned why he chose a particular route. Was it to avoid bumping into her? In her paranoid state she had been certain he was adulterous but had no proof. She wanted to know the truth but what if the truth meant he did have a lover? She was not at all sure she loved him anymore but she still needed him. She had even wondered if he was visiting the brothels except that they had been made illegal in 1947, so almost all had closed down. And in any case where would he have got the money? No, it had to be another woman!

*

So in addition to chronic depression and regular bouts of anxiety Marie had become excessively jealous. It was no wonder her relationship with Arnaud was breaking down. To relieve the egregious tension in the apartment Arnaud suggested they should go away to Précy for a summer holiday. Marie was hesitant because she did not know how things would be in Arnaud's parents' home given the tensions they had experienced in recent weeks but she desperately needed to escape the confined, oppressive atmosphere of their two-roomed apartment, and so agreed. Anyway, the thought of a train journey out of Paris travelling south through the dense forest of Fontainebleau before passing the magnificent Château of the same name one minute and journeying through the charming town of Montargis the next, would be a tonic for sure. Marie remembered being told by her teacher that Joan of Arc had passed through Montargis on her way to Gien after her unsuccessful attempt to besiege Paris during the Hundred Years war. She also remembered that Renée of France, daughter of King Louis XII, sheltered in her home (the Château de Montargis) many Huguenots fleeing from persecutions in Paris during the sixteenth century Wars of Religion.

On the train Marie sat opposite her husband and alongside

her daughter, but said nothing to either of them. She sat motionless, gazing out of a window streaked with rain that had fallen relentlessly since leaving their apartment. Next to Arnaud was an elderly woman who was continuously wheezing and coughing, something that in her current state Marie was unable to tolerate.

'Do you have to sit there spreading your germs over my daughter. I've already lost one child to illness! There's a seat further down the aisle; why don't you cough and sneeze to your heart's content over there?' she retorted, unsympathetically.

The frail old woman muttered something under her breath, and with the aid of two walking sticks tentatively and slowly made her way down the aisle to the seat she had been directed to. Arnaud gave Marie a stern look but said nothing. Marie continued the journey in silence, absorbed in her own thoughts.

The journey south took them along the banks of the Loire to Gien, which had been a Protestant stronghold during the time of the Wars of Religion. Marie noticed that some of the charred remains of the old town that had been destroyed in fires in 1940 — following the bombardment by the Luftwaffe in their attempt to destroy the town's bridge across the Loire in order to prevent the French Army from retreating — had still not been rebuilt[19].

The Rousseau's journey continued through the countryside of endless vineyards and past, in the distance, the hill-top village of Sancerre, the site of the infamous sixteenth century Siege of Sancerre that took place during the Wars of Religion. Again, Marie recalled what her teacher had told her. The Huguenot population had held out for nearly eight months against the King's Catholic forces, during which time the Royalists had attempted to starve the Sancerreans into submission, having failed to defeat them in battle. She knew from her studies that the inhabitants had survived during the lengthy time under siege by eating horses, dogs, rats, mice, leather, parchment, grass and roots. She could not help but compare this with her family's plight and their wretched struggle for survival, particularly during the three years her father was away in Germany carrying out forced labour, while

France was under the iron-fisted influence of Germany's Third Reich[20].

As they continued their journey southward Marie had plenty of time to dwell on the occasion nine years earlier when she undertook that journey, only in reverse, when, albeit for different reasons, she had been just as tense and perturbed. But at that time, on the brink of what was to become the oppressive occupation by the Nazis, the journey had been incredibly stressful and painstakingly slow. In peace-time it was quicker and an altogether more therapeutic experience. And of course, undertaking this journey meant that Arnaud would not be seeing that other woman.

By late morning they pulled into the station in Nevers. It is in the town's surrounding forests that some of the finest oak trees grow. Traditionally, the wood was used by coopers for their casks, including English coopers. Fine-grained French oak from near Nevers was considered particularly apt for wine-making casks, but had it not been for Napoleon Bonaparte there would be little left to sustain the cooperage industry. When felling thousands of oaks for the construction of his fleet he at least had the good sense to commission the planting of new forests, unlike in England where, as early as the days of the sea battles with the Spanish Armada, Drake and his contemporaries stripped the forests of oaks without replanting at least as many as they had felled, so leading to the demise of English oak.

From Nevers it was a sixty kilometre bus ride through the winding country roads to Chateau-Chinon. She recalled with inquietude that Raymond had undertaken that journey daily from his home in Chateau-Chinon when preparing for the Concours des Arts et Metiers at the lycée in Nevers. Once there they walked through the town passing familiar haunts before arriving in Précy by mid-afternoon. It was early summer 1954. The wild flowers were still a mass of colour in the meadows, but the cherry blossom had fallen and the fruit was beginning to set. The air was warm and yet fresh; the intense heat and humidity of the Burgundian summer was yet to arrive.

'Can you smell that Nathalie? Can you Arnaud?'

'Smell what Maman,' asked Nathalie.

'It's that lovely fresh smell of linen drying on the line.'

Nathalie and Arnaud looked at each other and frowned in bewilderment.

'But I've so missed that lovely fresh linen smell while we've been in Paris. It's never the same when I bring the washing back from the launderette you know.'

Nathalie sniffed the air. 'I can't smell any fresh linen Maman.'

As they walked up the path Arnaud's parents were already at the open door. Marie saw lettuces, tomatoes, onions and garlic growing in the field at the side of their house and there were raspberry canes and blackcurrant bushes too. All of a sudden she was overcome by the sensory memories of her early childhood and felt a burning desire to throw caution to the wind and run off and across the meadow and into the forest, but thinking they would all take her for a mad woman she suppressed that urge and instead stepped forward and kissed each parent-in-law on each cheek twice. They looked pleased to see the three of them. Grand-père picked Nathalie up under her arms from behind and swung her around again and again until she was parallel to the ground like a flag in a gale. Nathalie was very excited and giggled incessantly while her long hair covered her pretty little face.

'Do it again Pépère. Do it again.'

They stayed for a week. Marie was happier being there in the country air, Nathalie was enjoying the attention of her grand-parents and Arnaud seemed quite at home helping his father in the vegetable field and re-varnishing the window frames ready for the winter. Marie did not have nightmares whilst there and neither did she feel so anxious, though she still found it difficult sleeping. When silence fell in the dead of night she thought of nothing but Daniel, remembering his visits to Précy and seeing him laughing and giggling as he was pushed to and fro on the swing Grand-père had hung from an old oak tree in the back garden.

Back in Paris Marie's 'black dog' was champing at her heel, threatening to gnaw into her very soul. She was on a knife edge trying to fight the pain and anguish if only for Nathalie's sake. As for Arnaud, he went out as usual and Marie was left to speculate who that woman was that he so loved to visit.

It was still evident that Marie was suffering from separation anxiety disorder, a characteristic of which is an obsessive attachment to a spouse, friend, relative, particular place, or even the sufferer's own child. The circumstantial evidence suggested Marie was obsessively attached to her husband, and it became abundantly clear from Arnaud's behaviour that he could not cope with such an intense level of attention, so chose to go out rather than stay at home with his very needy wife. Whilst this may have been understandable given it could not have been easy for him to cope with someone so depressed, anxious and jealous, for sure it was a further obstacle for Marie to have to navigate.

The separation from her father when he was imprisoned in Germany and then from her mother caused by her untimely death, her numerous forced changes of abode during childhood, including being 'fostered' out to a virtual stranger rather than live with her father at a time when she was most in need of his love and support, the separation from her little boy after he died tragically in hospital and then followed two months later by the gruesome and yet not fully explained death of her father, had all left her excessively anxious and disturbed. And then to cap it all she was becoming rapidly detached from her husband, and at a time when she needed him. To cope, she returned to her only known therapy: dusting and cleaning and polishing her way through the days once more.

Not knowing the truth was something that had haunted Emeline, Marie and Colette ever since their mother's death. Whilst trying to cope with all her problems, along with her sisters, Marie had been trying to find the murderer of their mother as well as dig deeper into the circumstances of their father's death.

There had been times when the three girls had even wondered if their father had been murdered. After all, the grenade had been thrown in 1944 by a person or persons who had felt the need to punish him, not his wife. Perhaps someone had finally seized the opportunity to finish the job. They did not think for one moment the incident had been caused by Laurent, but they had wondered if, unbeknown to the two woodcutters or Jacques, someone else had been in the forest and had pushed Jacques at the time the tree was being felled. The perpetrator could have escaped under the cover of the forest and even if Jacques had cried out at the time he had been pushed — if pushed he was — Laurent and his assistant would not have heard because of the hammering in of the iron wedge, the creaking and splitting of wood and the fluttering of birds and sound of broken branches as the tree fell. They had no proof and the police had simply not taken their ideas sufficiently seriously to open an investigation.

However, they did feel there was a greater chance of getting to the bottom of their mother's death. Their mother had died at the hands of thugs who, without good reason the town's Comité had judged in 1944, had suspected that Jacques was a collaborator. The girls wanted justice and sought to obtain exactly that.

Quite by chance, at a dance in her home town of Chateau-Chinon in the summer of 1954, Emeline stumbled across an opportunity. She was introduced to Police Inspectors Chalot and Rossi of the Judicial Police of Clermont-Ferrand, whose responsibility it was to seek justice for suspected collaborators that had been wrongly convicted under épuration sauvage (savage purge) that took place illegally immediately after liberation. She was able to arrange a meeting at which she persuaded them to re-open the case of the unlawful killing of her mother. After several weeks of badgering them and furnishing them with the gruesome details, and with reports established by the gendarmerie of Moulins-Engilbert at the time of the murder ten years previously, and having taken statements from members of the public, they eventually succeeded in unmasking the guilty: the two teenage boys, Eric and Michel.

However, their euphoria at having unearthed the truth and been on the brink of exonerating their family was short-lived. The two men were never brought before a court of law and therefore they were never punished for their reprehensible crime. One explanation for this was that the conclusion of the police investigation had taken place after a lapse of ten years from the date of the crime, as well as the fact that the main perpetrator was not eighteen at the time he threw the grenade; he was just four days short of eighteen. The three sisters went through the rest of their lives knowing this to be a travesty of justice.

So once again it can be deduced that the French authorities could not — or would not — confront the past to ensure justice be done. And without a lawyer with the ability and persistence of Serge Klarsfeld, who eventually brought Bousquet, Papon and Touvier to justice in the 1990s, their chance of succeeding was very slim indeed. But the sisters were to gain some justice because in October 1954 a local journalist reported on the case, publicly naming the two murderers. The article was discovered in Marie's papers in 2015 by her husband, eight months after her death. He had never seen the article before. In fifty-five years of marriage she had never wanted to talk openly about the circumstances that led to the death of her mother and she never returned to Villars where the deed had been carried out.

It is believed that both murderers are still alive today with one living near Paris and the other still in Burgundy. Do they carry a heavy burden or do they still feel their actions were justified, even though the police decreed there was sufficient evidence to bring them before a court of law for the illegal killing of Rosine? Interestingly, the journalist signed his article XXX. From this the inference is that even ten years after Rosine's death, there were some who were still gravely concerned that reprisals had not ended.

And what of Brigitte, the woman who groomed the two teenage boys and sent them to do her loathsome deed? So immersed in guilt and remorse was she that life for her was no longer worth living, and so the woman who dressed in black and remained in the shadows at the funeral of Marie's mother, took her own life just one day later. But what emerged as a result of the years of digging and delving following the tragedy, was not only that Brigitte was very obviously insanely jealous of the Duvals, but that at the same time she callously and vociferously accused Jacques Duval of collaborating with the enemy, all the while she was prostituting herself with Nazi officers on her frequent jaunts to Chateau-Chinon. No wonder she felt insanely guilty and remorseful.

CHAPTER EIGHTEEN

The greatest happiness of life is the conviction that we are loved; loved for ourselves, or rather, loved in spite of ourselves.
— *Victor Hugo*

Life did not get any better for Marie over the next three years. She and Arnaud lived in the same home but not as a married couple. Arnaud found every opportunity to go out to cafés and bars, to help Fernand with his bikes or take Nathalie to the park. During the working week he was at the Ferodo factory in Saint-Ouen just north of Paris, in fact only a few kilometres from their apartment. At the time Ferodo was the world's largest commercial researcher into friction, paving the way to new revolutionary vehicle brake-linings. Arnaud had by then been promoted; he was a white-collar worker with the company, a supervisor of engineers.

Marie still worked hard to keep a clean and well-run home, put food on the table and look after Nathalie, and of course by her own precept she visited her son's grave every single day with Nathalie, even after her daughter had started nursery school in 1956, aged four. Of course, school for Nathalie caused Marie further consternation; she felt decidedly ill-at-ease being alone during the day, and separation from her daughter and husband, even though for only a short while each day, fuelled her anxiety, making her fretful and at times hysterical.

Marie looked forward to the school holidays when Nathalie was at home with her but increasingly she had become paranoid about the safety, health and welfare of her daughter. This may have been understandable given the death of her son that had been triggered by a childhood illness, but at five years of age Nathalie was too young to understand why her mother was constantly checking on her, almost never letting her out of her sight and being over-zealous when it came to washing her hands and wrapping up warm in winter.

During the long summer holiday Marie took Nathalie to Précy to see her grand-parents. In spite of the strained atmosphere between her and Arnaud she enjoyed being in Précy; she felt as though she was going home every time she made the journey and Arnaud's parents were very kind. She suspected they knew there were difficulties with Arnaud but she was thankful they never broached the subject with her. These visits were the only times she did not attend Daniel's grave, which made her feel guilty even though she made Arnaud swear that he would go in her place.

*

In June 1958 Marie received a letter from her older sister Emeline, telling her that she could not stay at Arnaud's parents' house over the summer because there was insufficient room. She was perplexed by this because she was not aware Emeline saw Arnaud's parents even though she knew they were acquainted, given they lived in the same area. She was also perplexed as to the reason why there would not be sufficient room because on all previous occasions there had been. Perhaps Emeline had got wind of the fact that they were getting a little uneasy about having Marie stay with them, knowing she was somewhat estranged from their son. Anyway, without a telephone to make a simple call to verify the facts, she accepted what Emeline had written and proceeded to make a booking at a small hotel in Chateau-Chinon for the holiday. Given that Arnaud was still working during the long summer break from school, she and Nathalie went alone. They made the journey, settled in to the hotel and walked around the town visiting familiar haunts.

The following day they walked through the town and down the lane to Précy to see Nathalie's grandparents. They would have been upset to know they were in town and had not called in to see them. When they arrived her parents-in-law greeted them joyfully but were a little baffled.

'But why did you not tell us you were coming? We would have put you up Marie. We love having you stay and Nathalie as well of course.'

'But, I thought ....' Marie stopped in her tracks and did not finish the sentence.

'But what did you think Marie?' said Nathalie's grandmother.

'Oh, nothing. How are you both? Are you both well?'

Marie had been confused but in a flash had assumed Emeline had been up to her tricks again. She had written to put her off staying with Arnaud's parents, but why? Just for the devilment of it, no doubt. She would confront her about it later in the week.

Nathalie enjoyed the day following her grandfather as he toured his three fields. The small one near the house was where they kept the hens and grew vegetables, and where they tethered their donkey. The other two were more distant from the house, the result of successive divisions of land following Napoleon's revised inheritance laws. They rode to those two fields in an old wooden cart that was pulled by his ageing donkey. Arnaud's father was hoping to plant conifers in the smaller of the two fields, thinking it would provide an income twenty years hence for his children and grand-children, but at the time it was where he grazed two goats. The other field had been left fallow but the following year he intended growing grass in the field in order to let it to a nearby farmer for cattle grazing. After lunch of cold cured meats, cheeses and freshly stone-baked bread Nathalie watched her grandmother perform the particularly difficult task of churning butter from their goats' milk. Preparing butter and cheeses was normal practice in remote rural areas; it was a way of extending the life of milk. As they left Précy Nathalie's grandfather called out that he intended to drop by in a day or two to take Nathalie off Marie's hands for an hour or so.

Since it was more or less on their way back to the hotel they called in to the woodcutter Laurent's house in Allée des Bleuets. She had not seen him since her father had died. He was out but she popped a note under his door telling him where she was staying and asking him to call by in a couple of days so they could catch up with news.

The next day they took a bus to Lac de Pannecière, the product of a dam constructed in the 1940s, barely ten kilometres north of Chateau-Chinon, to control the seasonal variation in flow of the Yonne into the Seine in order to protect Paris from flooding. Ironically, farmsteads were flooded to create the reservoir, and during times of particularly low water, even today there are stone remnants that can be seen protruding up above the surface of the lake. Apart from swimming there are beautiful walks nearby, including into the Bois de la Faye on the western side of the lake where alder, ash and willow are to be found near the river and along the lake shore, and elm and lime trees further inland. Like Marie when she was a child, Nathalie had developed a fascination for nature and always enjoyed strolling through woodlands looking for wild flowers, though to her disappointment there were no lily of the valley in flower at the time they were there. Back home she had to make do with the well-manicured flower beds of the Bois de Vincennes Parc, but here there was wildlife aplenty.

They alighted the bus just outside Les Vouas and like a dog with two tails Nathalie scuttled through the wood on her way down to the lake shore. It was a hot summer's day and Marie enjoyed lying in the sunshine reading her book while her daughter played and swam in the lake. Periodically she stopped reading, closed her book and thought about her childhood. She remembered the valley before the dam was there and recalled seeing the rising water slowly submerging the two abandoned villages. Inevitably her mind drifted back to the unhappy times she experienced in Villars and La Vallée de Cours, but as was the case on so many occasions previously, she found it impossible remembering the happy times she had as a young child, and this troubled her gravely. It was as though the immense traumas of the post-war years had become so ingrained on her mind that they had masked utterly the joyful occasions she had experienced earlier in her life.

They were back in the town by late afternoon. Marie took Nathalie to a café for a treat and while she sipped a diabolo-menthe through a straw, Marie drank a strong black coffee.

Later, back in their room at the hotel, Marie received a call from reception.

'Madame Rousseau, I'm so sorry but I forgot to tell you earlier that when you were out someone called by to speak to you. He said he would call back at about nine o'clock and hoped you would meet him here in reception.'

'Oh! Did he leave his name?'

'No, and I didn't think to ask. Sorry.'

'Okay, not to worry. I'll be there.'

Marie looked at the clock. It was already half past eight and nearing Nathalie's bedtime. She was a little puzzled. It could be Emeline's husband or it could be Arnaud's father. He had said he would call by to arrange a time when he could take Nathalie out. However, she felt it was more likely to be Laurent, paying her a visit having seen her note. Marie helped Nathalie get ready for bed and explained that she would need to leave her alone for a short while, but would be just one floor down in reception if she needed her. Nathalie was fine with that. She had her doll Lily for company and would read her book in bed while waiting for her mother to return.

At the allotted time Marie straightened her dress, tidied her hair and renewed her lipstick, though she did not know quite why she did that. She made her way out of the door, calling out to Nathalie that she would not be long as she did so, walked across the landing and down two flights of stairs to the hotel reception.

She saw nobody. She asked the receptionist if anyone had asked for her in the last few minutes, but nobody had. She turned as if to make her way back up to her room when she heard a man's voice calling her.

'Hello Marie. It's been a very long time.'

Marie knew instantly who it was. She spun round, smiled quizzically and approached him, tentatively at first, but then quickened her pace until she stood but an arm's length away from him. Marie stood motionless and looked into his eyes as if trying to read his motive for wanting to meet her again, hoping above all hope that he was about to tell her he had made a terrible mistake all those years ago and that he still loved her. There had never been a moment since the day he walked out of her home when she was just fifteen years of age, when she had stopped loving him; and this in spite of all that had happened in the ensuing years. She felt her pulse racing. She closed her eyes momentarily just as she did the very first time they stood facing each other in the autumn of 1946, when they had left the dance hall to steal a few moments together by the big plane tree. Raymond touched her face with the palm of his hand, gently tracing every contour as he moved his hand down to her neck. Marie said nothing and remained as still as the vision she had held of him since the moment they first met. She again closed her eyes hoping he would kiss her. She felt his warm hand on her neck and so lifted her head, ever so slightly, as if to offer ingress. Light-headed, and as though in suspended animation and far away from her world of evil daemons, she was in heaven, oblivious to all else around her. Tear drops moistened her eyes, but unlike those that had formed before, and that had been an indication of unhappiness, these were tears of sheer joy.

But she was suddenly shaken from her trance by the calling of a young voice. 'Maman, you said you were only going to be a minute. Are you coming upstairs now Maman?'

Marie stepped back a pace or two, turned and reassured Nathalie she would be up in a moment. 'Upstairs now darling,' she said. 'I'll be there in a second'.

Nathalie took the right hand of her doll and said, 'Come on now Lily, up we go. I told you Maman would be up soon. I told you there was nothing to worry about.'

And with that she was out of sight. Marie once again turned towards Raymond. He said nothing but touched her soft flawless lily-white forehead with his lips, and when she did not resist he kissed her trembling mouth ever so gently, and as he did so Marie placed both her hands to the back of his head and drew him in closer, so prolonging the moment. The second they withdrew, without a moment of delay she put her arms around Raymond and held him ever so tightly, and he did likewise, and they kissed passionately. In all that time, though it was but a few minutes, not a word had been exchanged: there was no need for words; their loving embrace spoke volumes.

Marie hurriedly broke away, straightened her dress and tidied her hair. 'I must go now Raymond. Shall I see you again tomorrow? Please say yes.'

'Yes, yes please Marie. I really want to see you tomorrow. Let us meet in the Café du Château on Place Notre Dame for coffee. Let's say eleven o'clock? Bring Nathalie of course.'

'Yes. I'll be there Raymond.'

She then strode up the stairs two at a time, turning once to smile at Raymond before she was gone. As she approached the landing she saw Nathalie sitting on the floor outside their door cuddling Lily and talking reassuringly to her.

'I'm sorry I was a little while Nathalie but I'm here now. In we go. I'll read to you and Lily while you both snuggle down for a good night's sleep.'

'Maman, who was that man? Was he the friend you said you were going to meet?'

'Yes, my little flower. He was the man I was going to meet. Now brush your teeth and then it's in to bed for you my little one.'

That night Marie slept longer and more peacefully than for a very long time. The next morning she bathed and got ready for the day. She explained to Nathalie that they were going to meet the man for a drink in the café. And so they did. As they made their way downstairs and out of the door, across the square and towards the café, Marie was in a state of heightened expectation. She was trembling a little and was unsure how she would act when she saw him, or indeed what she was going to say to him, especially with Nathalie alongside her. Had it all been a dream? Would he still feel the same this morning? How did he know she was there at the hotel?

Raymond caught up with them just as they were entering the café and kissed Marie on each cheek twice, while giving her an unobtrusive gentle squeeze across her shoulders as a reassuring gesture that he was very glad to see her. He introduced himself to Nathalie as an old friend of her mother's, and kissed her once on each cheek. They entered the café and ordered two cafés allongés and a juice for Nathalie. They took their drinks to a table on the terrace looking over Place Notre Dame. They chatted but given Nathalie's presence rather prosaically, asking after each other's families and general circumstances.

A little disinterested and restless Nathalie asked, 'Maman can I go and explore?'

'Yes my darling but do not wander too far. Keep within the square here, where I can keep an eye on you.' Nathalie finished her drink, left the table and skipped off looking in the shop windows as she did so.

'Raymond, how did you find me?'

'It was Emeline who told me you were unhappy at home. It was she who told me about your son and your father. I am so very sorry you have had such a terrible time. She told me you had a daughter and that you were married to Arnaud and lived in the suburbs of Paris.'

'Do you mean Emeline set this up? So the letter she sent me telling me I couldn't stay at Arnaud's parents' house in Précy was to make sure I booked in at a hotel so we could meet?'

'Yes, that's right. That was the only way I could get to see you Marie. I'm so glad we have found each other again. You see, all those years ago, I said we would meet again?'

'It's not going to be easy with Nathalie here too. Arrr! Where is Nathalie? Can you see her? I can't see her anywhere.'

Marie hurriedly rose from her chair, knocking it over in the process, and strode off to look for Nathalie. Raymond settled the bill and joined her.

'I can't see her Raymond,' she said in an agitated manner.

'She'll be here somewhere. She can't have gone too far away.'

But they looked everywhere. They even returned to the café in case she went back there. They looked in the shops, crossed the square to the library and the town hall but could not find her. Marie was by then panic-stricken. The sensitive and perceptive person that he was, Raymond realised she would be more concerned than most parents given her ordeals of the past few years. They again returned to the café and then Raymond had an idea.

'Is your daughter an inquisitive little girl? Does she like exploring unusual places? I ask because I notice that the wooden trap door leading beneath the fortified walls is open.'

They looked in and saw in the strong sunlight the stone staircase that led down to the basement. They entered, calling as they did. When at the foot of the stairs the basement opened up into a chamber with a stone floor and walls of granite, no doubt a couple of metres thick. There was another smaller staircase in the corner lit only by the little bit of sunlight that penetrated to the corner of the basement from the pavement above. They peered in and descended to the dungeons below. Raymond had visited the dungeons as a child, as had most of the town's youngsters at some time or another, so he knew they were there, how to access them and the fact that they were used in medieval times to lock up petty criminals. Down they went and there hiding in one of the cells was Nathalie, giggling by then, knowing she had found the most fabulous secret place for 'hide-and-seek' imaginable. Her mother was naturally very pleased and relieved to see her, but none-the-less scolded her for running off and causing her so much distress.

They returned to the café for a spot of lunch and then it was time to part. Marie did not want to alert Nathalie to the idea that she and Raymond wanted to spend time together. With 'la bise' as a parting gesture they went their separate ways, but not before Raymond slipped Marie a note.

Within a few minutes they were back in their room at the hotel getting ready for their visit to Lac de Settons, north east of the town on the River Cure. While Nathalie was using the toilet down the corridor from their room Marie opened the note.

My dearest Marie

I am so very glad I have met up with you again. I know life has been very difficult for you and I don't want to make things any more complicated than they are already but I'd like to see you again. I know you have Nathalie with you and must be careful she does not raise suspicion with Arnaud when you both return to Vincennes. I've never stopped thinking about you since the minute I walked out the door all those years ago. I'm so very sorry I hurt you then; but if you can find a way to forgive me and let me back into your life I promise never to hurt you ever again. I will come to the hotel reception at 9 o'clock on Tuesday evening.

I love you Marie. Raymond.

She folded the note, closed her eyes and held the note tightly against her chest. She heard Nathalie returning to the room so popped the note under her pillow, collected what they needed and the two of them left the room and walked to the bus shelter.

'Is that man coming with us to the lake Maman?'

'No, he won't be with us this afternoon. It will be just you and me my darling.'

'Do you like him Maman? I do.'

'Yes, my little flower, I do like him and I'm very pleased that you like him too.'

During that long hot summer's afternoon at the lake with her daughter Marie thought of little else but Raymond. She remembered the time she first set eyes on him at the dance hall. She remembered when he stole a first kiss by the big plane tree and how intoxicated it made her feel. She remembered the many lovely times they had spent in each other's company while dancing, walking in the countryside or enjoying a meal together in a simple restaurant. She remembered how happy and secure she always felt in his company. She remembered how patient and understanding he had always been. She even remembered him telling her exactly four thousand, four hundred and seventy days earlier that they may well meet again someday. In all that time she had hung on to the belief that in life one must never give up hope and that so much can be achieved by following one's dreams, however difficult they may be to acquire and however long they may take to materialise; in fact the very sentiments encountered while reading Antoine de Saint-Exupéry's *The Little Prince* when she was fifteen years old. And now her dream was about to become reality. She closed her eyes and re-lived the beautiful moment twenty-four hours earlier when Raymond kissed her and they had embraced so intensely that she knew then that their feelings for each other were unequivocal; neither of them being left in any doubt about how each felt about the other. Could it be that waiting almost twelve long years for that one kiss made it what is was: unbelievably exquisite and affectionately libidinous?

*

When Marie and Nathalie arrived back in Vincennes she told Arnaud she wanted a separation. She told him she had met up with Raymond again and they had rekindled their love for each other. Arnaud was not surprised. There were no harsh words exchanged and within days Arnaud moved out of the apartment and went to stay with his sister in nearby Champigny, which meant he remained in the same employment and could see his daughter regularly.

Thereafter Raymond visited most weekends and gave Marie the love and attention she had coveted for so long. He showed unquestionable affection for Nathalie and on numerous occasions took her into Paris to visit the Jardin des Plantes, Paris's main botanical garden on the left bank of the Seine a little upstream from Notre Dame Cathedral. He also took her to museums and galleries, like the Musée Grévin and the Louvre. They walked the Champs Elysées and saw the obelisk of Luxor at the Place de la Concorde, and the Arc de Triomphe, learning that it commemorates the French victories of the Napoleonic era. She climbed the Eiffel Tower, the Basilica of Sacré-Cœur and Notre Dame. In fact it was probably Raymond above all others that started Nathalie's interest in the arts, historical buildings and French urban culture, which she nurtured in later life.

Marie and Arnaud were divorced in November 1958 and Marie married Raymond the following year. The ceremony was conducted in Chateau-Chinon by the then newly elected maire, François Mitterrand. It was a quiet, simple ceremony. Florence was their witness. In May 1960 Marie gave birth to a baby girl, Beatrice. She continued to see Florence from time to time, though by then Florence was just a little preoccupied: she was married with five children of her own and five more she had adopted.

Though it was untrue to suggest that Marie's 'black dog' had been utterly tamed and held to heel, it was true to say she was bitten less often and less savagely. Marie continued to suffer from occasional night-tremors and her psychotic state often led her to believe that family and friends were critical of her. But these delusional episodes had been established in her distant past, when time after time she had endured painful separation from her loved-ones. In later life the delusions took a different course: an obsession with ailments, diseases and what she thought were life threatening conditions, when in actual fact they did not exist. But unquestionably she was happier and more contented than ever before; and above all secure in the knowledge that Raymond was there for her.

In October 2009, after fifty happy years of marriage, Marie and Raymond renewed their wedding vows in the presence of their daughter Beatrice and her husband, Marie's daughter Nathalie and her husband, her grandson Stéphane, and all their close friends.

Very sadly she became debilitated by illness early in 2014 and this time it was not hypochondriacal. But to the end she continued to take a pride in her home, something she had learnt as a young girl from her mother, and had practised in the years that followed when others were so very dependent on her for their well-being. Despite being in her eighties and suffering from illness she still cooked sumptuous meals and continued to dust and clean and polish her way through the days.

Marie died in July 2014. She had lived through many traumatic experiences, and though in her late twenties she had become resigned to the thought that she would never again find true happiness and lasting security she had been proved wrong: she was rescued from the abyss by her first and perhaps her only true love, Raymond.

EPILOGUE

To die, to sleep -
To sleep, perchance to dream - ay, there's the rub,
For in this sleep of death what dreams may come...
  — William Shakespeare

Is Marie now in a better place? Let us assume for now that there is no such thing as an afterlife and people are not reincarnated. In that Marie cannot any longer fear separation from her loved ones and all the anxiety associated with such paranoia, then yes most certainly she is. Thus holding on to the notion that good is the final goal of ill there's a relatively happy ending to this tale.

But perhaps we should not assume that when we die there is no afterlife. Of course some will argue that consideration of an afterlife will never be anything more than philosophical conjecture, some that it has never been anything other than a myth, and others will see it as part of their religion and belief in the control by a super being, but the majority will probably only accept that talk of an afterlife is pure fiction.

However, there are men and women who have devoted their professional lives to the study of the paranormal and the afterlife. One such pioneering researcher was Professor Ian Stevenson, a parapsychologist from Virginia University. Stevenson studied in excess of 2,000 cases of children's recollections from situations that in all probability must have occurred in a different incarnation. For example, reported in *Scientific American*[21] was the case of a toddler from Sri Lanka. Stevenson had overheard the girl mentioning to her mother the name of an obscure town (Kataragama) that the girl had never been to.

The girl told her mother that she drowned there when her 'dumb' (mentally challenged) brother pushed her in the river, that she had a bald father named Herath who sold flowers in a market near the Buddhist stupa, that she lived in a house that had a glass window in the roof (a skylight), dogs in the backyard that were tied up and fed meat, that the house was next door to a big Hindu temple, outside of which people smashed coconuts on the ground. Stevenson was able to confirm that there was, indeed, a flower vendor in Kataragama who ran a stall near the Buddhist stupa whose two-year-old daughter had drowned in the river while the girl played with her mentally challenged brother. The man lived in a house where the neighbours threw meat to dogs tied up in their backyard, and it was adjacent to the main temple where devotees practised a religious ritual of smashing coconuts on the ground.

The little girl did not get everything correct, however. For instance, the dead girl's father was not bald but her grandfather and uncle were, and his name was not Herath, though that was the name of the dead girl's cousin. Otherwise, twenty seven of the thirty distinctive statements she made were verified as having been true. Because the two families had never met and did not know of each others existence, the details the little girl mentioned could not have been acquired in any obvious way. Further, the number and variety of correct pieces of information suggested to Stevenson that it was unlikely to have been merely a coincidence.

From this example, and those from many of the other 2,000 cases he reviewed, Stevenson concluded there was creditable evidence for the existence of an afterlife in the form of reincarnation. Over a billion Hindus and almost half a billion Buddhists, as well as countless Jains and Sikhs, believe in reincarnation, that is the rebirth of the soul in another being in the physical world.

The notion of an afterlife can be explored further via the experience of Eben Alexander[22] [23] who grew up in a scientific world, the son of a neurosurgeon. He followed in his father's path and became an academic neurosurgeon, teaching at Harvard Medical School and other universities. Being a neurosurgeon he understood what happens to the brain when people are near death, and he had always believed there were good scientific explanations for the heavenly out-of-body journeys described by those who narrowly escaped death.

In the fall of 2008, after seven days in a coma during which the human part of my brain, the neocortex, was inactivated, I experienced something so profound that it gave me a scientific reason to believe in consciousness after death. On the morning of my seventh day in the hospital, as my doctors weighed whether to discontinue treatment, my eyes popped open. There is no scientific explanation for the fact that while my body lay in coma, my mind — my conscious, inner self — was alive and well. While the neurons of my cortex were stunned to complete inactivity by the bacteria that had attacked them[24], my brain-free consciousness journeyed to another, larger dimension of the universe: a dimension I'd never dreamed existed and which the old, pre-coma me would have been more than happy to explain was a simple impossibility.

He argued that the dimension he had experienced was roughly the same one described by countless subjects of near-death experiences. He said what he saw and learned when in that coma placed him in a new world.

A world where we are much more than our brains and bodies, and where death is not the end of consciousness but rather a chapter in a vast, and incalculably positive, journey.

The principal arguments against near-death experiences normally suggest that they are the result of partial malfunctioning of the cortex. However, Alexander's near-death experience took place not while his cortex was malfunctioning, but while it was simply completely shut down.

He was able to describe very clearly what he experienced. He said he was in a place with big billowing clouds in a deep blue-black sky. Above the clouds were living forms arcing across the sky — flocks of transparent shimmering birds, but not like any he had seen on earth. He heard a booming sound like a glorious chant. He was accompanied by a young high cheek-boned woman with blue eyes and golden brown hair. The two of them were surrounded by what looked like millions of butterflies, he said. He could see the two of them were riding on the wing of one of these butterflies. He even remembered what the woman was wearing: a simple outfit like a peasant's, but multi-coloured in powder blue, indigo and pastel orange-peach. She had given him an extraordinarily reassuring and loving look; not apparently in a romantic way, but a look that suggested a compelling friendship. He described it as a look of such magnitude that it surpassed anything he could imagine occurring on earth. She 'spoke' to him he said, but without using words. She conveyed her message unequivocally 'telling' him he is loved and cherished, dearly and forever, and that there is nothing for him to fear because there is nothing that he could do wrong. He said of this message that:

It flooded me with a vast and crazy sensation of relief. It was like being handed the rules to a game I'd been playing all my life without ever fully understanding it. We will show you many things here, the woman said, again without actually using these words but by driving their conceptual essence directly into me. But eventually, you will go back.

This struck him as odd and he pondered on this for some time before asking, 'back where?'.

236

Reflecting on this astonishing near-death experience Eben Alexander turned to modern physics for an explanation. Physics tells us that every object and event in the universe is completely interwoven with every other object and event. There is no separation. An occurrence in one place and time will in major or minor ways impact upon others. This is the essence of chaos theory: small differences in initial conditions yield widely diverging outcomes for dynamical systems, so rendering long-term prediction impossible. This theory is perhaps best illustrated by the so called 'butterfly effect', first described by Edward Lorenz[25]. He suggested that the flapping of a butterfly's wings somewhere in Brazil (for example) represents a small change in the initial condition of the atmospheric system, which in turn causes a chain of events that eventually leads to large-scale phenomena occurring elsewhere, such as a tornado in Texas. The point being that had the butterfly not flapped its wings, the trajectory of the system might have been vastly different. From this we learn that just because people may not fully comprehend why something happens as it does, that is not to say it does not in fact occur. This may be why people like Eben Alexander, who describe near-death experiences, are rarely taken seriously. It is not necessarily that they have not happened, it is more because we cannot comprehend them.

This idea can be explored more fully by examining the work of Professor Robert Lanza[26] from Wake Forest University School of Medicine in North Carolina. He claimed that there may well be an afterlife and he used quantum physics, specifically the theory of biocentrism, to prove it[27] [28]. He argued that the evidence lay in the idea that the concept of death is an illusion created by our consciousness.

We think life is just the activity of carbon and an admixture of molecules — we live a while and then rot into the ground.

He further claimed that as humans we only believe in death because we have been taught we 'die', or more specifically, our consciousness associates life with bodies — physical entities — and we know that bodies die. But there is more to human life than the body.

When a person dies the energy that operates in the brain does not disappear at the time of death. Science tells us that energy never dies; it can neither be created nor destroyed. In terms of how this affects life after death, Professor Lanza explained that when we die:

Our life becomes a perennial flower that returns to bloom in the multiverse.

He referred to 'multiverse' and not 'universe' because quantum physics suggests that there are numerous universes operating alongside each other, what some have called 'parallel universes'. From this it may be gathered that when something 'dies' in one place, elements of it may emerge in another.

Life is an adventure that transcends our ordinary linear way of thinking.

To fully understand we need to think beyond a simple linear dimension. Perhaps this can be understood by thinking of the difference between a food chain and a food web, the former illustrating progressing from one stage to another in a single series of steps sequentially, whilst the latter suggests that progression, or change, occurs within an infinitely more complex network of interwoven reactions in the dynamical system.

Our perception of something, like a single light particle passing through a multi-holed barrier, may be different from the reality of how it behaves. We only perceive something as a result of our consciousness Lanza argued. When we look at the light striking the barrier we see the single light particle passing through one of the holes much like a bullet would, but when we do not observe it directly, but instead measure the passage of the single light particle scientifically, we find that even though it is a single particle it passes through multiple holes, like a wave.

Professor Lanza also used colours to illustrate his point. He argued that the sky may be perceived as blue, but if the cells in our brain were changed to make the sky look green, the question may be posed, was the sky ever truly blue or was that just our perception of it?

Lanza makes a compelling argument for suggesting that whilst we may deduce death to be a termination of life, because this is what we perceive it to be, in reality this may not be so for it may be existing elsewhere in the multiverse. Perhaps it is true that the concept of death is, as Lanza suggested, a mere illusion created by our consciousness, with life being fundamentally immortal.

*

So, if the doubters are ignored and the thought that there is an afterlife — as academics like Stevenson (reporting on the experiences of others), Alexander (directly from his own near death experience) and Lanza (using the theory of biocentrism) suggest — is pursued, with the assumption that an essential part of an individual's consciousness lives on after the death, then what of Marie? Has she entered another world much like the one Eben Alexander was on the verge of entering himself? If so, for Marie surely, her afterlife will bring comfort to replace trauma, joy to supersede sadness and contentment to displace turmoil.

It is comforting to presuppose that Marie has been reunited with her nightingale, her lost son Daniel, after all she waited 63 years for the moment. Further, at some time in May each year it may be assumed she will be somewhere in a beautiful wildflower meadow with her loving mother. Perhaps she is being cared for by none other than those who took advantage of her in 'life'. If this is so then her world beyond the grave has reunited her with an angelic Emeline, a healthy and cheerful Colette, an apologetic first husband and a doting father, desperate to make up for his failings at the time Marie needed him most — 'Just one more time Papa, please' — and so he would play his accordion and serenade his angelic daughter with *Mon amant de Saint-Jean*. And of course she is waiting patiently for Raymond. Remember there is room for another in her burial place.

And let us not forget one more key player in this story: a lost and repentant soul, working out the years of a penance. Her coming face to face with Marie in the afterlife will provide her with an opportunity to devote time to ensure that while in her other place Marie will be blissfully happy and contented. By 'cleansing the fire' in this way the reprobate who caused so much distress to Marie by orchestrating the death of her mother will be able to end her perdition, and by so doing make the first steps to the procurement of the holiness necessary to enter the joy of heaven. So the punishing guilt endured by sinners for their mortal sins can be remitted, even Brigitte's!

I believe there are two sides to the phenomenon known as death, this side where we live, and the other side where we shall continue to live. Eternity does not start with death. We are in eternity now.

— *Norman Vincent Peale*

ACKNOWLEDGEMENTS

I wish to record my gratitude to my wife for sharing her memories of the first few years of her life when the principal character, her mother, was living in Paris. I also wish to thank her step-father for sharing his memories of the time he spent in the Morvan during the Nazi Occupation.

I am indebted to my wife and brother for reading the draft of this novel and for their invaluable advice.

ABOUT THE AUTHOR

K R Chapman graduated from London University and became a secondary school teacher of Geography. He retired in 2014 after 43 enjoyable and rewarding years in the profession. He now lives in Essex with his French wife, whose mother was the inspiration for this, his debut novel.

Notes

[1] Trotsky was a major figure in the Russian Bolshevik revolution of 1917. He led a failed struggle of the Left Opposition against the policies and rise of Joseph Stalin in the 1920s and against the increasing role of bureaucracy in the Soviet Union for which he was removed from power, expelled from the Communist Party and deported. He wrote his paper encouraging a united front against the rise of German extreme right-wing movements while in exile in Turkey. Interestingly he was given exile in France for a brief period from 1933-35.

[2] There had been no love lost between the Communist Party of Germany and the far more liberal Social Democrats between the wars — they were bitter rivals. The communist party in Germany was in fact remodelled to become the Socialist Workers' Party of Germany from a nucleus of more radical left-wing Social Democrats.

[3] Kaplan, Alice (2006). *The Collaborator: The Trial and Execution of Robert Brasillach*. Chicago: University of Chicago Press.

[4] Richard Corliss (2000). *Killing for his Words*. Time Magazine, 15 May 2000.

[5] Don Lawson (1984). *The French Resistance - The True Story of the Underground War Against the Nazis*. New York : Julian Messner.

[6] Dr Simon Kitson (2008). *The Hunt for Nazi Spies: Fighting Espionage in Vichy France*. University of Chicago Press.

[7] Antony Beevor (2014) *D-day - The Battle for Normandy*. Viking Penguin.

[8] Jean Guéhenno. *Diary of the Dark Years, 1940-1944 : Collaboration, Resistance, and Daily Life in Occupied Paris*. Translated and annotated by David Ball (2014). Oxford University Press.

[9] Alan Riding (2011). *And the Show Went On: Cultural Life in Nazi-Occupied Paris*. Vintage Books.

[10] Maurice Chevalier (1960) *With love: the autobiography of Maurice Chevalier*. Cassel.

[11] Hal Vaughan (2011). *Sleeping With the Enemy: Coco Chanel's Secret War.* Random House Books, Australia.

[12] Kim Willsher, Journalist. *Louis Vuitton's links with Vichy regime exposed.* The Guardian (3 June 2004).

[13] Clive James (2012). *Cultural Amnesia: Notes in the Margin of My Time.* Picador.

[14] Carole Seymour-Jones (2009). *A Dangerous Liaison.* Arrow.

[15] Mary Louise Roberts (2013). *What Soldiers Do: Sex And The American GI In World War II France.* University of Chicago Press.

[16] Mike Thomson - presenter, *Document*, BBC Radio 4 (6 April 2009). *Paris liberation made 'whites only'.*

[17] Friedrich Nietzsche (1883) - *Thus Spoke Zarathustra.* Penguin Books (March 1978 edition)

[18] In fact it is still a hospital for children but now specialising in genetics, treating children with developmental anomalies and malformation syndromes.

[19] Today Gien has gained a reputation as a centre for the manufacture of fine dinnerware; in fact it had been an Englishman (Thomas Hall) who in the early nineteenth century set up the town's first factory. Gien pottery became a favourite of Marie's and her best Gien tableware was still being used shortly before her death.

[20] The wine of Sancerre became a particular favourite of Nathalie's from her late teens. She worked as a grape-picker there on her return from her gap year in England. Courtesy of the owners she and the other workers were offered al-fresco breakfasts in the vineyard and white Sancerre was always served with them!

[21] Jesse Bering. *Ian Stevenson's Case for the Afterlife: Are We 'Skeptics' Really Just Cynics?* Scientific American (2 November 2013).

[22] Eben Alexander (2012). *Proof of Heaven: A Neurosurgeon's Journey into the Afterlife.* Simon and Schuster Paperback.

23 Eben Alexander. *Proof of Heaven: A Doctor's Experience With the Afterlife.* Newsweek, 8 October 2012.

24 He had developed a very rare and serious form of meningitis.

25 Edward N. Lorenz (1995). *The Essence of Chaos.* Washington University Press.

26 Dr Robert Lanza was named one of TIME Magazine's 100 'Most Influential People in the World', selected as one of Prospect Magazine's 'World Thinkers' in 2015, and in 2013 was voted into the 'Top 50 Global Stem Cell Influencers'.

27 Robert Lanza with Bob Berman (2010). *Biocentrism: How Life and Consciousness are the Keys to Understanding the True Nature of the Universe.* Paperback.

28 John Hall (2013) *Is there an afterlife? The science of biocentrism can prove there is, claims Professor Robert Lanza.* The Independent: 15 November 2013.

Printed in Great Britain
by Amazon